Assassin of Nova

(second editon)

by

Prudence MacLeod

Book Two of the Nova Series

I0672178

Escape

"When you are fully aware that death stalks you, only then are you truly alive." Rathbone of Urn the Elder.

———◉———

"I SPARED NO EXPENSE to help you assemble your team, Doctor. You were supposed to give me super soldiers, not dead bodies."

"Mr. O'Loran, Sir, I did try to warn you; we need to hold back a bit with the strength of the mechanical augments. By pushing the boundaries so hard, we made them too strong. Their bodies are tearing themselves apart. Four of the nine are already dead and I doubt the rest can survive more than a few more days."

"This is unfortunate, most unfortunate."

"Sir, with what we've learned from this trial, we can assure you of complete success with the next series."

"Very well. Terminate the rest and start over." The tall man turned and stalked away. "Do not fail me again, Doctor." His voice faded as he stepped into the elevator.

A powerfully built man had been hiding in the shadows, listening, his instincts screaming at him to run. He slipped silently away as those elevator doors closed. He had just heard his death warrant issued, and he didn't plan to stick around for it to be carried out.

As he reached the corridor to the sleeping quarters, he smelled the gas. Taking a deep breath, he held it as he raced through the gas cloud to the locked door at the end of the hallway. A leaping kick tore the door from the hinges and hurled it against the opposite

1

wall. He had only hoped to kick it open; he still wasn't sure of how much additional strength the mechanical augments had given him. He would soon learn.

Two armed soldiers had been stationed on the other side of that door and both had been knocked unconscious. He snatched up their weapons and fled down another corridor.

Suddenly, the alarms sounded, and steel blast doors began to close and lock down. He would soon be trapped.

A squad of soldiers came out of another corridor; they'd found him. Before they could raise their weapons he was on them. The battle was terrible and swift. Five dead men lay on the floor as he fled on, but he was trapped.

There was only one possible way out; the garbage chute. Without hesitation he plunged in head first. It was quite a drop but a soft, if smelly, landing. He scrambled over to the side of the container and waited. As soon as it was wheeled into the hold of the ship he climbed out and found the air lock. He had barely enough time to get inside before the ship lifted off.

As the ship rose through the atmosphere, the vid screens all over the central cluster of planets came alive with the news. Rathbone of Urn had gone rouge and escaped the authorities. The manhunt was on, but there were few who wanted to encounter the legendary assassin.

At this point, the ship's pilot stepped through a doorway, his eyes on the hand-held vid screen in his palm. He looked up to see a large man, heavily armed standing in front of him. The armed stranger held his finger to his lips in a sign for silence. "You're him, aren't you?" said the pilot, as he lowered the vid screen to his side.

"Him?"

The pilot held out the vid screen and he lowered his weapon as he took it. A glance at the screen told him all he needed to know. He passed it back. "Damned media never gets anything right," he sighed. "Rathbone of Urn, the assassin, is my grandfather."

"So, who're you?"

"Rathbone of Urn, the mechanic."

"Right. So, you're on this scow because...?"

"I have some repairs to make on the refuse planet."

"Of course you do. You'll be staying behind then, right? Because I just unload then return to Elliston Prime."

"That's right, I'll be staying behind."

With a soft chuckle the man put his back against the wall and slid to the floor. He pulled some ration bars from his jacket pocket and tossed one to Rathbone. "Might as well take a load off, Mr. Mechanic. We've got some time to kill."

Rathbone slid to the floor as well, then began to chew thoughtfully on the ration bar. "How many on the ship?" he asked after a long silence.

"Just me," came the reply, "She's all on auto. All I really need to do is takeoff and return landing. Pretty much everything else is automated."

"Can you do manual override?"

"Sure, but why bother? Tell me you're not really going to steal my poor old scow. They'll shoot you down as soon as you hit open space. She's far too slow to outrun the R.I.M. special police."

"I won't steal your ship," chuckled Rathbone. "I just want you to get close enough so I don't break my neck when I hit the ground."

"Fair enough. So, have you got a plan for getting off the refuse planet?"

"Not yet. I take life one step at a time, my friend. They were trying to kill me, so I escaped. Once I'm on the planet I'll look for the best way to take the next step. What can you tell me about this place?"

"Well, you can survive there, if you call it surviving. It was originally terraformed so you can breathe the air and scratch out a living from the soil. There are a few people living there. I'm supposed to report the human rats, as they call them, but I don't."

"Why not?"

"These folk don't do any harm to anybody; they just scavenge what they can from the refuse. If I report them they'd be exterminated."

"Why do you care?"

"I've seen far too many people die for no reason, friend. I won't add to that."

"You're a veteran?"

"Yes. I was flying the ship that wiped out Nova Prime."

"The plague planet?"

"There wasn't any plague, brother. It was a war. Nova rebelled and we gassed the whole damned planet. Everything died, men, women, children, animals, you name it. When my tour was up I got out and bought this old scow. Now I haul garbage. I get paid damn near the same and I can sleep at night. I won't see folks die needlessly again if I can help it."

Rathbone was silent for a while. At length he laid aside his weapons and relaxed fully back against the bulkhead. "Friends call me Rath," he said, as he held out his hand.

"Deke," replied his host, as he accepted the offered hand.

"Deke, why the hell have you not installed a few comfortable chairs for your passengers?"

"There's a chair in the cockpit," chuckled Deke, "but I promise you're more comfortable here on the floor."

Rathbone grinned at that then twisted a bit to ease the pain in his body. "You're carrying wounds," observed Deke.

"Yeah, a few, but I'd wager yours are deeper." Deke just nodded and didn't reply. "Deke, what are my chances of getting back off that refuse heap?"

"Well, I could take you off again, but you'd just end up back on Elliston Prime."

"Not at all where I want to be. Are there any other options?"

"There is a spot where they dump a lot of old useless ships. A good mech-tech with lots of time on his hands might be able to restore an old speeder or some such. There's nothing military there, though."

"A speeder would be more to my liking anyway," sighed Rathbone. "I just want to get back to Urn, to my companion and child. I'll take them out to the rim; find a little backwater planet where I can set up a mechanic's shop and stay out of the way. I just want to live long enough to see my baby girl grow up."

"All right, Rath, I'll set you down an easy hike to the ship scrapyards." Just then an alarm sounded through the ship. "That's the signal to get to work. We're almost there. Come on, we'll go put her on manual and find a soft spot for a landing."

———◦———

RATHBONE STOOD WATCHING the old ship lift off and fade into the evening sky. With a deep sigh he turned to the endless acres of junk piled just behind where he stood. As he turned a ragged woman scurried away from her hiding place, but she stumbled and fell at his feet. Holding out her hands defensively, she cowered there on the ground. "Please don't kill me," she begged.

"Now why would I want to do that?" he asked, a grin playing at the edges of his mouth.

"You're a soldier; soldiers always try to kill us. We hide, but they find and kill most of us."

"I'm not a soldier anymore, so I have no reason to kill you; any of you, so you can all come out of hiding." At that several others stood and brandished crude weapons.

"We won't share the food," declared one man. "There's not enough to feed a man your size. We only grow enough for ourselves."

"Now that presents a problem," replied Rathbone. "You see, if you won't share the food with me, then I have to find my own. The easiest thing would be to eat one of you. Hell, if I'm stuck here long enough, I'll probably have to eat the lot of you."

They were horrified at that. The men edged closer together, fingering their crude weapons. The woman laughed as she regained her feet. "That's the idea, big fella. I'll help you. Let's start with him, he's the fattest." She cackled again, then her voice evened out with a note of command in it. "Of course we'll share the food with him. He's a human being; we'll share."

"But Etta..."

"No buts, we share what we have." She turned to Rathbone and stuck out her hand. "I'm Etta of Naith. I'm elected leader of this sorry group of misfits."

"Rathbone of Urn," he grinned as he shook her hand. "I won't rob you folks of your food, Etta; I can look after myself."

"We'll share the food, Rathbone, come on."

She took his hand and led him into a maze of boulders and junk piles. They soon found themselves in the belly of an old cargo ship. It'd been made into a rather homey kitchen. The smell of cooking food was everywhere, and it was delightful, pulling at him, reminding him he was still alive.

"It's all vegetarian, I'm sorry to say," she said. "We don't get a lot of meat around here."

"Oh, why not?"

"It's too big and we have no way to kill it," said one of the men.

"Understood. Old Deke gave me a handful of protein bars. If we add those in with that soup we all get one full meal; what do you say?"

"You'd share your ration bars?" asked the man.

"I told you he was a human being," said Etta. "Let's eat."

The next morning Rathbone set out. It was late in the afternoon when he spotted what he wanted, the hull of an old style speeder. She'd been gutted, but the hull was still sound. He had his ship.

He was returning to the human encampment when he saw the creature. It was a huge mass of fur, fang, and claw, easily weighing over 300 kilos. It charged at him and he brought it down with his blaster. The humans came out of hiding then, staring at the dead bear.

"That thing could have killed us all and destroyed our home," muttered one man.

"Is it fit to eat?" asked Rathbone.

"Who knows? Let's find out," chuckled Etta, as she appeared with a knife and started skinning out the carcass. "Looks like meat's back on the menu, folks." With a rousing cheer the others pitched in to help.

"You people need to set up defenses," Rathbone observed, as he set aside the bowl he had just emptied for the second time. "You also need ways to catch your meat and protect yourselves."

"Yes, we do," replied Etta. "Will you help us?"

"Sure, if you folks will help me."

"What do you want?" asked one of the men suspiciously.

"I've found the ship I want, but she's been gutted. I'll need help to locate and transport the parts. You folks help me with that, and I'll show you how to protect yourselves from the bears, kill them for meat, and hide yourselves from the soldiers. Will that work for you?"

"It will," replied one of the men. "You'll have to teach us first."

"Understood. We can start at first light."

Several weeks later, the small village was completely hidden, both from above and from the ground. There were several escape routes, but the only way in was through several narrow passages. A bear or a big man would have to squeeze to get through and there were traps along the way. For the first time the people felt safe. There were also several deadfalls set up around the surrounding area. There would be meat.

"I'd like to start work on the ship tomorrow," said Rathbone, as they enjoyed an evening meal.

"Fair enough," agreed Etta. "We'll get at it in the morning, right folks?" There was a round of agreement. Everybody knew they owed their current good health and relative prosperity to Rathbone and what he had taught them. They were also in complete awe of his strength as well as his seeming endless knowledge of tactics and stealth.

"Etta, how long have you folks been on this planet anyway?"

"About ten years now," she replied. "We were refugees from a war zone in Sector Six. The Company sent in soldiers to kill everybody in the camp. The bodies were scooped up and put on a refuse carrier then dumped here. Some of us managed to survive.

"That's our story, now how about yours?"

"Much the same," he sighed, as he leaned back on his elbow. "I was a mech-tech stationed on Elliston Prime, but my home, companion, and child were on Urn. When Gen and Ari took sick I couldn't afford the medicines. The military was recruiting for a new program. Cyborg implants. They said they'd pay for the medicines if I volunteered, so I did.

"The implants were way too strong and some of the guys tore themselves apart. I overheard CEO O'Loran tell the surgeon to terminate the rest of us and start over. I fought my way out and escaped on the refuse hauler. The rest you know."

"So that explains the pain I see in your eyes, Rath," sighed Etta. "Your body is tearing itself apart."

"Yes, it is. I don't know how long I'll last. I just want to see Gen and Ari one more time before I self-destruct."

"We'll do all we can to help you with that. What's the plan?"

"Rebuild that speeder and get off this rock. Go home to my family. Do you want to look for a slightly bigger ship, one big enough to take us all off?"

"You'd do that? You'd help us escape?" Etta's tone betrayed the hope they had not dared to allow themselves.

"I will. It should be easier to find parts for a freight hauler than for that speeder anyway. You folks help me build a ship, then we get out of here. You drop me off at Urn and then head out to the rim."

"I'm not going anywhere," declared one man. "You've made this place safe for us. We can survive here. Out there we'll be hunted outlaws again." The argument was on then. In the end about half of them decided to stay, while the rest wanted to go. They all agreed to help as much as they could. It took nearly three years before they managed to get a ship ready for lift off.

Everyone waved as the battered old freight hauler lifted off and wobbled its way out into space. A week later it set down on Urn. Rathbone quickly traded his two blasters for food supplies for the ship then it lifted off again, Captain Etta at the helm and Rathbone's well wishes ringing in her ears.

Three days later, Rathbone stood staring down at the graves of his companion and daughter.

On the Run

The information on the gravestones was slow to sink in to his grief fogged brain. They'd been dear for over three years? That meant they'd died of the fevers. The medicines hadn't worked. Why was that? They'd assured him the meds would bring his family back to health within days. As he tried to process the information the sounds of someone's slow painful approach reached his ears.

"Rath? Is that you, boy?" It was his grandfather's voice, and he was frail. He turned to see the old man approach, leaning heavily on his canes.

"Poppa? Poppa, what happened to you? What happened to Gen and Ari?"

"I'm so sorry, Rath," sigh the old man as he embraced his grandson. His voice choked up as he spoke. "I'm so very, very, sorry. The bastards never did give them any medicine. They were dead within days of you volunteering for that program, whatever it was. I went to Elliston Prime and stole the meds, but I didn't get back in time. Gen and Ari were already gone.

"R.I.M. soldiers were hard after me. They caught me and destroyed my knees; put an end to my career. Once you escaped they came back. I was held hostage in your house for over two years until they finally gave up on the idea that you might return.

"I can see the pain in your eyes, Rath. What did they do to you in there?"

"It was a cyborg program, Poppa. They made us way too strong and some of the guys tore themselves apart. I overheard O'Loran tell Doc to terminate the rest of us and start over. I made a run for it. You made me work at getting strong and it paid off, I guess. I'm still alive for now."

"Come on home, son, you're looking a bit peaked. When was the last time you ate regularly?" Slowly they made their way back to the old man's land transport, then headed for home.

The old assassin gave Rathbone only three days to mourn, during which time neither man spoke often. When they did it was of Gen and Ari. After three days the old fellow sadly broached the subject. "Rath, you can't stay here. They'll know by now that you're home. It won't be long before they come for you. We need to make a plan."

Rathbone sighed deeply and shifted in his chair. The pain in his body could not compare with the pain in his heart. He shook his head slowly, sadly, as he pushed his grief away. The old man was right. He had no time for mourning. The bastards wouldn't even give him that much. Slowly the loss and heartache were pushed aside, but a deep rage and thirst for vengeance seeped in to fill the void in his thoughts. "Agreed." He said at last.

"What's the objective?"

"Payback," he snarled, allowing the pain in his heart to add fuel to the desire.

"Who's the target?"

"O'Loran, if I can get to him, R.I.M. military if I can't."

The old man thought for a moment before he spoke again. "If you want to hurt O'Loran, go after R.I.M. hard and fast. Kill as many of his pet projects as you can."

"The cyborg program," growled Rathbone. "That one killed Gen and Ari, and it'll kill me. What's my best move?"

"Our best move."

"Poppa, you're in no shape to..."

"True, I can't run and fight anymore, but I'm a long way from useless. I have a lifetime of experience, hundreds of inside contacts, hidden caches of weapons, and I can still fly a ship. I also know where to get my hands on a fast speeder. I'm in."

For the first time in three days, Rathbone smiled. "All right, you're in. What's our first move?"

"We get off Urn before they get here. I have a speeder fully fueled and stocked with food. We get off planet and stay on the move while we work out a plan of action."

With a nod Rathbone rose and swept up the weapons his grandfather had provided. The old fellow grabbed his canes and they headed for the transporter outside. As they drove away the house exploded behind them. "We're not coming back?" grinned Rathbone.

"Not in this lifetime." They rode on in silence.

Several hours later, a troop of heavily armed soldiers stood gazing at the wreckage of the once magnificent house. "Must have blown themselves to the nine hells trying to rig booby traps," muttered their commander. The others just nodded their agreement, happy they didn't have to face the two assassins in a pitched battle.

———⊙———

THE OLD CARGO HAULER hung in orbit behind one of Elliston Prime's dead moons. Inside a group of hard-faced men were preparing for the final run at R.I.M.'s capital city.

"One last time," growled Rathbone, "where's your spot?" Each man silently stuck his finger on the map laid out before them. "Very good, remember what you're carrying. Don't be late. You don't want to be anywhere on the planet when I set it off. Just plant your package then get to the rendezvous point. Poppa will pick you up in a land car then get you off planet in the freighter."

"What about you?"

"I have another errand. I'll meet you back on Refuse with your pay. Stick to the plan, don't mess it up, and you'll all be richer than you've ever imagined."

The old man's voice came over the intercom then. "Settle down, we're going in." Everyone shifted to a seat and grabbed hold; they were expecting a rough ride.

They listened to the crackle of the comms as the old freighter was challenged and the pilot gave their prearranged codes. The codes were accepted, and the ship moved on, eventually settling down at a small port outside the city. A large land car was waiting there for them. It was swiftly loaded, and the old man slipped into the seat at the guidance panel. They set out for the city center.

The big car slowly circled the main office complex of R.I.M., making several stops. At each stop a man got out and walked away; first Rathbone, then the rest. Rathbone watched from the shadows, waiting, nursing his grief, feeding his desire for revenge with the pain in his body. Finally the big car drove slowly by, the driver giving him the success salute. The charges were set; all was ready. Rathbone slipped away into the shadows of the city.

By the time the men were back on board the old freight hauler and leaving the planet, Rathbone had reached his target. He disabled the sensors and leaped over the high fence, ignoring the lights. Ten heavily armed men were guarding the armoured car, but they had no chance against the cyborg assassin.

Rathbone pulled the bodies out of the way then mounted the cabin. As soon as the vehicle engines started, the alarms went off in the compound. He gunned the engines and blasted through the gates and off into the city. The entire military payroll for the planet had just been stolen.

The hunt was soon on, but he had a good start. The search was around the city perimeter; no one would ever expect to find him deeper in its heart. A mere two hours after the robbery, the armoured truck was driven at speed through the main doors of the R.I.M. office building.

The security guards were no match for the maddened cyborg they faced. Some fought and died, the rest fled. As they fled the building, Rathbone grabbed the intercom microphone. "Attention, flee the building, repeat flee the building. I'll kill anyone in my path."

Dropping the mic, Rathbone leaped to the elevators. He softly cursed the insipid music that played as the machine rose. Stepping out of the elevator, he placed a small charge on the door to O'Loran's office. Once it blew open, he tossed in a grenade then ducked away. The office was shattered by the blast.

"I wish you'd been in there," he muttered, as he took the elevator back down to the mail lab in the basement. "One day you will be."

Rathbone stepped out of the elevator, blew open the lab doors, then set his charges. As he fled the lab he heard the big trucks arriving outside. He could hear the soldiers above and the speed of their movements. As he'd hoped, the cyborgs had been sent after him. He sped to the garbage chute and jumped in. It was a hard landing, but he rolled to his feet and climbed out of the near empty container. They'd search the building first, starting with the top floor. That would buy him the time he needed.

A land speeder was waiting for him as he vaulted off of the container wall. He jumped in and the woman at the controls moved the machine swiftly away from the area. When she finally stopped, he opened the door and got out, dropping a huge bag of money on the seat.

"Get as far away from here as you can, as fast as you can," he said, as he closed the door. She sped away in one direction and he ran the other.

He hadn't run far when another car stopped for him; Deke was at the controls. Neither man spoke as Rathbone pulled out a small transmitter and pressed a button. Several explosive devices detonated simultaneously, shaking the entire city. With a massive shudder, the monstrous R.I.M. office complex collapsed in on itself, killing the cyborg soldiers inside and destroying the secret cyborg labs.

The car sped away, heading for the service area of the outer spaceport. They left the car there and boarded the old refuse hauler. A few hours later the ship rose into the air. Rathbone lay on the floor, grinning as Deke chatted with the controller.

"You're a bit early today, Deke; clearing you now."

"Thanks, Jim. This'll be my last run. I can't afford the repairs on the old girl so I'm retiring. A friend will pick me up on Refuse and I'm gone to my gardens on Apex."

"Happy gardening, you lucky bastard. You're clear to Refuse."

"Thanks, Jim. Deke out."

He switched off the comm and Rathbone stood up. He grinned as he settled into the new plush seat beside Deke's. "Nice chair."

"Yeah, I had to upgrade. I was getting too many complaints. It won't take them long to figure it out, Rath."

"Long enough. Did you get the new engines put in?"

"Yep. I don't know how you managed to get that engine or the guys who put it in, and I don't care. She's purring like a kitten, but she still can't outrun the military, and that's who will come after us."

"I know, but we're putting that engine into another hauler. By the time they figure it out and get to Refuse, all they'll find is this ship, gutted. You'll be half a sector away with a new ship, new identity, and a lot of money."

"Why did you bother with me, Rath? You could have easily bought a faster ship and a woman to fly her for you."

"You're a friend, Deke. I've got damned few of those, and I look after the ones I do have. Can we take these seats to the new ship? This is really comfortable."

"You're a crazy man, Rathbone the Mechanic. I'll bring the seats over myself."

Over the next two years the hunt for Rathbone intensified, but all to no avail. He was elusive as a breeze, yet as deadly as a hurricane. Lab after lab was destroyed over the three inner sectors. O'Loran's summer home was destroyed, as was his apartment in the city, yet he always seemed to elude his pursuer.

The office was still new and O'Loran fussed in the new chair. He hated these temporary offices. Worse yet, Rathbone had destroyed the new office building before it was halfway up causing another delay. Finding this man was eating up a lot of resources.

O'Loran was not a happy man. A snarl crossed his face as his assistant knocked softly on the glass door. He jerked his head to indicate the man should enter.

"Well, what is it now?"

"Sir, we've lost all control in Sector Nine. The witch has appointed a new viceroy from the Borelian Clans and she is rebuilding Nova Prime."

"How is that possible?"

"Unknown, Sir, but they've managed to cleanse the atmosphere and re-establish a community there."

"We'll have to deal with that, but there are other priorities. What else?"

"Sir, there's a group of mercenaries operating out of Nova Prime. They're tough, efficient, and led by a boy barely out of his teens. Sir, your daughter is on that crew."

"What is that child thinking? First a dispatcher in a war zone and now a merc? Is there any word on the search for that damned assassin?"

"No, Sir, as near as we can determine he's fled. Some say to Sector Five and others say to Sector Nine."

"It'll be Nine. The bastard is going after my daughter. We need a plan to finish that witch, end Nova's rebellion *again*, and bring Brenna home where we can protect her from this madman. Dammit anyway, why is that man not dead? His body should have destroyed itself long ago."

As he settled back into his chair, muttering to himself, his assistant recognized that the meeting was over. He quietly withdrew and closed the office door behind him.

———◦———

NOT FAR AWAY, A FAST ship hung in space, all systems powered down to shield it from prying eyes. Inside Deke and the Rathbones sat reviewing the situation.

Rath shifted uncomfortably in his plush chair. Wordlessly, his grandfather passed him a syringe of pain killers. "What's our next move, Rath?" asked Deke.

"We're done," sighed Rathbone, as he felt the painkillers begin to do their work. "They're tightening security everywhere; we can't get close to anything right now. If I had time, I'd lay low for a few years then go at them again, but I don't believe I do."

"So we just quit?" snorted the elder Rathbone.

"Come on, Poppa, admit it, we're done here for now."

"Yes, I guess we are," sighed the old fellow. "This'll be the first time in forty years I failed to complete a contract. We sure raised hell with them for a while though, didn't we?"

"Indeed, we did," chuckled Rathbone.

"So, what now?" asked Deke.

"Now we split up," said the elder. "You get lost out in Sector Seven. It's nice and peaceful out there and a rich man like you will have a good life. Enjoy your retirement."

"Are you sure about this? Rath?"

"He's right, Deke, you've risked enough. You go on, enjoy your ill-gotten gains and your retirement."

"What will you fellas do?"

"Poppa will leave a false trail for them to follow then disappear into retirement too. I'll head out to the rim in Sector Nine."

"Why Nine?"

"O'Loran's daughter is out there somewhere, and he's lost control of that sector. He'll be sending agents or troops out there so I'll have no loss of possible targets."

"We should go with you, Rath."

"No, Deke. Both of you have a lot of good years left in you, but I don't. I want to see the both of you safely away, then I can go meet my fate with a clear mind."

"Understood. All right then, suit up."

Deke dropped the ship down to the surface of a nearby moon and landed near a jumble of giant boulders. The two Rathbones hugged and said a sad goodbye, each knowing he'd never see the other again, then they donned space suits and left the ship.

The two figures walked to the hidden one-man speeders and climbed aboard. Soon three ships rose from the moon's cold surface and shot out into space, each going in a different direction.

Rathbone grunted as he eased the pain in his shoulders. There wasn't a lot of room in the speeder, but it would do. "Well, Gen, looks like it's just you and me now," Rathbone said to the ghost of his dead companion. Talking to her as though she were beside him always seemed to ease the pain. He'd talk to her a lot in the months that followed.

Brenna

Rathbone sat on the floor of his cave hideaway, his mind foggy with the pain. He'd been without the drugs for a while and was having trouble. "This could be it, Gen. It's getting pretty bad. Maybe here on this barren rock is where we'll finally be reunited." As usual he got no response, nor did he want one. It was just comforting to talk to her.

The cave was littered with bits and pieces of technology he'd salvaged or stolen. His food was long gone, but he managed to survive by hunting and stealing food from nearby farms. That was wearing thin though. He knew he'd soon have to leave this area, but he'd need to find a transport. Rathbone wasn't about to leave all these weapons behind if he could help it.

Suddenly the sounds of a ship close by reached his enhanced hearing. Snatching up a weapon, he bolted outside. A ship was landing nearby, a ship of military design. He ran toward it. R.I.M. soldiers meant targets and perhaps even a fast ship.

Reaching a vantage point, Rathbone took out field glasses and checked it out. There were soldiers setting up a field camp. By the speed of their movements he knew they were cyborgs. "So, some of you escaped, or that bastard has made more of you. We can't have that, now can we, Gen?"

As he passed the glasses over the soldiers on the flats below Rathbone saw a familiar face. "Jorge? Jorge, you damned fool, what have you done to yourself? Don't worry, Gen; I won't shoot your baby brother unless I have to. Maybe we should get closer and see what these buggers are up to."

Slowly, carefully, he worked his way closer until he could hear their conversation. He listened for a while then carefully withdrew. "O'Loran's daughter. Well I'll be damned, Gen. These lads will bring her right to us. We just got lucky."

Rathbone returned to his cave for a long-range projectile weapon with a powerful scope. He then sought out a vantage point. He had to move several times as they shifted their camp several miles away. Obviously they didn't want O'Loran's daughter to see a Company ship.

It was two long days of waiting before the second ship landed. Rathbone watched through the scope, waiting for his target to show herself. When she did, he got a shock. It was his Gen. In the moment it took him to process what he had seen, the woman exploded into action.

Rathbone watched in admiration for a few moments until the woman was captured. He nodded his head and slipped away from his vantage point as the second ship rose into the air.

"I think we should go back and pay a visit to that ship the soldier boys landed in. They marched quite a way to meet this girl. They didn't want the second ship to see it for some reason. Let's go see why, Gen."

THE SMALL DARK WOMAN sat quietly, not fighting her bonds. There was no point; she was surrounded by over twenty hard faced soldiers. These weren't the ragged soldiers of the endless tribal wars of Sector Nine. These were well fed, well trained, and well equipped troops wearing crisp new uniforms of the R.I.M. Company; professional soldiers. They were also cyborgs, men who had been greatly enhanced with powerful mechanical implants.

Such things had been illegal for generations. Obviously someone in a position of authority had decided it was time to revive the practice. Brenna had strong suspicions about who'd sent them, but why had they attacked her instead of approaching as normal envoys?

She felt certain she would soon be freed for, by this time, there would be an angry witch and a crew of super enhanced mercenaries on her trail. She needed to gather as much information as possible before Lessa arrived. Her reverie was broken as she sensed the eyes upon her.

Brenna looked up to see the commander watching her, studying her. As their eyes met he arose from the ground and approached, stopping just outside her reach. He had a blaster in his hand. "Do you fear me so much that you need a blaster, even though I'm bound hand and foot?"

"I do not fear you, Miss O'Loran, but I'm a cautious man. You killed three of the finest soldiers in the Company's employ, men with families. Those families are now without resource."

"You attacked me; I defended myself. When I'm attacked I don't take time to consider the fate of my attacker's children should he be killed. Why didn't you just approach and introduce yourself? Had you done so your men might still be alive."

"My orders are to bring you in, unharmed, but I was told you'd resist."

"You were told the truth, Commander. I assume my father sent you, and it was his agents who brought the tale that called Lessa away from Nova just as I was summoned here. She'll come for me, but then, that's the real plan isn't it? Your orders were to bring me back after you've killed Lessa."

"You're a very astute woman, Miss O'Loran. I'll never gamble at cards with you."

"Sorry, Commander, but that game is already in progress; you dealt the first hand yourself." He studied her for a moment longer then grunted and walked away.

Another man soon approached and stood facing her from a safe distance. He also was holding a blaster. "Are you afraid of me as well?" The man made no sound, nor did he give any indication he had heard her at all. Brenna studied him for a moment before she spoke again.

Squirming to loosen her tunic enough to show a bit of cleavage, Brenna gave the young soldier a smile that nearly melted his knees. "Won't you even tell me your name, Handsome?"

He didn't respond but swallowed hard and blushed. The bulge in his trousers showed clearly that she had his attention. "These bonds are too tight; can't you loosen them just a tiny bit?"

The soldier swallowed hard and took a step toward her. The woman was so incredibly beautiful, and it had been so long... "Hextall!" That was the commander; he too had seen the effect Brenna had on the young soldier. "Relieved!" The man turned and walked away; his face still crimson. The commander made a signal and another soldier approached.

Brenna watched as he took up his post, then sat and smiled at her. Brenna shrugged her shoulders, and her tunic went back into place. "So, you prefer the company of men and will be immune to my charms, is that the idea?"

His laugh was rich and genuine. "Oh, you are the perceptive one, aren't you? Yes, you're quite right about that. Now, since you're in such a talkative mood, talk to me for a while. You're trying to gain information, and so am I, so let the games begin."

"Shall we play a game of questions then?"

"As long as a refusal is considered an answer, I agree."

"Agreed. I'm Brenna of Nova, who are you?"

"I'm Dav of Elliston. What are you?"

"A deep question, Dav, elaborate."

"You killed three highly skilled and greatly enhanced soldiers. A normal woman couldn't do that. What are you?"

"I'm a Dispatcher. I used the tools of my trade to defend myself against attack. Now it's my turn. How did such a sweet boy get mixed up with these ruffians?"

"I have certain skills," he grinned. "Why did you break your oath?"

"I've broken no oath. Of what oath do you speak?"

"Your oath of dispatch. You used the tool of dispatch to take the lives of three men who didn't ask for passage. How could you do that?"

He was stunned at the change in her as she answered, the coquette vanished and a stone cold warrior was looking back at him. Involuntarily he shrank away from her as she replied. The ice in her voice and the hardness of her eyes sent a shiver up his spine.

"I learned my trade on the battlefields of Kora Six. It's my duty to grant a painless and respectful death to those who desire and need it. I will also grant passage to any who lay unfriendly hands upon me. Those three were not the first; I doubt they'll be the last. I'm a Novan Dispatcher; my oath also requires me to use any means available to defend myself. That is what I am. I broke no oath."

"This is Sector Nine. Did you think war here would be as pretty and sanitary as training camp on Elliston?" Brenna had seen the shift in him as well and understood his place in the troops. He was the interrogator, highly skilled at gaining information without seeming to do so.

There was a harsh remark on his lips, but he bit it back. "No, I guess it isn't. Tell me, how is it you can move with such speed and skill, yet you have no enhancements? If you did our instruments would have shown them."

"I studied the ways of personal combat with a great master. There are more ways to enhance skills than with forbidden technology."

"The tech's no longer forbidden, thanks to CEO O'Loran. Who's your skills master?"

"His name shall remain a mystery. The other companies went along with this?"

"There are only two others left, R.I.M. has absorbed the rest. Those two fear a hostile takeover so they made no opposition. Where does he hold his classes?"

"Classes were held on the farm on Kora Six. It was bombed out of existence by the Arlen invaders. Tell me, how do you fools expect to overcome Lessa?"

"There'll be no need, the witch is already dead."

Further conversation was stopped as a man hurried into the camp. "Report," barked the commander, swiftly rising to his feet. The others had already moved into defensive positions.

"The ship is damaged beyond repair, the fighter ships as well, and the two guards are dead, Sir." The man paused as he struggled for breath. He had obviously run a long way. "We're stuck on this rock until we can find another way off."

"So, do you still think she is dead?" Brenna smiled cruelly at Dav and again he shrank back from her. "Here's some friendly advice for you, Dav, get as far away from here as you can as quickly as you can. Abandon your post and companions, for they're already doomed, just run for your life." Brenna lay back on the hard ground and closed her eyes.

Realizing the conversation was finished, Dav returned to the commander to report. "Well?"

"She's a Novan Dispatcher, her oath requires her to defend herself at all cost any way she can. She has studied the arts, but didn't say with whom. She spent two years on the battlefields, and I get the impression she's seen more work than most dispatchers do in a lifetime. She believes the witch is still alive."

"Your impressions?"

"She's old O'Loran's daughter all right. She's a stone cold warrior as well as an exceptionally beautiful woman. She'll use all her skills as well as her feminine wiles to escape us, and she'll kill any or all of us in a heartbeat if she gets the chance."

"I see. Marx, move her into the shade then watch her, but stay out of her reach."

"Sir." The soldier walked over and gently lifted Brenna into his arms and moved her into the shade. He laid her carefully on the hard ground. She hadn't opened her eyes or made a sound. He moved off a bit then sat watching her carefully.

The commander was busy organizing his troops. "What killed the guards at the ship?"

"Unknown, Sir, but they put up one hell of a fight. There was blood and damage everywhere. The camp was trashed in the battle. Whoever or whatever it was it took the food and weapons then disabled the ship."

"How bad is it?"

"Some small, but vital engine parts are missing as well as some important pieces of the command console. We can probably rig something for a console, but we need those engine parts."

"Options?"

"There's a town about five days hard march to the north. We might be able to get parts there."

"Take Morse and Hextall with you. We'll go back to the ship and try to keep it in one piece until you return."

The three men trotted away without a backward glance. The rest gathered their gear and prepared to leave. They didn't know, couldn't know, that Death stalked them. Rathbone was on their trail; he'd stalk and kill all stragglers. He wouldn't allow them to get off planet. They were O'Loran's pride and joy, the last of the cyborg program. He'd finish destroying that program.

The commander approached Brenna. "I know you're not sleeping, Miss O'Loran. We're moving out, you can run with us, or you can be carried. Choose." She didn't move or show any indication she had heard him. "Carried then." He ground his teeth as he turned and signalled for one large man to carry her.

Brenna was a small woman, fifty kilos of body-weight at best, but it was another fifty kilos they'd have to carry, and that would put an extra drain on the men's strength. The commander knew this and so did she. She also knew he had orders to bring her back to Elliston unharmed. They had to be careful with her. Brenna had no such restrictions.

The big man scooped her up with ease and tossed her across his shoulder. He had huge shoulders, and she wasn't all that uncomfortable. His stride was fairly smooth, and her mind slipped back to how she'd been taken.

Brenna and her lover, Arlessa, high priestess of Nova, had been having tea at the newly built temple on Nova Prime when two ships had landed nearby. One was a larger freighter and the other a small rundown mail hauler. The freighter brought news of a group of Novan mercenaries pinned down and being pressed hard by Arlen troops in the last of the trade wars. The mail ship brought a farmer who told of an old woman in great pain, her bones broken, who begged for a dispatcher.

Reluctantly, Arlessa had agreed to take her crew of mercenaries and bring the Novans to safety while Brenna went with the mail carrier. "Brenna, I don't like this, it feels wrong. I don't like the idea of being parted from you."

"Nor I, my love, but I can't see an old woman suffer if I can help. If I can't heal her injuries, I will ease her passing to the next life. Be careful and return to me as swiftly as you can."

They had embraced and reluctantly parted, Lessa and her crew boarding their ships to follow the freighter while Brenna had climbed onto the mail carrier. Three days later she had descended to find herself on the wrong planet, surrounded by soldiers. One reached out and grabbed her by the shoulder.

She'd moved faster than they had expected. Brenna dropped to the ground and spun away from him, stinging him as she fell. He fell without a sound. Two more pounced on her at frightening speed, trying to haul her to her feet. As fast as they were, she easily matched their speed.

Using their strength as leverage, she leaped high in the air. Stinging them as she leaped, she turned a backward somersault and landed behind them. Even as they fell dead to the ground, she had been seized from behind and her arms pinned at her sides.

Brenna had been swiftly bound, hand and foot, and placed in the dirt beside the three men she'd killed. A dispatcher uses an injection of swift and deadly poison to relive a person of their pain and then their life. The passage is swift, taking mere seconds. There was a syringe stuck in each of the three dead bodies. Brenna lay beside them, a prisoner.

Brenna's reverie was broken as she was lowered gently to the ground. "You all right, Miss?" the big man's voice was gentle, just as his handling of her had been.

"Yes, thank you. You're a good man; you should run now while you can. She'll come and she won't be gentle."

"I can't, Miss, but thanks for the warning." He smiled at her then walked away.

"What's your name, Soldier?"

He paused and turned to face her again. "I'm Jorge, Miss."

"You really should run, Jorge." He smiled sadly then walked away, wishing he dared to take her advice. Another man came to watch.

Brenna sat thinking, what could she do now? She had to do everything she could to harass these men, to keep them off balance, create discord, doubt, and to gain further information. She remembered how she'd first met Lessa. Even as a prisoner Lessa had kept pressure on her captor. Brenna had been terrified at the time, but that was long ago, and she'd been quite young and naïve then; not anymore. Two years of working at a field hospital in a war zone had changed all that.

Deciding to take a page from Lessa's book, she called out to the commander.

"What do you want, Miss O'Loran?"

"I need to relieve myself; you have to remove my bonds and allow me privacy."

"Denied," he said flatly, as he turned away from her.

"My father won't be pleased if you allow me to soil myself and be cleaned up by your men."

The commander stopped, his jaw clenched tightly and his shoulders bunched. He muttered a foul oath before turning to face her again. "Fine."

He pulled some rope from a pack on the ground and approached warily. First he tied a harness around her torso then released her bonds. He stood back as she rose and stretched out her aching muscles. "You can go behind those rocks. I'll hold this line snug, so if you try anything I'll know."

"Understood." She went behind the rocks and relieved herself. Oh gods, that felt so good. Brenna dawdled as much as she dared then returned. The commander put the shackles back on her hands and feet then removed the rope harness.

He started to walk away, but her voice stopped him. "Commander."

"What now?"

"Have you a sanitizer for my hands?" With a sigh he pulled one from his pocket and allowed her to use it. She passed it back as soon as she finished and again he started away.

"Commander."

"Now what?" he was clearly annoyed now and Brenna was a bit surprised at how much she was enjoying this game.

"I'm hungry; will you not feed me?"

"Jorge, get her some rations. Maybe the chewing will shut her up."

The big fellow came over with a handful of ration packs and a grin on his face. "These are my favorites, Miss O'Loran. There's lots of protein in them, but enough fiber to keep you from getting backed up, if you know what I mean."

"I do, and thank you, Jorge. Please call me Brenna," she smiled. "Jorge, do you have a mate or children back on Elliston?"

"I do."

"Should the worst happen here, will they have resources?"

"No, I couldn't afford the insurance payments. Are you so sure I can't survive?"

"An entire army couldn't survive Lessa when she's angry, and without me there to help her control the rage, well, I fear the worst for you all. She'll come like an avenging goddess with her hunting hounds at her side. They'll find us and destroy you all. Run away, Jorge, your family needs you."

"Brenna, you know full well what your father would do to me if I deserted," he chuckled. "It was a good try though." With that he rose to leave.

"Jorge, I'll do my best to protect you." He gave her a puzzled smile then walked away. "If I fail I'll see your family has resource."

She lay still, trying to sleep. A tear leaked from her eye and made its way down her cheek. "Lessa, please be alive," she prayed softly, "please come for me."

———◉———

FAR FROM BRENNA AND her captors, a battle was about to erupt. Suddenly a speeder appeared and shot straight at the two fighter ships following the freighter. "Incoming," bawled the pilot as the small missile bore down on them.

The communicator began to crackle on an odd frequency. "Micha, trap! Run!" It was a woman's voice and it spoke only once as it sped by too close for comfort.

"Go!" barked the young leader, and both ships pulled a tight turn that shouldn't have been possible. They pursued the tiny ship at full speed. Once they were turned Micha grabbed the comms. "Kella, respond, Kella."

"Kella here."

"Who?"

"R.I.M. special forces."

"Skeeter." They could only want one or two people. Brenna or Lessa; they probably want to kill Lessa and capture Brenna. "Kella."

"Kella here."

"Is there room in that missile of yours for a passenger?"

"I can take one, Micha."

"Lock up with me." The small ship dropped back and locked to the fighter.

"Be careful, Lessa," he said as she prepared to board the small speeder, "they've probably got her by now. We'll keep the rest off your back as best we can."

"Micha, be careful."

"I will. Go now." The tall woman slipped through the air lock and into the cramped speeder. The locks hissed and it shot away from the two Arcalian ships that turned to fight. There was nothing to engage, just the freighter waiting for them.

"How's our fuel?"

"Both ships were topped up, Boss," grinned the pilot. "Are we going in?"

"I'd really like to see what's going on here. You got anything on instruments?"

"Nothing but the freighter."

"So, where is the war zone we're supposed to be rescuing Novans from?" He picked up the com again. "Zartah, you know this area?"

"Something big is wrong, Boss. There's nothing out here worth fighting over. Should we ask our friends in the freighter?"

Micha was the youngest and most successful crew boss in the sector, for good reason. All the witch's enhancements aside, his crew followed him because they trusted him, and he was lucky. He was also fearless and eminently practical.

"Good idea, Zartah. Watch my back. Keira, jam their comms then put a missile into their engines. Gorda, lock us up with them; I want a word with the captain. As soon as we're aboard, break away; I don't want to be caught off guard."

The freighter tried to run, but a freight hauler is no match for an Arcalian fighter. The engines were shot out and the fighter locked on. Micha and his mate, Edie, dived through the air lock then the fighter broke away.

As they boarded the ship five armed men were waiting, but they came through so fast the men didn't have time to shoot. In less than a heartbeat the defenders were unconscious. The two intruders made their way to the bridge where they encountered more resistance.

The heavy door was shut and braced. Micha slapped an explosive charge on it and turned away. As the door was blasted open Micha and Edie leaped through. A short battle ensued. Moments later three men were kneeling on the floor, their hands clasped behind their heads. The captain was trembling as he stared down the barrel of Micha's gun.

"Tell me who paid you to draw us into a trap."

"What are you talking about?"

"Who is the first man here?"

"I am," replied one of the men on the floor.

Micha's gun flashed and the captain fell. "Now you're captain. Tell me who paid you to draw us into a trap."

"They're Company soldiers," the man stammered.

"How many?"

"At least fifty in five fighter ships."

"Where are they?"

"Behind that next moon. Please don't kill us, we're not soldiers."

"I can see that. Are there lifeboats on this tub?" The man nodded. "Very well Captain, get your men into the lifeboats. I'm commandeering your ship. Take the former captain with you; he'll have quite a headache when he wakes up."

"Wakes up?"

"It was set on stun. Get busy now." While the men hurried away towards the lifeboats, Micha set the controls to continue course on thrusters, then disabled them. Grabbing the com, he called for his own ship.

"Gorda, pick us up now. Zartah, bring your ship in behind the freighter as well. We'll go in with a shield. We're facing Company soldiers, five ships."

"See Gorda, there's always something exciting to do on this crew," Zartah's voice laughed.

"Shut up, Zartah," growled Gorda as he snapped off communications.

A few moments later five ships swept past the freighter, but there was no enemy to engage. The two Arcalian fighters attacked from behind, destroying four instantly. The fifth managed to turn and start firing, but the Arcalian fighters pulled some incredible turns and he was suddenly targeted from both sides. "Surrender or die," commanded a voice over the comm.

"Why are you still alive?" he asked. "The artificial gravity should have ripped you in half trying to keep up with that turn."

For an answer one ship shot off his gun turret. "Last chance."

"I surrender, I surrender."

"Eject, we'll pick you up." The ten men in the crippled ship barely had time to lock their helmets and eject before the two fighters opened fire. They were hauled through the air locks then both ships shot away. The pilot struggled out of his suit, careful of the two hard eyed women training guns on them. A young man, barely more than a boy, was watching him closely.

"Where to, Boss?" asked the fighter's pilot.

"Back to the freighter, Gorda. We'll dump off our passengers then be on our way." The young man hadn't taken his eyes off the captives.

"Aye, Boss, back to the freighter."

"Who is in command here?" ask the youth.

"I am," replied the man in the fancy uniform as he tried to rise to his feet. One of the women kicked the back of his knee and sent him to the floor.

"Who sent you? What were your orders?"

"Commander Orlic of Elliston, 85977469867."

"O'Loran sent you. What were your orders?"

"Commander Orlic of Elliston, 8..."

The boy moved so fast it was hard to see. With one hand he grabbed the man and threw him back into the airlock and then shut the door. "Who is second in command here?" he asked, turning back to the rest of the men. He was all the more terrifying for his complete lack of emotion.

"He's on your other ship," replied one of the men.

"Fine, who among you?"

"Me," replied the man.

"What were your orders?"

"It no longer matters. We were to lure the witch off Nova and destroy her along with her small band of Mercenaries."

"You failed. What else was supposed to happen?"

"There were three groups. One was to capture O'Loran's daughter and take her home. She's probably halfway to Elliston by now. The third group was to destroy everything on Nova."

"Thank you." The young warrior opened the air lock and let the commander back inside. A short time later the men were on the crippled freighter and the two fighters were on their way back to Nova at full speed. Micha relayed a message to the Borelian Command, telling them where to find the freighter. The viceroy and high priestess would have a few questions for the Company soldiers.

———◆———

"THAT WAS A TIMELY WARNING, Kella," said Lessa as she wriggled into position in the tiny speeder. "I must ask, how did you know, and why did you risk warning us?"

"I owe Micha my life, Lady; I will always do whatever I can to repay that. My father learned, through his special channels, that a big freighter from Elliston had slipped past the Borelian Guard. Father made a few less than subtle inquiries and learned that R.I.M. Special Forces were on board with orders to kill you, capture Brenna, and destroy Nova. I grabbed our fastest speeder and ran. I'm just happy I arrived in time."

"As am I, Kella. What else can you tell me?"

"The troops sent to bring Brenna back to Elliston are super soldiers, cyborgs with greatly enhanced abilities. They won't hurt her of course, but they'll be hard to defeat."

"Just get me to her, let me worry about the soldiers."

"Yes, Ma'am, where to?"

"Back to Nova Prime, we'll pick up the trail from there. I'm curious, Kella, your father's reputation would suggest a more prudent man. I'm a bit surprised he wouldn't just stay out of this."

"Father doesn't like newcomers moving into his territory without permission. He also likes being able to haul freight in and out of Nova without having to dodge the authorities or to pay huge bribes," grinned Kella. "He's even talking about retiring to Nova in a few years."

"I'm sure we can arrange something." Lessa fell silent then, reaching out with her mind, trying to find Brenna. She wasn't able to do so. Her lover had been taken from her; the most powerful witch in history was not happy. She knew full well who had taken Brenna. The account she had to settle with CEO O'Loran was growing.

———◦———

WHILE THE WITCH NURSED her fear for her lover and her hatred for O'Loran, Rathbone staunched his fresh wounds and searched the pockets of the three dead men. As soon as he had the painkillers they all carried he injected himself. Gathering up the rest of the painkillers plus the spare parts for the ship, he set out at a run. He had to catch up with the soldiers again.

Castoff

Lessa arrived back on Nova Prime to find the people cleaning up after a battle. There were several small fighter ships down, and it looked like her people were trying to see how many they could salvage. "What happened here?" The words were out of her mouth before her feet hit the ground.

"We were attacked, Priestess." The big fellow was grinning as he stopped work and dropped to one knee. He rose quickly as she signaled for him to come to her.

"I assume Norlene was up to the task."

"Aye, Lady, that she was. The Lady Norlene knocked them down before they could fire a shot. We fought them hand to hand until they were no more."

"Are there any left alive to question?"

"There are a few, but Lady Norlene has them at the temple."

"Kella, will you help me further?"

"Of course, Lady Arlessa, I'll stay with you until Micha can return."

"Thank you, Kella. This fine gentleman here will help you refuel your ship while I see what I can learn at the temple."

There was nothing more to be learned from the captives so Lessa returned to the speeder. They set out after the mail ship at full burn.

BRENNA SLEPT FITFULLY the first night, and spent much of the next day trying to drive her captors crazy. They'd come expecting to capture a spoiled rich girl, and that's what she was giving them. They knew what she was doing, but it still irritated them.

The day was nearly done before they reached the ship. The area had been a battleground. Two battered and mangled corpses testified to that. The commander set a detail to burying the two dead soldiers. Another man was sent to scout about and see what he could find. It was the third morning before he returned.

"Report."

"One man approached from the south and engaged the guards. He killed them and disabled the ship. I found where he camped and waited."

"Waited?"

"Yes, when our man returned and found the damage he went to report. The killer followed. When the men left for the town, he followed again. I signalled to warn them but got no reply."

"We must assume they were out of range. Only one-man, what sort of man could do this?"

"Perhaps a cast off, Sir?" suggested the tracker.

The commander's shoulders slumped. "They should all be dead by now."

"One escaped in a garbage scow a few years ago, so they say."

"Until right now I never believed that," sighed the commander. "There's only one man who could have done that and survived this long."

"Rathbone of Urn, but even if he survived, how could he have gotten way out here in Sector Nine?"

"I don't know, soldier, but we must assume it's him. There's no time now to wait for repairs to this ship, we'll have to find another."

"Sir, do we have enough funds to buy another ship?" asked one of the other men.

"No. We'll commandeer a ship and get off this rock as quickly as possible."

"What of Hextall and the others?"

"We'll meet them on the way if they're still alive. Break camp." He strode over to Brenna and spoke. "Miss O'Loran, we have no more time for your games. Your survival is at stake here as well as our own."

Brenna rose to her feet in spite of her bonds. "If you want me to run with you my bonds must be removed. I can't run or defend myself when I'm bound."

"I'll release your legs, but your hands will remain bound."

"I can run much faster and farther with my hands free, you know this to be true."

"Swear that you won't try to escape and put yourself in danger."

"I swear I will do all in my power to remain alive, safe, and to return to my home."

"On Nova?"

"Yes."

"It's already been destroyed. Your hands remain in shackles." He turned and stalked away.

Jorge soon appeared and released her leg bonds. He tied a rope from her waist to his belt and smiled. "You'll be able to keep up if I pull you along a bit." On a barked command they all set out.

A cyborg can run fast and for a long time. It was a surprise to the commander that Brenna was keeping up and wasn't tiring at all. She almost seemed to be at ease. With a snarl he picked up the pace.

By the third day Brenna wasn't keeping up so easily. She was tiring, but so were the men. It seemed the human parts couldn't keep up with the machine parts. They finally slowed to a walk about noon. An hour later they found the bodies of the three men. Two had been shot cleanly and the third had died in a bloody hand to hand battle. The commander gathered the ID tags and the men buried their dead.

They moved a short way from the battle scene then made camp for the night. When they awakened in the morning, Brenna was gone. Her boots were still in the leg shackles, but she was nowhere to be found.

———⊛———

MILES AWAY BRENNA WAS struggling. She had complained about her bonds being too tight so they'd loosened them slightly. Darkness fell; she rolled on her back, put her feet up on a rock, and went to sleep. Brenna knew this uncomfortable position would do two things for her. It would only let her sleep a short while and it would drain the swelling from her legs caused by a day on the run.

She awakened to pain in her back and rolled quietly from the rock. Her shackles were no longer tight, and Brenna was able to wriggle out of her boots. With her legs now free she crept silently away from the camp. She waited a long time near the outer guard, waiting for him to need to relieve himself. Her patience was rewarded.

Finally the man stood and stepped away from his hiding place. At the sound of the zipper she made her escape. Brenna was well out of sight by the time he returned to his position. Barefoot, she ran on through the night, stumbling often, but always regaining her feet to run on.

Rathbone

B renna hid herself in a clump of tall grasses, screened slightly by a jumble of rock. Breathing deeply, she winced as she inspected her torn feet. Perhaps she should have carried the boots and seen if she could get the shackles off them. Too late now, with her feet torn and bleeding, all she could do was wait for them to re-capture her again. Hopefully this would delay them long enough for Lessa to catch up. She couldn't bring herself to believe that Lessa had been killed.

"You should probably keep moving," said a deep voice behind her.

Brenna spun around, bracing her back tightly against a rock. There was a huge man squatting on the ground. He was armed to the teeth and had obviously been in battle recently. There were several wounds crudely bandaged, blood dried in a number of places on his fatigues, and a look of pain in his eyes. He wasn't actually looking at her, but scanning her back trail with those dark eyes.

"Who are you?"

"Rathbone of Urn."

"That's an unusual name."

"We're an unusual folk, we people of Urn. Who're you?"

"Brenna of Nova, companion to Arlessa, dispatcher and teacher."

"Long name, how about I just call you Brenna?"

She chuckled at that. "Fair enough. May I ask a question?"

"Sure."

"Are you going to kill me?"

"I did consider that when I first heard them say you are old O'Loran's daughter. After I watched you drop three of them, and then drive the rest crazy for days, I thought better of it."

"Oh?"

"It seems we have a common purpose, at least in the short term. We can help each other."

"And after that?"

"Go our separate ways."

"Forgive me, Rathbone, if I mistrust that."

"Understood, but it's time for you to take a leap of faith. Your hands are bound, you're barefoot, your feet are in bad shape, and your former captors are coming. Will you let me carry you to safety where we can discuss a better plan than getting re-captured?"

Brenna turned her gaze to where he was looking. The soldiers were still a long way off, but they were moving swiftly. Her time was up. She nodded her head in agreement and he swiftly knelt beside her. A quick pass of a laser knife and her bonds parted. "Climb onto my back. I can run faster with you on my back than I can with you in my arms."

"And they won't shoot at us because they dare not harm me," she said as she climbed onto his broad back.

"Exactly." Tucking his arms under her knees he leaped away at terrifying speed.

Brenna clung to his back as he ran. He was moving faster than even she could run, and she doubted the soldiers could ever catch him, but how long could he keep it up?

She could feel him beginning to tire when a wide chasm loomed ahead. Her eyes widened in horror as he picked up one last burst of speed. Launching himself skyward at the edge of the ravine, a screaming Brenna clinging to his back, Rathbone sailed through the air to the other side.

His feet landed on the edge then slipped back over the loose stones. Flinging his arms forward he managed to stop their slide into the abyss below. "Climb over me."

Brenna willingly obeyed. As soon as she reached solid ground she turned. He was slipping. Bracing her poor battered feet against a rock, she leaned forward and grasped the collar of his tunic and heaved with all her might. It was enough. He scrambled and rolled up beside her. "Climb on," he gasped, as he struggled to his knees, his heaving lungs fighting for more air. "Quickly. No time."

Brenna climbed onto his back once again. He levered himself to his feet then staggered away toward a large outcropping of jumbled rock. A few moments later they rounded a boulder and were well out of sight of their crossing. Rathbone slowed to a walk and soon entered a cave where he knelt so she could descend to the ground. "Welcome to my humble abode on this god forsaken rock."

The cave was dry and a fair size, filled with bits and pieces of technology salvaged from who-knows-what. One wall had a tidy space set up as sleeping and eating area. It actually looked fairly comfortable. "Sit, rest. Here's water and food."

"R.I.M. rations?"

"Compliments of your former hosts. Your dispatch kit and med kit are over there. Your feet are pretty banged up; I'll bring the kits." He stepped away, gathered the two kits and returned, setting them gently on the ground beside her.

"You trust me with my kit, even though you've seen me use it to kill innocents?"

"Point number one: they weren't innocents. They attacked you and you defended yourself. I'd have done the same. Point number two: I've lived the past five years with pain. It grows worse with each passing day and I don't expect to last much longer anyway. Put me down if you need to. It'll only bring relief."

Brenna set aside her dispatch kit and opened the med kit. "Let me start by cleaning those wounds." He sighed deeply and removed his tunic. His torso was heavily muscled and a mass of scars, some old, some new and red looking still. There were open wounds as well. Brenna set to work cleaning and bandaging him up.

"That's a fine job, Brenna," he smiled. The pain never left his eyes, yet he smiled. Brenna liked this man.

"I was a medic first," she replied softly as she turned her attention to her feet. "I trained in a field hospital as a medic."

"But what they needed more was a dispatcher, right?"

"Right. No one would take the job so I did. I couldn't just watch those people die slowly in excruciating pain if I could help them."

"You see lots of action?"

"Over two years of battlefield action."

"That'll change a person."

"It did. How about you? What happened to you? What is causing the pain?"

"Now that's a bit of a story."

"I have time."

"All right," he chuckled. "I was raised and trained on Urn by my grandfather, a professional assassin. He expected me to go into the same line of work, but I had other ideas. I love tinkering. If it has moving parts, I can fix it. I left home and joined the military, becoming a fighter ship mech-tech. I chose a companion and she bore a daughter. Life was good for a number of years, and then it all went to hell."

"Tell me."

"My companion and daughter contracted some sort of rare disease. The cost of the medications was out of this universe. I couldn't afford it and was frantic. A man came and told me about this new program. Volunteer for the cyborg implants and they'd pay all the expenses for Gen and Ari. I signed up.

"They went overboard on the first nine of us. The implants were too strong. Three of the guys tore themselves apart, two more died within a week and they terminated the rest."

"You escaped."

"Grandfather's training came in handy that day. I fought my way clear and escaped on a garbage scow. On the refuse planet I managed to build a small ship from bits and pieces, but it took years to do it. By the time I got back to my home on Urn, Gen and Ari were long since dead. They'd never been given any medication. They died shortly after I volunteered. I fled Urn and eventually found myself here."

"Why did you attack the soldiers?"

"Those men represent the people who killed my family and tried to kill me. Any chance I get to hurt the Company, I'll take. I slipped in close when I first spotted them. I overheard them talking about capturing old O'Loran's daughter and hauling her spoiled ass home where she belongs. O'Loran's Company killed my daughter, so I thought I'd kill his.

"I had you in my sights when suddenly you took down three cyborgs. That was impressive. I decided to see what would happen, so I spied on you. My grandfather would be proud of you, Brenna."

"Oh?"

"If you're captured, keep your captor under stress as much as possible, wear him down, and never let him rest. That's what he taught me, and that's what I saw you doing. I slipped back with the notion of disabling the ship to keep them here until I could get you away from them."

"What do you plan to do with me now?"

"I need to know what you want to happen here. If we can work together at a common purpose we have a better chance of success. So, are your feet feeling any better?"

"Yes, they are, thanks; but I won't be doing any running for a while. All right, what I want to happen here is to stay away from those men until Lessa can come for me. How are your wounds?"

"Much better, Brenna. You're a good medic. I think we can manage that, but I'd also like to know what else they're up to."

"So would I, but Lessa will get that out of them once she gets here. We just have to keep them busy and on this planet until she arrives."

"Are you so sure she's still alive?"

"Oh yes, she's alive. When we first joined, Lessa cast a spell on us. She always knows how I'm feeling and I know the same about her. Somewhere out there is the most powerful witch in history, she's angry, she's losing control of her temper, and she's hunting for me."

"All right, so the object of the game here is to keep them busy for a while. We can do that, but we need to keep moving."

"Rathbone, what do you want to have happen here?"

He winced slightly, in pain, as he sank down beside her. Laying his head back against the cavern wall for a moment, he paused before speaking. "If we're going to succeed here, there can't be any secrets between us, Brenna. I'll tell you the truth. Best case scenario is I kill them all, take their ship back to Elliston where O'Loran will welcome it. I then use that ship to blow him to hell and back."

"You'd be shot down long before you got that chance."

"I know, but I'd rather go out in a blaze of futile glory than be torn apart by my own body."

"Lessa may be able to help you with that. She's a healer above all else."

"Her reputation would lead a man to believe otherwise."

"Perhaps, but reputations can be deceiving."

"Like your father's?"

"That's a sad and heartbreaking story. When I was a small child, he was always loving and gentle with me. In the end, our views on the social welfare of the galactic populations came between us. Only after I arrived in Sector Nine and learned of the genocide on Nova Prime did I understand the reach of his convictions. I won't try to hinder you, Rathbone. Neither will I help you in that."

"Understood and accepted. Can we work together?"

"I think so, but considering the condition I'm in right now, it is you who'll be doing all the work."

He chuckled at that. "You sound just like Gen."

THE SPEEDER CLOSED on the fleeing mail carrier ship like a striking falcon. Pulling alongside the aging craft and matching speed, Kella reached for the communicator. "Mail carrier Argus, slow your rotation. We'll lock on."

"No." The reply was short, but the voice sounded fearful. The captain had an idea who might be in that small ship, and he wanted only to be anywhere she was not.

"Look at your screen, Captain. Do you see the woman with the tattoos? Do you know who this is?"

"Yes." He was terrified now.

Lessa moved closer to the screen and spoke. Her voice left no room for argument or dissension. "Slow your rotation if you wish to survive."

"Yes, Lady." The ship's rotation slowed and the speeder locked on.

The air lock hissed open and Lessa slipped through. She was instantly hit with a blast of energy from a high powered pulse weapon. Anyone else would have been killed instantly; Lessa staggered, but remained on her feet.

She thrust out her hand and the man screamed in pain as the weapon burst into flame, severely burning his hands. A twist of her hand and his clothing caught fire. He screamed again, but she closed her fingers tightly and the flames vanished. Her hand flew open again and he was hurled against the bulkhead where he hung in the air.

"Where is she?" That voice was deep, filled with hate and rage, and clearly not the voice of a human woman.

"Not here," he gasped out.

"I know that. Where did you leave her? Speak."

That terrible voice sent waves of fear and pain through his body, and he whimpered as he answered her. "PX19. They were waiting on PX19."

"Your hands are ruined, and your eyes no longer see." At that dread pronouncement his world went dark and he fell to the deck, whimpering in fear.

Lessa stepped past him and made her way to the bridge. A quick scan of the ship's auto log showed her the co-ordinates on PX19. She sent them to Kella then returned to the loading bay where the hapless man lay on the floor.

"I will contact the Borelian Guard; they'll come for you." With that she turned and slipped gracefully back through the air lock.

The speeder peeled away from the mail carrier and hurtled off into space. Lessa sent her message to the Borelian officials as they sped towards PX19. It had taken far too long to catch that mail carrier, for he'd changed his route in an attempt to escape. She didn't expect to find Brenna on PX19, but she hoped to pick up the trail.

Lessa closed her eyes and focused her mind. She sent a message to Brenna with all the strength she had. "I'm coming, my love."

⟶◉⟵

THE TWO ARCALIAN FIGHTER ships touched down lightly. Norlene strode towards them as the crew dropped to the ground. The crew set about refueling the ships and replenishing their weapons and supplies while Micha conferred with Norlene.

"She's nearly out of control, Micha," sighed Norlene. "Without Brenna or you there to help her stay focused, the gods alone know what she might do. You have to catch up to Lessa and take control of this situation."

"That's not going to be possible, Lady. There is no way our fighters can catch that damned speeder. We need a better plan."

"I'm open to suggestions."

"Our best chance is to find Miss O'Loran first. If we can retrieve her unharmed, Lessa will be fine."

"And if you can't, Arlessa will probably head straight to Elliston and blow it to hell. Go ahead, Micha. May your hunt be successful."

"Yes, Lady. Gorda, Zartah, join us."

The two men approached, Gorda giving Norlene a smile and a wink. That gesture wasn't lost on Micha. "These are dangerous times, Lady Norlene. Shall I leave Gorda here to protect you while we're gone?"

Norlene grinned as she pointed a threatening finger at him. "Be very careful, Young Micha, it is dangerous to tease a witch."

"What's the plan, Boss?" Gorda was grinning and Norlene gave him a playful poke in the ribs.

"We'll never catch Kella's speeder; we need to find Brenna. How would you have planned this if you were the ones after her?"

"Well," mused Gorda, "they used a mail carrier as the bait, so they'll know the mail route won't be safe. They need to take her alive and get her back to Elliston Prime. I'd guess they'd have the carrier veer off the standard route; drop her at some remote spot. What do you think, Zartah?"

"Northern hemisphere of PX19?"

"That would be my best guess. They won't want her on the mail carrier any longer than necessary; they want her in custody. PX19 is the closest. There's nothing in the north except a few scattered dirt towns and the odd farm."

"PX19 it is, let's go." With that Micha leaped towards the ships where the rest of his crew was waiting. The ships rose from the ground in moments.

Cat and Mouse

+

Brenna had slept fitfully for a few hours, but the pain in her feet kept waking her. Finally, Rathbone roused her. "We'd best be on the move, Brenna. How are your feet doing?"

"I can walk." She stood up and took a few painful steps, her badly swollen feet protesting at carrying her weight.

"We won't outrun many folks at that speed." He grinned in spite of the pain in his body. "Climb on." He knelt so she could climb onto his back again.

Rathbone swept up an old-fashioned projectile weapon as he left the cave. He walked swiftly away from the cavern, always stepping on hard rock to hide his passage.

"Should we swing back towards their ship, Rathbone?"

"No, they'll be expecting that. They've probably booby trapped it by now. No, there's a small dirt farm nearby. We might be able to get boots for you there, provided they don't shoot me on sight."

"Shoot you on sight? You've been there before?"

"A man gets hungry, and when they won't share food, nor barter it..."

"You steal it. Did you kill any of them?"

"Of course not, woman. Dead farmers can't produce more food. Angry farmers can be a problem though. Here's a good spot to take a look and see if our friends are on our trail yet."

He knelt. Brenna slid off his back and stood, working the kinks out of her back. Rathbone took the binoculars from his belt and scanned the open lands behind them. Suddenly he froze, muttered something, and reached for the projectile weapon. "These guys are

50

good, and they probably know who they're tracking. I've got to slow them down a bit."

"Are you going to kill some of them?"

"No, only wound them. Wound one man badly and another has to slow down to help him. That removes two from the chase."

He was resting the long barrel of the rifle on a rock and sighting carefully. Brenna watched through the field glasses as the soldiers came on swiftly, one man fixated on the ground before them and the rest watching the terrain for ambush. They were good. Then the rifle barked beside her, and a split second later the tracker fell to the ground clutching his leg. The rest dived for cover.

"That should slow them down a bit. Shall we press on?" Brenna climbed back to her perch on his back and away he went.

Rathbone had changed directions several times, always keeping to the rocks and hard packed ground. It was well into the afternoon by the time he stopped to rest. Brenna was amazed at the man's stamina, but also concerned about the pain in his eyes. There was blood seeping out of one of his wounds and she began to dab at it with her shirt.

"There's no time for that now, Gen. Sorry. Brenna." He sighed as he gently pushed her hand away. "The farm is near, and we need a plan."

"Show me the way to the farm, give me something to trade with, and then stay here and rest until I return."

"Oh, stay here, just like that?"

"Listen, mister, you're injured, and you've been carrying me all day. Your wound has reopened, and you're exhausted. You asked me to take a leap of faith with you; now you have to trust me. Those farmers want to shoot you. It's better if I go in alone."

He gazed into her eyes for a moment then chuckled. "Yes, Ma'am. I'll wait right here. Take this to trade." He passed her a bag with several small sugar packets in it.

"Sugar?"

"A rare and expensive item around these parts. It's about all we have unless I trade some of our weapons. I'd rather keep those."

"Agreed. Which way?"

"Up this hill to that rock outcropping. There's a well-worn path on the other side that will take you into the small valley and the farm hidden there."

"You're not really going to stay here, are you?"

"No, but I'll keep this place in sight and watch for your return."

"And if I don't come back?"

"I'll find you." He was grinning and she just shook her head and smiled.

Brenna set out slowly. She had makeshift sandals on her battered feet, but walking was painful, and she made slow progress. The sun was setting as she found the farm.

Three huge dogs spotted her instantly and charged, barking furiously. Brenna froze and didn't make eye contact with them. She knew she had only one chance here, for there was no way to outrun those beasts. The dogs reached her and began snuffling her all over. Eventually she felt a lick on her hand and gently began to scratch behind a floppy ear.

A man appeared from the house and began shouting for the dogs. He was armed with a primitive projectile weapon. "Get away from here. We don't want strangers on our land."

"I'd be happy to, but I can't walk much further. My feet are badly blistered, and I have no boots."

"Why not?"

"I'll be happy to tell my story over a meal."

"No, get away."

"I have sugar. I'll trade for boots and a meal."

"Did you say you have sugar?" asked a woman, as she stepped out of the house.

"Yes."

"Hiram…"

"Dammit, Meg, last time you talked me into bringing in a stranger, he stole half the farm."

"She's only small, Hiram, and she's not armed. She's hurt and she has sugar, she's coming in the house." She marched past him, pushing aside the weapon as she did. "I'm Meg," she said as she reached Brenna.

"Brenna," she smiled, accepting the offered hand.

"Come on girl, lean on Meg and we'll get you inside where it's warm." Brenna leaned against the woman's strong arm and hobbled along beside her. In a few moments she was seated by a warm fire, a mug of hot soup in her hand.

"Let's take a look at those feet," said Meg, as she knelt before Brenna, carefully unwrapping the bandages. Some of the blisters were bleeding again. "Hmm, I've got just the thing for this. You wait right here. She hurried away, but soon returned with a jar of salve which she began to spread on Brenna's feet.

Brenna winced once or twice, but the salve was cool and refreshing. "It's numbweed; it'll heal you right up by morning. Hiram, she's pretty small. Perhaps an old pair of Lian's boots will fit her."

"Hmm," he muttered. "We'll take a look in the morning."

A number of people had gathered for the evening meal, men, women, and children as well as the three dogs that lay down by Brenna's side. Meg helped Brenna to the table then began to serve the food. This was a poor farm, but the fare was hearty enough. "You'll want this, Meg," smiled Brenna, as she passed the bag of sugar packets to the farm wife.

"My gods, Brenna, you can't give us all of that," gasped Meg as she dumped the pile of precious packets out on the table. "That's worth two year's harvest."

"Take it all, good people, just remember, I need those boots. I have to get going."

"Stay the night, girl," said Hiram. "It's dark out now and it'll be morning before your feet have healed."

"There are men following me, Hiram. They won't harm me, but I don't know if I can protect you from them."

"Men? What sort of men?" asked Meg.

"Soldiers of R.I.M. Company. Super soldiers."

"Hmm, we've met one of them already, the thieving bastard," said Hiram. "What do they want with you, did you steal the sugar?"

"No, the sugar was given to me to trade for boots. They were sent to capture me and take me back to Elliston."

"You don't want to go back," grinned Meg. "Wanted by the law?"

"In a manner of speaking, but I won't go willingly. My mate will come looking for me. If she comes, you must tell her the complete truth. She won't harm you if you do."

"Harm us? Is she a witch or something?"

"Yes, Meg, she's Arlessa, high priestess of Nova Prime."

"The Black Witch herself," breathed Hiram and everyone at the table made the sign to ward off evil.

"Yes, and there are others. A band of mercenaries may be with her, or they may come on their own. They're led by a young man, barely more than a boy. Never lie to him and he'll treat you well, but don't anger him or Arlessa. It is too dangerous."

"Just who are you, young miss. Why are so many dangerous people looking for you?"

Brenna sighed and sat back in her chair. She looked down as she scratched a dog behind the ear for a moment. These folk had been kind to her and she didn't want them in danger.

"I'm Brenna O'Loran, hand mate of Arlessa of Nova, and daughter of R.I.M. CEO O'Loran."

Hiram gave a long slow whistle. "Well I declare, Meg, look what you've done now. You've brought the Angel of Death into our home."

Brenna looked up at that. "I haven't been called that since Kora Six. Were you there?"

"My younger brother was there. The man who brought news of his death described you and the gentle kindness you showed as you gave Walt release from his pain. You're welcome here, Dispatcher."

"Thank you, Hiram, but there are dangerous men after me and I won't bring their wrath down upon you. You've tended my hurts, fed me well, and with decent boots so I can walk, I'll leave and take the danger with me."

"Ah, you can leave in the morning, girl," sighed Hiram as he rose from the chair at the table and walked to the fireplace. "Your feet need more time to heal, and you need rest. If your friends come they'll be happy to find you well, and the dogs will tell us if an enemy is near. Big Jip there hasn't left your side since you showed up. No one will get past that lad in one piece. You rest, Brenna of Nova, and we'll find your boots in the morning."

Brenna didn't argue; she was nearly asleep already. She returned to the chair by the fire and snuggled down. The big dog paced over and, with a deep sigh as only a dog can do, flopped down beside her feet. Brenna wasn't even aware of Meg covering her with a blanket.

Outside the farmhouse, and not so far away, Rathbone nodded then slipped away, back towards his cave. He had errands to run and things to do. Rathbone planned to lead the soldiers away from Brenna then kill some of them once they were far enough away. He just hoped he could talk sense into Jorge. Damn fool kid, what madness had made him volunteer for the cyborg program?

Next morning, after a hearty meal, and wearing a pair of comfortable boots, Brenna took her leave of the farm. Jip trotted along at her side even though she tried to send him back. "Might as well take 'im with you, Brenna," called Hiram, as he waved from the farmhouse door. "You might need a guardian and he's the best." Brenna waved back and trotted away, Jip right at her heels.

She reached the place where she'd left Rathbone, but he was nowhere to be found and he'd left no mark for her to follow. "Well, it looks like we're on our own now, Jip. I've got enough food for a day or two, but I have no idea what I'll feed you."

The big dog just gazed adoringly at her and wagged his tail. "All right then, I guess we'd better keep on the move. Let's go in that direction and see if we can't find a way across this ravine. I want to stay in the area so Lessa can find me easier. I dreamed of her last night, Jip. I know she's coming."

Brenna continued to chat softly to the dog for quite some time. It made her feel less alone. She didn't see Rathbone following her, but he was there, between her and the soldiers hunting her.

Planet Fall

"There she is, Boss, PX19," said Zartah, pointing to a small dot of light on the screen.

"All right, we'll set down at the most likely spot and make a plan." The two fighter ships closed on the planet and shot into the atmosphere over the northern hemisphere. They settled gracefully to the ground and the warriors dropped out to stretch their legs.

"There's nothing here," sighed Micha. "What's your best guess, Gorda?"

"Boss, they could be anywhere, if they're still here."

"All right, we do it the hard way. Zartah, take Murtah, Ena, and Gorda with you. Fly a search pattern around the planet's equator. Edie, Keira, and I will fly just north of you. Stop at every town and farm you see for information. Let me know if you have any luck. We'll meet back here and move the search further north and do it again. Sooner or later we'll find her or we will find out where they took her."

"Right, Boss. We're on it."

They boarded the ships again and set out. They made a careful circuit of the planet, but saw nothing of interest, no life signs that could have been a group of soldiers, no farms and no towns. It was late in the day when they set out on the second circuit. They hadn't gone far when Micha found a town. Keira set the ship down right at the edge of the dusty street.

Micha dropped to the ground and rolled away, coming to his feet with weapons at the ready. There were a few people nearby, but no one made any sudden moves so he relaxed his stance. He rapped his knuckles on the ship and the two heavily armed women dropped out.

Micha strode easily towards the few people brave enough to be outside. "Hi folks, how's everybody doing?" he asked amiably as he slung his rifle over his shoulder.

One man began to raise a weapon, but Micha leaped at him. The move was so fast the man had no time to react. Micha had his wrist in a vice-like grip and a blaster right at the man's temple. "Easy now," he said softly," just relax your hand and give me the weapon."

With an audible gulp, the man let go of the weapon. Micha stepped back as he put the safety on the man's firearm. "You've got to watch these old Hemmings. Dang things can go off and take your hand if you're not careful." Micha smiled as he passed the weapon back to its owner. Completely bemused, the man accepted the now safe weapon.

"Folks, we're not here to steal anything, or to hurt anybody. We need information, that's all."

"Information about what?"

"I'm looking for a certain woman. She's small, full black, and very beautiful. She may be on her own or she may be a captive. If she's a captive she'll be held by a group of Company soldiers. Have any of you seen her, Company soldiers, or a Company ship around here?"

"There's been nobody like that around here," said the man who had pointed a weapon at Micha. "I'm the lawman here and I keep a close eye on things. If there's been anybody like that hereabouts, I would've known."

Micha sighed and gazed around. Everybody made eye contact and shook their heads. "All right," he said at last. "Thanks anyway. Lawman, if a tall woman with golden hair comes here looking for the dark girl; don't point a weapon at her. It will just make her angry; bad things happen when she's angry."

"She a witch or something?"

"That she is, my friend, and it's best not to annoy her. Okay, looks like we're done here. Let's go." He returned to their ship, followed closely by Edie. Once Micha and Edie were in the ship, Keira backed slowly to the hatch, her weapons at the ready in case anyone tried to be a hero. No one did. With a smile and a wave she leaped aboard. A moment later the ship rose gracefully into the air and moved away.

<hr />

"ZARTAH, LOOKS LIKE a town over there. Set her down?"

"Yep, drop right into the edge of town, Gorda. You stay with the ship and be ready. You know, just in case the folks here aren't friendly."

"Still looking for excitement, Zartah?" Gorda was grinning as he set the ship down lightly at the end of the single long street.

"Yep, that's why I love this crew; always something exciting to do," chuckled Zartah, as he dropped to the ground and rolled away.

He saw no threat so he rapped his knuckles on the side of the ship. Murtah and Ena dropped down then all three headed down the street, looking for someone to talk to. The street was empty; the sight of a fighter ship landing had driven everyone inside to hide.

Suddenly a shot rang out and dust puffed up right in front of them. "That's far enough, Slaver. Get back in your ship and take off. Only death waits for you here."

Zartah spread his arms wide to show no ill intent. "Hold your fire; we're not slavers. That's a fighter ship, not a cargo hauler. There's no room for slaves in there. All we want is information."

"Fine then. Drop all your weapons on the ground and step away."

"I've got a better idea," replied Zartah, as he turned to the communicator on his shoulder. "Gorda, lock and load." There was a metallic sound as several big blasters and two launchers leaped into view on the ship. "Gorda, next time someone fires on us, level this whole dung heap of a town. Pound it back into the mud it was built on."

"Understood!" replied the voice over the communicator. The street was deathly quiet.

"All right now," Zartah went on, "how about somebody come out here and talk to me before I start getting bored. Don't make me come find you."

"We don't want no trouble here, Stranger," said a big man, as he stepped from behind a corner, his weapon relaxed in his arms.

"We didn't come for trouble, friend," replied Zartah, his arms wide again. "We just came for information. We're looking for somebody, somebody pretty important to us."

"Most folks will be at the pub now; that's the most likely place to ask. Listen, we don't allow folks to wear weapons in town. It helps to keep the place peaceful; if you get my meaning."

Zartah unhooked his weapons belt and passed it to Ena. "Ena, take our toys back to the ship and man the guns for Gorda. Murtah and I'll go see if these nice folks can help us."

"He's lying, Zartah." Ena hadn't looked away from the big man and his eyes snapped up to her face.

"Is he now? So, it's going to be like that, is it?"

"I'm not lying..." He sputtered, but Murtah interrupted him.

"Ena's witch trained. She knows when you're lying." Before the man could respond, Murtah was at his side with a blaster at his head. "I'll just carry that rifle for you, friend; I wouldn't want you to shoot yourself in the foot. Now, since this is your town, you lead the way."

Sullenly the man led the way while Zartah strapped his weapons back on. As they pushed the doors aside and entered they saw every man there wearing a sidearm. Murtah shoved the man inside ahead of them. There wasn't a sound to be heard.

"Now folks, we're just here looking for a bit of information," said Zartah, as he stepped forward. "How about I buy a round for the house and we all make nice-nice?"

"We don't want your kind around here, bounty hunter. Take off while you still can." The voice had come from the people to the side.

Zartah didn't even look in that direction. "Why does it always have to be the hard way?" grumbled Zartah, as he reached to the communication device on his shoulder. "Gorda, you hear all that?"

"I heard," came the voice. "You know what the Boss would do."

"Yes, indeed. Looks like we have to do this Micha style. Lob a shell or two into those buildings across the street from where we are."

"Lobbing," laughed the voice, as the sudden scream of shell fire split the air, then the building across the street exploded into kindling.

"Stop, stop. What do you want?" It was a woman who had stepped forward.

"A friend of ours was taken captive by a bunch of R.I.M. soldiers. We want her back. She's small, full black, exceptionally beautiful, and extremely dangerous. Her name is Brenna, but we call her The Dispatcher. Have any of you seen anyone like that?"

"I have," said another voice. All eyes were suddenly on the speaker. "I was up north in Attica two days ago. I saw three soldiers there. They were trying to buy parts for a ship. I didn't see any woman who looked like you described."

"Attica. Where is that from here?"

"North by northwest and straight on; town's a fair size and the only one in the area. You can't miss it."

"Ena, is this fellow lying to me?"

"No, Zartah, he's telling the truth."

"Much obliged, friend. We'll just be on our way then." Zartah flipped a handful of script onto the floor. "There's a few rounds on me folks. Be warned; don't step outside until you hear the ship lift off. You do and old Gorda is likely to blow the whole building up just for fun." With that Ena, Murtah, and Zartah backed slowly out of the building.

Once aboard the ship Zartah relayed the news to Micha. Both fighters ships swung north.

Evading Capture

B renna found the ravine and followed it for much of the day. She didn't find a likely place to cross, but that didn't concern her a great deal. Her plan was to just stay out of the soldier's hands as long as possible. The day was nearly gone when she finally stopped to rest and to eat. Jip was still beside her.

"Well, Jip old dear, looks like we'll have to share the food. Hope you like nuts and berries." The big dog just sniffed at her offering then snorted and trotted away. He was soon lost in the scrub brush and tall grasses amid the jumbled mass of boulders. Brenna was chewing thoughtfully when she heard the scream of an animal in pain mixed with the savage growls of the dog. A moment later Jip returned with a dead animal in his jaws. It was nearly as big as he was.

"I see," she sighed. "Well, I guess you can hunt, but is it fit to eat?" For a response Jip put a paw on the carcass and tore off a front shoulder with his massive jaws. "Ok, I guess it's fit to eat. I'll see if I can get a fire going; there's lots of dry brush here."

As Brenna was coaxing her fire to life, she heard the scream of engines high overhead. She looked up to see a pair of fighter ships streak by. She jumped up and waved her arms, but they were too far away to see her.

"Ah well, Micha's here, it won't be long now. They went that way so we'll head off in that direction first thing tomorrow. Right now I have to cook my dinner then put the fire out before dark. We don't want the soldiers to see the flames." The big dog just grunted as he gnawed contentedly on a leg bone.

Brenna used the small knife Rathbone had given her to skin out and cut several strips of the meat. Jip just grunted and slapped a huge paw over the main carcass, unwilling to share too much. Brenna grinned at him as she poked long sticks through the meat and began to cook it over the fire. Once it was cooked she began to kick dirt over the fire to put it out. Rathbone's voice stopped her.

"Let it burn, Brenna."

"So there you are," she smiled, as she offered some of the meat to him. "Hungry?"

"Famished," he grinned, as he accepted the meat and squatted by the fire to eat it. Jip growled and pulled his kill farther away from him. "Easy there, big fella, I won't steal your dinner." The dog sank to the ground again, and with a deep sigh, began to gnaw on the bones once more. "Looks like you have a friend, Brenna. The farmer let you take him?"

"He wanted to come and Hiram said it was okay. He's a good provider, my buddy Jip. So, where have you been all day?"

"Right behind you; I really have to teach you some stealth, Gen. Sorry. Brenna."

"That's the second time you've called me by her name. Do I remind you of her?"

"You could have been sisters. Your face, voice, even some mannerisms invoke the memories."

"I'm not your mate, Rathbone," she said gently.

"I know, Brenna. Part of the problem is I've been alone so long I have fallen into the habit of talking to her constantly. I mean no offence."

"None taken; now tell me why you want the fire. Shouldn't we put it out so the enemy can't see it in the darkness?"

"These guys are so smart they're dumb," he grinned. "There's a bit of light left. We can make good time, but they'll be drawn to the fire."

"So you can ambush them?"

"No, but that's what they'll think. They'll waste most of the night securing the area. We'll find a sheltered spot to sleep.

Tomorrow they'll be tired and we'll be rested. Tired men make mistakes."

"We may not have to elude them much longer anyway. Did you see those fighters fly over?"

"Uh-huh."

"Did you get a good look at them?"

"Arcalian Guard, I have no idea why they'd be here. I just hope they're not on the Company payroll."

"That's not the guard. That's Micha's crew."

"The witch's hounds?"

"Yes, but I don't think she's with them."

"Oh?"

"I couldn't feel her..."

"Brenna..."

"She's alive, Rathbone, that much I know. I have no idea why she's not with the crew, but I know she's alive; I can feel her searching for me. Oh well, we'll find out as soon as we connect with Micha."

"Are you certain that's your crew?"

"Oh yes. Two Arcalian Guard fighter ships; that's the crew all right. We won't be outnumbered much longer."

"Are you sure they won't shoot me on sight?"

"Don't worry, Rathbone; we'll protect you. Won't we, Jip?" The big dog looked up at her, snorted then went back to his pile of bones.

Rathbone chuckled at that, then rose to his feet. "We should be going. Build up the fire a bit, then we'll cover some distance. There's a place we can cross the ravine first thing tomorrow." He threw a few more sticks on the fire, then set out with Brenna close behind. Jip sighed and rose to follow, abandoning his bones.

———◉———

"I DON'T TRUST IT, SIR. It's too easy."

"Trap. Spread out but be careful; we know that bastard's out there somewhere. He's probably drawing a bead on us right now. Goddam nightmare, this is."

"Commander?"

"It's all gone sideways since she set foot on this planet, Dav. First she caught us by surprise and killed three men, and then she nearly drove us mad for days. To make matters worse, we had to stumble onto Rathbone of Urn. Somehow, he managed to spring her loose and has kept her out of our hands while seriously diminishing our numbers.

"We've got two healthy guards and two wounded men back at the ship, which that bastard crippled, and now we're walking into a trap because we have no choice.

"This should have been an easy assignment, but instead we're being cut to ribbons."

"No one could have known Rathbone would be here, or that he'd get involved."

"Doesn't matter, Dav. It's my responsibility, and it's not looking good. Why the hell did that damned assassin have to get involved anyway?"

"Revenge, Commander. Pure and simple."

"Revenge?"

"O'Loran had his wife poisoned to coerce him into the cyborg program, and then double crossed him by letting her die anyway. Rathbone probably saw our uniforms and decided to kill us all."

"Then why he didn't kill her? She's O'Loran's daughter after all."

"He's probably saving her for last. As long as he keeps her alive he knows we won't leave the planet; he'll still be able to get at us."

"So it boils down to this: If we kill Rathbone and get her back, we go home heroes. If we fail, we die here on this god-forsaken rock."

"Military luck, Commander." They sat in silence for a long time, until the other soldiers began reporting in. They'd found nothing and the fire was dying down. "Come back in, men." The commander spoke over his communicator device, "It was just a ruse to make us waste time and let him get farther ahead. We'll camp here and pick up his trail at first light."

———◦———

THE TWO FIGHTER SHIPS swept down on the town like avenging angels. This was a larger town, with several streets, a central core, and a space port with a half dozen or more ships of varying descriptions parked in a ragged row. The crew came in low, well below the scanners abilities to track.

At the sound of those engines, some of the townsmen gathered to mount a defense, but by the time they reached the port the ships were already on the ground. A crew of heavily armed mercenaries had already alit and were waiting for them.

"Easy folks," called Micha, as he spread his arms wide to show he meant no harm, "I just want some information, that's all."

The townsmen stopped, looking nervously at the mercs. These people looked extremely dangerous. Perhaps it would be better to see if a battle could be avoided. "What do you want?" asked a tall fellow, as he lowered his weapon and stepped forward.

Micha stepped towards him, his hands still empty. "A member of my crew was kidnapped by some R.I.M. soldiers."

"Why look for them here?"

"Is this the town of Attica?"

"It is."

Just then, another man stepped forward. "You're that Novan Crew, aren't you?" Micha just nodded. "Jesup, we don't want to mess with these guys; they're the ones who took down the old viceroy. Be very careful here."

"I was told the soldiers were seen here a few days ago," said Micha. "Did they have a female captive with them?"

"They were here alright, but there was no captive," replied the last man to have spoken. "They bought parts for their ship, paid with good Company script, then left."

"Ena, you there?"

"Right behind you, Micha."

"Is he lying?"

"He's telling the truth."

"Fair enough. Listen, Mister, the day's nearly gone and we're pretty tired. Have you got a hotel in town?"

"Murgie's, two blocks that way. You plannin' to stay long?"

"Just the night. We'll ask around, see if we can learn anything more about the soldiers, their plans, and where they went from here. In the morning we'll refuel our ships and be on our way. We'll pay our dues in scrip just as they did."

"Fair enough, Merc," nodded Jesup. "Try to stay out of trouble." The men began to disperse and one led them to the hotel. They asked around, met a few folks who had spoken with the soldiers, but learned nothing new of value except the direction their prey had taken upon leaving the town.

Next morning, they fueled up the fighters and flew away, following the general direction they'd been given. Shortly after they took to the air, the communicator squawked. It was Lessa. "Micha, are you within range of comms?" At the second repeat, Micha understood the message.

"You're coming through, Lessa. Keira, can you clear that up a bit?"

"Micha, are you there? Micha?"

"That's better. Lessa, Micha here."

"Micha, are you alright? Is everyone safe?"

"The crew is safe and well, Lessa. Where are you?"

"On my way to PX19, Micha. That's where they took Brenna. Where are you?"

"We're on PX19. We're on the trail now."

"I'm sending the coordinates of their ship. At least this is where it was."

"I believe they're still on the planet, Lessa. They've had some mechanical troubles. How far out are you?"

"Hours only."

"See you soon, Micha out. Got the coordinates, Edie? Okay, send them to Zartah, and then set the ship down."

The ship settled down and the second followed. Soon everyone was on the ground, making a plan. "Here's what I want to do," said Micha. "I want to send the ships ahead to meet Lessa and I want the rest of the crew on the ground here, following the soldiers' path. Any suggestions?"

"Should we separate, Micha?" asked Edie. "The lady didn't sound like she was in a very good mood, and we have no idea what we're up against here."

"Perhaps you're right, Sweetheart. All right, we'll play cautious here. We don't want to walk into a trap and we don't want to blunder into something that might get Brenna hurt. We'll head up and settle into an orbit right above those coordinates and wait for Lessa to join us. We'll make certain nothing gets off this rock until we have Brenna back safe and sound."

A moment later the ships rose gracefully into the air, then shot out into space. They didn't notice the two figures run out of the rocks and across the open space, trying to catch their attention.

Recaptured

A s they settled down for the night, Brenna squirmed to get more comfortable. "You all right, Gen?" A hand reached out to lightly stroke her cheek. She gently took the hand and moved it away.

"I'm fine. Rathbone, it's Brenna, remember?"

"I'm sorry, Brenna, I..."

"Tell me about her."

"What?"

"Tell me about Gen. What was she like? How did you meet her?"

"Gen was just a little bit, you know, small and all fire. I met her at a 'meet and greet' dance. All the guys were getting drunk and making fools of themselves. I always stayed sober and waited. The drunker the others got, the better I looked, if you know what I mean.

"I'd spotted her earlier, but she was pretty popular, and it wasn't easy to get near her, so I waited. Sure enough, as the evening wore on and the lads got drunker, she began to avoid them. Finally she tried to walk away from a dance, but the guy grabbed her arm and yanked her back.

"I was there in a heartbeat, but she'd already broken free. She stomped his foot then kicked him in the balls. Quite effective, actually. He looked like he would hit her, but then he saw me. 'I don't want trouble with you, Rathbone,' he said, backing off.

"Then go away," I replied.

"I don't need your help," she said, but I just smiled at her.

"I didn't come to interfere, I just wanted to ask you to dance," I said. We danced away the rest of the evening. She discovered I was wearing baby powder and teased me about it."

"Baby powder, Rathbone?"

"Yes, my dear Brenna, baby powder. All women like to cuddle babies, so I always wore baby talc instead of fancy scents. Worked every time."

"Rathbone of Urn, you're a thoroughly bad man," chuckled Brenna, slapping lightly at his massive shoulder.

"I am, and I admit it freely. Brenna, I am sorry. I warn you girl, sometimes the pain can fog my mind a bit. I'll try harder, I promise."

"It won't be long now, my friend. Lessa is drawing nearer, I can feel her. Micha is already here and soon we will be safe. I'll ask Lessa to help you with the pain."

"Thank you, Brenna, but I doubt there is much she could do."

"Perhaps. Rathbone, if she is successful, will you reconsider killing my father? I know you think your life is over and you want revenge, but if Lessa can give you relief and a longer life, will you reconsider?"

"Gods, you're like Gen. Alright Brenna, if your witch can give me a few more good years, I'll think it over as a favor to you. I'm not likely to change my mind, but I will think it over."

"Thank you, that's all I ask."

"The hell it is, Brenna. You're way too much like Gen. You'll keep at me until you get your own way."

"Then why not just give up and save yourself all the trouble?" giggled Brenna.

"Now where would be the fun in that?" he grunted, as he rolled over and settled down. Rathbone wanted that conversation over. He was growing far too fond of this woman; best to put a stop to that right now. She wasn't Gen and never could be. The damned pain in his shoulders was fogging his mind.

As they settled down, Jip crawled between them and gave a deep sigh, thumped his tail on the ground a few times, and instantly went to sleep.

The sun was nearly up before they awakened. Rathbone cursed as he roused Brenna. "Quickly now; we've slept too long. Behind those bushes and do what you must then we have to run. They'll be on our trail already."

Brenna relieved herself then reappeared to find Rathbone ready to go. He had the spare meat from the night before plus a few rations in a small bundle, as well as his weapons and ammunition. Without a word he raced away. To his great surprise, Brenna was able to hold the pace, Jip loping along beside her.

As they neared a narrow point in the ravine, Rathbone pointed then picked up speed. He leaped through the air to land on the other side, Brenna and the dog landing easily beside him. Grinning at her, he trotted away from the ravine until he found a jumble of boulders big enough to hide them from sight. He sank to the ground and pulled out the packet of food.

"We should eat a bit while we have the chance," he sighed. "They'll be along soon enough and we don't have the time to hide our tracks. Any idea what our next move should be, Gen? Sorry. Brenna?"

"Micha's on the planet," she replied around a mouthful of rations, as she tried to get more comfortable on the hard dry ground. "He was flying north and there is a town there. The commander sent men to that town to buy parts for the ship, but they never returned."

"I know."

"Yes, when they found the bodies they figured out who you were. No one else could have defeated their men, or so they believed. Anyway, Micha will learn of them in that town. By now he is tracking them back toward us. We just have to get onto that trail and meet up with him."

"Sure, nothing to it," chuckled Rathbone.

"I know, easier said than done. Skeeter, I wish I had a communicator."

"Gen, such unladylike language," he chuckled.

Brenna got the distinct impression she'd just done something else that reminded Rathbone of his lost love. She'd have to be careful about that. She also noticed he didn't correct himself about her name. The man was in great pain; that was easy to see in his eyes. Rathbone was a terribly efficient killer, yet there was a gentle warmth about him. Brenna was growing attached to him and that concerned her too.

The soft clink of a cast aside syringe caught her attention. "What was that?"

"The last of the pain control meds from your med kit, Brenna. This stuff works pretty fast. I can see by your face I've slipped again. Did I call you Gen? Did I touch you?"

"It's all right, Rathbone, the pain confuses you, I know. We need to find Micha. Edie will have a fresh med kit and we can dull the pain for you until Lessa has a chance to do a healing song for you."

"Sounds good to me. Do you want me to go back and borrow a communicator from the troops? I'm sure they're all carrying one."

"No," she chuckled, "let's just move on. The sun is up now, and Micha will be on the move. We should go soon."

"Tell me about this Micha."

Brenna smiled fondly at Rathbone as he absentmindedly fed the last of the meat to the dog. He scratched Jip behind the ears and the big dog wagged his tail as he enjoyed the attention. She was definitely liking this man too much. She needed Rathbone for protection, but the soldiers would kill him the first chance they got, and Brenna didn't want to get too close. The more she liked him, the harder it was going to be when he was killed. They had to find Micha quickly.

"Micha? He was a boy of about sixteen when we met. I had come out to the rim worlds to work with and help as many of the children orphaned by the wars as I could. Gods, I was so naïve. I made my way to Kuris Morn where I managed to gather about a dozen children together. My plan was to transport them back to Elliston Prime. Micha was an escaped slave and he had his young sister with him. I convinced him to come with me. Unfortunately, the ship I hired was a slaver."

"I assume that didn't go well for you."

"No, we were all about to be sold into slavery. Fortunately, a bounty hunter arrived with a captive. It was Lessa. Lessa, with Micha's help, got us free and to safety. Micha appointed himself Lessa's personal guard, learned combat arts from a Borelian champion, and then was enhanced by Lessa's magic. Physically, he is easily your equal, Rathbone. Mentally, he can be a bit frightening."

"Oh, how so?"

"Micha is like two people. There's the fun loving farmer who is so very gentle with his mate, Edie. There is also the crew boss and Lessa's guardian. He is as cold as space, terrible in the speed and efficiency of his mind, unfeeling and completely practical in the approach to achieving his goals. Micha is protective of his crew as well as Lessa, and something about him commands complete loyalty and obedience from everyone on the crew."

"Even you?"

"Yes, Rath, even me. Micha's overriding aim is to protect Lessa and the crew. If he asks it, then I know it is the best way to accomplish the goal. Even Lessa defers to him."

"The witch?"

"Yes. If she has an objective, Lessa will tell Micha, then step back and become another member of the crew until the task is complete."

"He sounds like quite a man. I'd like to meet him."

"All right, then let's get going." She smiled as she rose and headed out. Rathbone and the dog were close behind her.

About an hour or so later they saw the two ships settle gracefully to the ground. They were quite far away, but reachable given a bit of time. They did not get that time. As they raced out into the open, waving their arms and shouting, the ships rose into the air and shot out into space.

"Skeeter!" Brenna stomped her foot in frustration then sank to the ground, tears running down her cheeks.

"Gen..." the dog's deep growl alerted them. "Dammit, they've caught us out in the open."

Brenna leaped to her feet. "Split up. Run."

"No, Gen..."

"They won't hurt me, Rathbone, but they'll kill you. Split up, they'll chase me. Find a way to contact Micha, then find me again. Go!"

She pushed him then sprang away, the big dog at her side. Rathbone ran in the opposite direction. It was almost too late; the cyborgs were close enough to see clearly. Rathbone ran for the cover of the boulders and hillside while Brenna poured on all the speed she could muster and ran straight out into the open fields.

Cursing, the commander swung towards the fleeing Brenna. He was no fool. To send men after Rathbone was to send them to their death. She was leading them out into the open and that damned assassin would be behind them again. Worse yet, the woman was fast and seemed as tireless as they were. They would not run her down easily.

To the commander's great surprise, after she had led them a merry chase for a good while, she suddenly stopped and sat on a boulder to wait for them. "Good morning, Commander Darks," she smiled, as they approached cautiously and surrounded her. "Are you out for your morning exercise?"

The big dog at her side growled menacingly, but she laid a hand gently on his back to calm him. "Easy Jip, easy boy, these bad men would shoot you and I don't want that to happen. Go back to the farm now." She hugged the dog then gazed into his eyes. "Find

Rathbone. Rathbone. Go." She whispered. Jip wagged his tail then reluctantly trotted away. "Go back to the farm," she called after him.

"Now, Commander, it's safe to capture me again."

"Safe isn't a word I would use where you're concerned, Miss O'Loran. Why did you stop?"

"I was getting tired and hungry. Have you any of those good rations left?"

"There's a few, Brenna." chuckled a big soldier, as he tossed one to her.

"It's good to see you still alive, Jorge."

"It's good to still be alive."

"Enough of this," snarled the Commander. "Just what's your game now?"

"Since you chased off my last escort, I decided to let you escort me until I get picked up."

"Picked up? You're pretty sure of yourself, aren't you?"

Brenna sat back on her boulder. "Come sit with me, Commander, and I'll explain the position to you." With slumping shoulders he sat near her, indicating that his men could rest as well.

"Here's the situation," she smiled as he sat. "I'm sure you saw those two Arcalian fighter ships. That's Micha and his crew. They've tracked me to this general area."

"They left without you," he replied. "Now what?"

"They won't have gone far. I sensed that Lessa wasn't with them for some reason, yet I sense her drawing nearer. They must have split up to search for me. Micha has located the general area where I'm being held, now he's making sure no ships leave the planet before Lessa arrives. Once she's here, they'll come for me."

"How could you know all that?"

"Micha is here, Commander. Therefore, your people failed to kill him or Lessa, since she was with him. That means you're on your own with an angry witch on your trail. You're down to seven men left,

Commander. Rathbone himself may just wipe you out before Micha gets the chance."

"Rathbone of Urn. How, in the name of all that's holy, did you manage to get control of that assassin?"

"He likes me?"

"I've no doubt he does. So, why did you let us recapture you?"

"I'm just a small girl alone without food or protection. Since you chased off Rathbone, I needed someone to protect me."

"You mean it'll be easier for your people to find you if you are with a group rather than hiding in the wilds."

"Exactly, Commander."

"There is one small hole in your plan, Miss O'Loran."

"Oh?"

"Yes. Jorge, take what you need and head for that town. Steal a ship, any ship big enough to get us off this rock."

"Sir, with those Arcalian fighters out there, we won't stand a chance in anything I could steal here."

"They won't dare shoot us down; we'll have their precious Brenna as hostage. Go steal us a ship, Jorge."

"Sir." With that he swept up his weapons and sprang away towards the distant town.

"You've just signed his death warrant," sighed Brenna, as she watched Jorge disappear in the distance. "Do you know how to contact his family?"

"Why do you say that? And why do you want to know about his family?"

"Commander, Rathbone is between Jorge and the town. Jorge's chances of reaching that town are nil. Rathbone will kill him, then take his communicator. He'll contact Micha and lead Lessa to me. You are all as good as dead right now.

"I asked about Jorge's family because I promised to see they weren't left homeless when he gets killed."

"Why would you do that, Miss O'Loran?"

"He was kind to me, Commander, and gentle with me when he carried me."

"Was he the one who set you free?"

Brenna's laughter was sweet and genuine. "No, Commander Darks, you did that yourself."

"Explain."

"You forced me to run with my hands tied. This put additional stress on my legs causing greater swelling. My bonds had to be looser when we stopped because of that. I put my feet up and went to sleep. A few hours later I awakened and the swelling was gone. I pulled my feet out of the shackles with ease, then slipped away. The next morning, I bumped into Rathbone and we joined forces."

Suddenly the commander leaped to his feet, cursing himself. She had done it to him again. A swift look around showed a tall outcropping of rock nearby. He pointed to it. "We'll set up a defensive perimeter there," he barked. "Let's move."

Brenna ran easily beside the commander. She had no desire to escape them now. "Commander, what did I miss?" asked Dav, as he ran beside them.

"She didn't send that damned dog back to the farm, she sent it to Rathbone. He'll kill Jorge, use the comms unit to contact the witch, then the dog will track us. The best we can do now is set up a defensive position and try to negotiate our way out of this mess."

"I can tell by your smile that he's guessed right, Miss O'Loran," said Dav. "Why aren't you trying to escape to take away the last advantage we might have?" Brenna did not respond, but her grin widened.

Treason

The day was hot, and he'd been running for a while. Jorge slowed to a walk and looked back over his shoulder. His companions were lost to sight as he had covered a lot of ground. Turning back to his line of travel he looked for a shady spot to stop for water and a ration bar.

A jumble of rock with a lone tree near the top caught his eye. Jorge trotted over and plopped himself down in the shade. He took a long drink from his water canteen then sighed deeply as he re-corked it. He wiped the sweat from his brow and tore open a ration bar. Munching thoughtfully, he looked over his options.

They weren't good. He had to get past Rathbone, steal a ship fast enough to outrun the witch, and get back before the witch showed up. The witch's hounds were flying Arcalian Guard fighters. Jorge didn't hold out much hope of finding anything faster on this mud heap.

"It doesn't look too promising, does it, Jorge?" asked a deep voice from behind. Jorge stiffened but forced himself to sit still. "Gently now, brother. I want your weapons out of reach in front of you."

Slowly, deliberately, Jorge obeyed, tossing away his weapons. "Is that you, Rath?"

"Yes. Long time, no see, Jorge. Life been good to you?"

"Up until right now it has."

Rathbone stepped out beside Jorge and sat near him, a gun at the ready. "Got any more of those rations?" Jorge tossed over a bar and Rathbone ripped it open. He took a bite then whistled. The big dog appeared and Rathbone tossed him the rest of the bar. Jip caught it and sank to the ground to enjoy his treat.

"You going to kill me, Rath?"

"That depends. Did you notice how much Brenna looks like Gen?"

"Yeah, she does look a lot like my big sister. She's not though, Rath. Brenna's not Gen. She's O'Loran's daughter."

"I know, I know. I get a bit fuzzy now and then. I've called her Gen a couple of times but she doesn't get mad about it. She just reminds me of the difference."

"How the hell have you survived so long? Those over-powered enhancements should have torn you apart by now."

"Yeah, well, it's getting close to that these days. I don't expect to last a lot longer. Do you have any painkillers in your gear?"

"Sure, we all carry them, you know that." Jorge pulled out a small kit with three syringes in it. He passed it to Rathbone who pulled the cover off one and plunged the needle into his thigh. The drug was fast acting, and Jorge watched for a few moments as the relief spread across Rathbone's face. "So what now?"

"Now you have a decision to make."

"I do?"

"You do. You have a companion and one child that I know of, possibly more by now."

"No, still just the one. Economics and all that, you know."

"Indeed I do, Jorge my friend, indeed I do. So, I assume you don't have the death insurance."

"You're right about that. I couldn't afford the payments on the premiums."

"So that brings us to the crux of the matter. Get yourself killed and they're homeless and helpless. Your only chance to honor your oath to protect them is to remain alive at all cost."

"What are you getting at, Rath?"

"Jorge, if you were anyone else I would have just killed you and been done with it, but you're not. You're Gen's brother, a man I promised her I'd protect. Here's the best I can do for you. Work with me to help Brenna, and I promise I'll do everything I can to help get your family out here to the rim worlds. Hell, Brenna can probably arrange for them to live on Nova Prime."

"You mean, turn traitor?"

"No matter what you do now you betray, one oath or the other, Jorge. Fight me and you betray your family as well as the sister you promised you'd stay alive. Work with me and you betray R.I.M. So what will it be, true to your family or true to the Company and dead?"

Jorge sighed deeply and looked away across the hot barren land. He'd known for days now that this decision was coming, he just hadn't wanted to make it. No matter what he chose his carefully planned life was about to explode, or end. "All right, Rath," he said, nodding his head, "I guess we're both wanted outlaws now. What do you want me to do?"

"Swear on young Ander's life, Jorge."

Jorge gazed into Rathbone's eyes for a moment. There was a lot of pain there, but his mind was clear. Jorge nodded and relented. "I swear on Ander's life and Gen's memory that I'll help you if you promise to help me get my family out to the rim where I can protect them."

"Agreed." Rathbone offered his hand and Jorge shook it. "All right then, pass me that communicator then gather up your weapons." Jorge tossed the radio to Rathbone then reached for his weapons. He noticed the big dog watching him carefully. "It's all right, Jip," said Rathbone, "Jorge's one of Brenna's troops now." The dog relaxed and went to sniff at Jorge's outstretched hand. Slowly his tail began to wag.

Rathbone adjusted the frequency on the communicator then spoke. "Rathbone of Urn calling Nova Crew. Come in, Nova Crew."

He got no response so he adjusted the settings and tried again. On the third try he got an answer.

"Micha here, identify yourself."

"I'm Rathbone of Urn, and friend of Brenna, Dispatcher of Nova."

"Is Brenna with you?"

"No longer, but she is near and I can find her."

"What is her status?"

"She is fine, but prisoner of R.I.M. military. Nine men and two wounded left."

"Nine and two wounded left?"

"Brenna killed a few and so did I."

"Your status?"

"We're healthy and ready to fight. We can lead you to Brenna. Lock on to this signal; we'll stay put until you get here."

"I'll be right down. I warn you friend, if this is a trap you won't even hear the shell that takes you."

The signal went dead, but a few moments later one of the Arcalian fighter ships swept down on their position in the rocks. The big bird alit gracefully, and the hatch dropped open. A man and two heavily armed women dropped out of the ship, each rolling swiftly in a different direction. They were moving and into the cover of the rocks in a heartbeat. Rathbone nodded his head approvingly. "Come on, Jorge, time for us to surrender and see if we can enlist in a new army." Jorge just snorted softly and spread his arms wide.

As the two men walked into the open with their arms wide and their hands empty, Micha stepped out to meet them. Jip growled once and stepped in front of Rathbone, but one of the women whistled then slapped her leg. With a happy wag of his tail, the big dog accepted the invitation to play and bounded toward her.

"So much for my protector," said Rathbone, as he approached Micha carefully. The second woman had a clear line of fire at them both and as they moved, so did she. Rathbone decided he didn't ever want to mess with this one.

"Edie loves dogs," grinned Micha, "and they know it. Relax before your arms fall off. I'm Micha."

"Rathbone of Urn, and this is my brother-in-law, Jorge of Elliston. Brenna said to contact you."

"Why isn't she with you?"

"That's your fault."

"Explain."

"We saw you earlier and ran out from cover to join you. You took off before we reached you, but we were exposed then. She sent me away to contact you, then led them in the other direction."

"Why didn't she contact me earlier?"

"We didn't have a communicator," replied Rathbone, a grin on his face. His smile faded as he saw the shift in Micha. Micha had gone completely cold, and Rathbone could see in his eyes why the youngster was the crew boss. This man was dangerous.

Micha shifted slightly falling easily into a fighting stance, his hands hovering over his weapons. "Keira. If I don't get a straight answer to my next question, shoot one of them. I don't care which one.

"Now. Rathbone of Urn. You have a communicator. You called me with it. If Brenna was with you, why didn't she call herself?"

"He didn't have the communicator," said Jorge. "I did and I wasn't with them. Look, we'll tell you the whole story, but I'm frying out here in the heat. Can we get into the shade, at least?"

Micha had kept his eyes locked on Rathbone the whole time Jorge was speaking. He could see the pain in the man, but also a sense of mirth. Brenna was safe and this man knew where she was. The rest could wait until Lessa arrived. "Edie?"

"This big fella likes them; they can't be all bad," smiled the woman still playing with the dog. Rathbone gave her a nod of appreciation. Even though she'd been wrestling with Jip, her eyes had always been on him and her weapon ready.

"Keira?"

The warrior woman straightened up and lowered her weapon. She stepped close to Rathbone and gazed into his eyes for a moment then offered her hand. Amazed, he took the offered hand and shook it firmly. She nodded and moved away toward the shade.

At that, Micha slung his weapon over his shoulder. "Let's get in the shade before we cook."

"What just happened?" asked Jorge, as they strode back to the shade beneath the rocks.

"That beauty showed us her back, brother," said Rathbone, as he slid painfully to a sitting position on the ground. "I expect she doesn't do that often."

"She doesn't," said Micha, "not ever. Edie, is there a med kit in your pack?"

"It's on the ship. Why?"

Micha's gaze darted to Rathbone for a second. It was enough; Edie was instantly kneeling by Rathbone, searching his eyes. Her hand reached for his face, but he caught it gently, kissed her fingertips then moved her hand away. She nodded then stood. "I'll be right back."

She raced to the ship with a speed that impressed Rathbone. These people were enhanced somehow, just as Brenna was. He smiled as Edie leaped easily up into the ship. "She your mate, Micha?"

"She is."

"You're a lucky man."

"Yes, I am."

Edie was already on her way back. A moment later she was beside Rathbone with a med kit. She reached for a pain killer, but Rathbone stopped her. "Not that one girl, it'll relax me too much and my brain will get confused. We don't want that. Bad things happen when I lose focus. Use that one. It'll dull the pain and still let me function."

"It won't stop all the pain," Edie replied.

"Nothing can, but this will leave me functional and focused."

"As you wish," said Edie, as she gave him the injection, "but I'm going to ask Lessa to have a look at you."

"You're carrying old wounds," said Micha, as Edie closed her med kit and sat beside him.

"I am, but that's a tale for another time as well. Right now we need to get Gen back. Brenna, I meant Brenna. It's not going to be easy. I expect the commander knows by now that he has no hope of escaping this rock, so he'll have taken up a defensive position. What do you think, Jorge?"

"I agree. That's what he'll do. You can dig him out, but lives will be lost and Brenna could get hurt."

"Now, here's how I see our options..." Rathbone got no further as Keira grabbed his arm. He locked eyes with her, and she nodded her head at Micha. He looked at Micha then back to Keira. "He's the crew boss. He'll ask for options and opinions when he wants them." She gave him a smile that could melt polar ice and patted his arm. He just grinned and shook his head.

Rathbone studied Micha for a few moments. Neither man spoke. Finally Rathbone broke the silence. "No free thinkers on your crew?"

"They're all free thinkers," grinned Micha. "There's a time and a place for everything. Right now is a time for waiting. We'll discuss our options once Lessa arrives and you have told us the whole story."

"You don't trust me, and you're waiting for the witch to see if she can determine if I'm lying or not."

"I could have one of my crew do that, but you're right, I'm waiting for Lessa and for the rest of my crew. You say Brenna is well and safe for now, so we have the luxury of time. When you have time, you rest." Just then Micha's communicator squawked.

"Micha." He responded as he gripped the device attached to his shoulder gently.

"The Lady is inbound, Boss. We gave her your co-ordinates. Should we come down?"

"Yes, come down." He released the communicator and relaxed back against a boulder. Edie settled down beside him and Jip wriggled in between them.

"You're a bloody traitor, Jip," chuckled Rathbone. "I'm telling Brenna you abandoned me."

"He's just showing you that we're not enemies or a threat," laughed Edie. "You need to learn to speak dog."

As Edie spoke, Jorge pointed at the sky. The second Arcalian Fighter swept in at alarming speed then banked and settled gracefully to the ground. Three heavily armed mercenaries hit the ground running, two men and a woman. Seeing no threat, they stopped and sauntered over towards Micha and companions.

Rathbone was even more impressed as Micha reached for his communicator again. "Clear here. Come on out, Gorda, and bring some water." A moment later another mercenary dropped out of the ship, several containers of water in his arms. Without a word he passed around the bottles. Edie cupped her hands and Micha filled that cup with water. Jip lapped up the offering gratefully, then gave Edie a big slobbery kiss, causing her to shriek.

Micha introduced them and then looked up. A small ship was inbound at speed. Somehow the pilot got the ship slowed down for a soft landing. Two women came tumbling out of the speeder, one stopping to stretch out the kinks while the taller one with light hair ran to Micha, seizing him in a bear hug. "Where is she, Micha."

"She's safe, Lessa. We'll get her back, I promise. First we need more information and these men have it. Come into the shade now and we'll hold a council of war."

"You know where Brenna is?" asked Lessa, as she stepped past Micha.

"Well, not exactly," replied Rathbone. He was suddenly hurled against the rock face with a force that would have killed a lesser man. "Where is she?" demanded that voice from a distant hell. "Tell me. Where is she?"

Micha stepped between them and gently pressed her outstretched arm downward. Rathbone slid to the ground and groaned. "He can't help us if you kill him, Lessa. Here, have some water; you're all cramped up."

Lessa fought herself to keep from crushing Micha as well. The rage and fear were flooding her with power that demanded to be released at an enemy. Slowly she regained control, her eyes flashing as she finally relented. "That was foolish, Micha," she snarled, as she took the water bottle from his hand and stepped away.

"Understood. Let me do this, Lessa."

Her shoulders slumped and tears flowed from her eyes as she turned back and fell into his arms. "Micha, I'm so lost and afraid. Please get her back for me."

"Yes, Lady. It shall be as you desire." He guided her to a seat in the shade. "You rest here for a moment, and I'll be about the business." Rathbone had been watching and now fully understood why the crew followed this youngster as they did.

"Rathbone."

"Yes, Micha."

"Tell us the story now. Tell us all of it and tell only the truth. Ena will know if you lie and if you hold anything back."

"I won't hold back, Micha. I want Gen back safe and sound as much as you do."

"Who is Gen?"

"I meant Brenna. Sorry. My mind gets fuzzy with the pain sometimes. Gen was my mate and Brenna strongly resembles her. Gen was also Jorge's sister. O'Loran killed her and our child.

"A number of days ago I spotted a Company ship landing and I moved in for the kill."

"The kill?"

"I have a grudge against the Company, as you might expect. I kill their soldiers every chance I get. That story can wait. I saw the ship land and I moved in. I overheard them talking about capturing old O'Loran's daughter so I backed off to wait. It was my big chance; I could kill his daughter just as he did mine.

"The old mail carrier landed and dropped her off. As soon as she hit the ground she attacked and killed three of them before they subdued her. I saw her face in the scope and couldn't bring myself to shoot.

"She drove them crazy for days while I followed along, enjoying the show. I managed to kill a few during that time. Finally she escaped them, but she was barefoot and in bad shape. I found her and took her to safety."

"So, where is she?" demanded Lessa.

"Forgive me, Lady, I'm getting there. We led them a merry chase for a few days and finally we spotted Micha's ship on the ground. That was this morning. We ran out to meet them, but the ships took off before they saw us. Out in the open, we split up. Brenna led the soldiers away while I looked for a way to keep them on the ground and some means to get my hands on a communicator."

"What was your part in this, Jorge?" asked Micha.

"I was a member of the troop that captured her. I liked her instantly, especially when I saw how she was driving the commander crazy. I did what I could to make her comfortable. When we recaptured her this morning, I was sent to the town to steal a ship so we could get her off world."

"What changed your mind?" asked Lessa.

"Rath did," chuckled Jorge. "Rath's my brother-in-law. He's also the most dangerous man alive. He got the drop on me then explained that if he had to kill me, my companion and son would be left without resources. I couldn't afford death insurance, so they'd end up in the ghettos where they'd be dead or worse. Rath promised to help me get them out to the rim worlds where I have a chance to protect them."

"So you turned traitor?"

"Lady, I did what I had to do to protect the woman I love and her child. I owe the Company nothing. They murdered my sister. What would you do in my place?"

"Exactly what you did," sighed Lessa, the rage seeping out of her at last.

"Ena?" said Micha.

"They told the truth, Micha, but not all of it."

"Let's have the rest," said Micha, his eyes going hard. It was Rathbone who answered.

"We're cyborgs, and so are the men who have Brenna. I was part of the first experiments. They made the enhancements too strong and most of the guys tore themselves apart. They aborted that experiment, killing those few who had survived."

"But not you."

"No, I escaped. I was raised by my grandfather to be an assassin like him, but I chose to become a mech-tech. However, when Gen needed medicines I volunteered for the program. I had the skills and enhancements to escape. For the past five years they have hunted me, and I've hunted them."

"I was part of the second experiment," said Jorge. "They held back on the power of the enhancements, so we survived and were fine. There are seven, plus the commander left with Brenna. Two more and two wounded back at the ship. All are cyborgs and trained combat soldiers."

"What level are your skills compared to the rest?" asked Micha.

"I'm probably the strongest, but not the fastest or the most highly skilled. I'd say I'm about average for those who are left."

"Is there anything else?"

"They've got their wounded back at their original ship," said Rathbone. "I disabled it so they can't escape with that."

"They acquired repair parts back in that town," said Micha.

"I killed those men and took the parts. I hid them so I could steal the ship at a future point. I was planning to take Brenna back to her father myself. I thought that might get me close enough to kill him."

"What made you change your plan?"

"She did. Gods she is like Gen. She kept at me until I agreed to think over the plan to kill O'Loran. By the time we got that sorted out, you arrived. The rest you know."

"Ena?"

"That's all of it, Micha."

Micha paced around for a few minutes then stopped facing the rest. "All right people, the objective here is to retrieve our crew-mate unharmed. Nothing else matters at this point. If we go in shooting, she might get hurt accidentally. We could sneak up on them in the dark, but these men are enhanced as well. Jorge, Murtah, face off."

Jorge looked startled as the huge merc slid out of his weapon's belt and stepped into the open. Damn, the man moved easy; he was sure to be dangerous. Jorge dropped his weapons and stepped out to meet Murtah.

Murtah feinted with one hand and struck with the other. Jorge blocked easily and struck him a mighty blow to the chest. Murtah went sprawling backwards, but leaped easily to his feet. He grinned and nodded an acknowledgement then moved in again. Jorge was startled at the man's speed and strength. He was sent flying, but landed in a roll and came easily back to his feet again. Murtah attacked with hammer blows and lightning fast moves, but was surprised when Jorge managed to block most and shrug off the rest. A blow from Jorge sent Murtah sprawling. Jorge followed with a leap, but Murtah wasn't there when he landed.

Murtah was behind him and on his back. Jorge fought like a demon, but the big man clung to his back like a spider. Jorge couldn't dislodge him. Murtah managed to work Jorge into a choke hold and Jorge relaxed fully, tapping lightly on Murtah's arm. Murtah released him and helped him to his feet with a friendly slap on the shoulder.

"Murtah?"

"He's our equal for the most part, Micha. The only weakness I can see is the human parts aren't up to the strength of the machine parts. We could wear them down in a hand to hand battle, but it wouldn't be quick. A bystander could get hurt."

"Understood. Rathbone, options, opinions?"

Keira gave Rathbone a friendly punch on the arm and winked. He chuckled and shook his head. "I see it this way, Micha. Jip here can easily lead us to their position. You've got two fighter ships you can set down just out of weapon's range to let them know you mean business. They'll try to bargain their way out and you should be able to get her back unharmed in exchange for their lives."

"No, they won't," Jorge said, as he stepped closer. "They can't let her go. If they return without her they'll be tortured and killed, so will their families. They'll fight to the last man."

"So be it," declared Lessa, as she rose to her feet, the fire back in her eyes.

"Lady, they'll kill her at the end, rather than let you win."

"All right, everyone relax," said Micha. "Gorda, suggestions?"

"Well, Boss, it seems to me there is only one card we can play. They don't know Jorge here has defected, so they won't shoot him if he goes in. He can take a message in for us."

Micha grinned. "Keep going, Gorda."

"Jorge had to choose between death and protecting his family. I'm just wondering how many of them would do the same."

"How about it, Jorge, how many of the others do you think have the death insurance for their families?" asked Micha.

"The commander, maybe," he replied, "but I'm not so sure. None of the rest."

"I like it, Gorda, we'll do it."

"What's the back-up plan, Boss?" asked Zartah.

"Back-up plan is this. First we find them, then Jorge holds their attention while one of us gets Lessa in behind them. Lessa, can you freeze them if you get close enough?"

"I can."

"Their hearing and vision have been enhanced as well, Micha," said Rathbone.

"You've been eluding these men for days now," replied Micha. "Your task is to get Lessa close enough without being spotted. Can you do it?"

"I can, and if I screw up she'll blast me to pieces, right?"

"Right. Keira will go with you, just in case."

"I won't betray you, Micha. We have the same objectives here. Besides, I spent enough time with Brenna to know that wouldn't be a good idea anyway."

"All right, just you and Lessa. Let's go people. Jorge, here's one of our communicators. Tell the commander he can talk to me with this. Once you give him the comm we'll show ourselves enough to keep his attention."

Jorge nodded, swept up his weapons, whistled for the dog then set out. Rathbone grimaced as he swept up his weapons. "You're injured," said Lessa, as she stepped closer to him. She could easily read the pain in his eyes.

"Yes, Lady, but it can wait for another time. We have to keep Jorge in sight, but we have to stay hidden as we travel. Quickly now." He set out up into the rock jumble and away, Lessa right on his heels.

Jorge ran easily, setting a gentle pace. He didn't want to tire the dog and he wanted Rathbone to be able to keep up. Rathbone and Lessa had to work a bit harder to keep him in sight while remaining hidden themselves. Micha and the crew waited near the fighters. Micha would show himself, but he'd take no chances on a sniper getting lucky.

The day was well on when Jorge stopped and gazed around. He'd reached the spot where Brenna had been recaptured. "Find her, Jip, find Brenna." The big dog wagged his tail as he put his nose to the ground then set out at a trot. He headed straight for a rock formation nearby. Grinning, Jorge followed closely.

Farther back, just on a ridge, Rathbone sighed and sat back. "Bugger and damn."

Lessa snickered for a moment. In spite of everything, there was something about this man she liked. "What is it?"

"They're dug in there pretty tight. That commander is no fool; he's not going to be easy to get at. Ah well, there was no promise it would be easy. Let's go."

He slipped back below the ridge line and set out again, Lessa close behind. They hadn't gone far when her communicator squawked softly. Lessa was startled at the speed he turned with a weapon drawn. He lowered it instantly and held a finger to his lips. She turned it down further but left it where they could hear the exchange between Micha and the commander.

"JORGE, WHY IN THE NINE hells aren't you flying a ship?" demanded the commander, as Jorge climbed the last few meters to the soldier's defensive position.

"I was captured by the mercenaries, Sir. They sent me back with this communicator so you can parley with them."

"Why would I want to do that?"

"Sir, you can't beat these mercs. They're like nothing I've ever seen. Sir, they're faster and stronger than we are, they have years of actual combat experience, they're heavily armed, and they have Arcalian Fighter ships. Commander, I've seen the witch; I suggest you talk to them. There might be a way to keep the rest of your men alive."

"I want a full report, Jorge."

"Yes, Sir. I was taken by Rathbone long before I could reach the town."

"Did you put up a fight, or did you just make him tea? He is family to you, isn't he?"

"Rath's my brother-in-law as well as a friend, yes, but he is what he is. He took me from behind and I knew I was dead. There's no way I could ever defeat him. He took my weapons and comm unit, then called the mercs down. They gave me a choice; the same choice they're going to offer you, all of you. I suggest you take it."

"Oh you do, do you, traitor. Why shouldn't I just kill you right now?"

"Commander Siemon Darks, always in command, always so damned much smarter than dumb old Jorge; use your damned head for a change," sighed Jorge as he tore the R.I.M. patches off the shoulders of his uniform. "You owe it to these last few men to keep them alive." He dropped the communicator Micha had given him at the commander's feet then stepped over to sit beside Brenna. She gave him a bright smile and a friendly squeeze on the arm.

His face flushed with rage, the commander jerked his hand at a soldier. The man rose and grabbed Brenna by the arm, hauling her to her feet and placing a gun to her head. Scooping up the fallen communicator, the commander turned it on. "All right, Merc, I've got O'Loran's daughter with a gun to her head. You people make a wrong move and the game's over."

———⊙———

RAGE LEAPED TO LESSA'S eyes as she heard that message. She surged to her feet, but someone grabbed her arm, trying to hold her back. Savagely she turned and blasted him with unholy pain and fear, driving him to his knees. To her amazement, he gripped her even tighter. He was speaking to her, urging her to listen.

"Stop it, woman," he gasped through the pain. "Stop it. You'll get Gen killed."

"Who is Gen?" she snarled. "And why would I care?"

"Brenna, I meant Brenna. Stop this. Get control of yourself, woman. That damned temper of yours will get her killed. Is that what you want?"

Lessa's eyes bored into his as she poured on the pain, but somehow he held on to her and fought through the pain. "Dammit, woman, get control of yourself. If you haven't the strength to control the power, you should never have embraced it."

That stung her and the rage flared higher within her. Somehow, a small voice at the edge of her reality spoke softly. Lessa heard her mother's voice. "Lessa, never let your temper control you; you must control it. It is a powerful weapon, but it can destroy you as well as an enemy."

Lessa shuddered with the effort to gain control over her emotions, but she managed it. She released her grip on Rathbone and stepped back. He let go of her and sagged to the ground, his mind lost in the fog of pain.

"I kept her alive and safe for many days without you," he gasped. "I wanted to take her off this rock to safety, but she was determined to stay here so you could find her. Is death the reward she's earned for her faith in you?

"The power you wield is like my weapons, useful but deadly. I have to be in control of mine so I don't shoot off my own face. You need to control your temper before you tear out your own heart." He was struggling to speak through the pain and finally began to lose the battle. With a soft moan he sank onto the ground, holding his head.

Suddenly a warmth like liquid sunshine washed through him, erasing most of his pain and leaving him feeling better than he had in years. The witch was gazing at him, only compassion and regret in her eyes. "You're right, Rathbone. Enough time has been lost and wasted to this temper of mine. They have a gun to her head; what should we do?"

"I'll put a stop to that gun to her head, Lady," he grinned, as he flexed his hand. "You keep going along this ridge until you're close enough to do your thing."

"What are you going to do?"

"Get rid of the gun at her head," he growled, as he swept up his rifle and crawled to the top of the ridge. Rathbone sighted along the barrel then squeezed the trigger. The gun in the soldier's hand exploded away and, howling in pain, the man fell to the ground, clutching his hand to his chest.

"You shot the gun from his hand?"

"If I'd shot him his body might have pulled the trigger. Hurry Lady, they'll be on their guard now. I'll keep their attention off you if needs be."

"We'll talk later," she said, as she patted his arm and slipped back out of sight.

AS THE MAN LAY ON THE ground, clutching his injured hand, Jorge chuckled. "You learning anything, Commander Darks?"

Before the commander could respond, the radio squawked in his hand. "That was a bad idea, Commander. My name is Micha, friend of Lessa, Boss of Nova Crew. Release my two crew members and you live. We can then negotiate the terms of your surrender."

"I have a strong position here," replied the commander. "You can't get to me without harming your own people."

"I just did," was the response. The commander blanched white. There was no denying the truth of that statement.

"I prefer to keep them while we negotiate. You bring me one of your ships, and then I'll release Jorge to you. As soon as I'm safely away I'll put Miss O'Loran off on another planet and let you know where to find her."

There was no response to that, but a few moments later, to the commander's great surprise, an Arcalian fighter swept into view then settled down gracefully. One lone man dropped out of the hatch when it opened. He gripped the communicator at his shoulder and spoke. "Here's your ship, send out Jorge."

"Walk away from the ship." The commander pointed at Jorge and grinning, Jorge rose and walked away. They all watched while he climbed down and walked over to join Micha, who had stepped well away from the ship.

The Commander turned and saw Brenna grinning at him. "What's so damned funny, Miss O'Loran?"

"Jorge was right, Siemon, you're not half as smart as you think you are. Don't you recognize a distraction when you see one? Look behind you."

He spun around to see his men hanging several feet in the air and an angry woman standing there, her golden hair flowing back in a wind he could not feel. He swept up his weapon, but it exploded in his hand and he howled in pain as he too was raised into the air.

The men were moved through the air at great speed, then dropped unceremoniously to the ground where they were instantly surrounded by armed mercenaries.

Brenna was in Lessa's arms, tears streaming down her face as she hugged Lessa tightly. Cooing softly, Lessa kissed Brenna's hair and rocked her back and forth. "Shhh, I've got you, Sweetheart. It's alright now, Lessa's got you."

"Oh Lessa, they kept saying you were dead, but I didn't believe them. I was starting to worry that you might not be able to find me in time."

"I will always come for you, my darling Brenna. Besides, you seem to have found a very capable guardian."

"Rathbone, yes. You met him?"

"Yes, and he saved all our lives, I do believe. Somehow that man withstood my power and reached past my rage to find me. I owe him much."

"The poor man lives with constant pain, Lessa. Can you help him?"

"I believe I can. Come, my love, darkness is falling, and Micha's set up camp below. Let's join them."

A New Plan

The other fighter had landed with Kella and her speeder close behind. The smuggler princess was preparing food when Lessa and Brenna arrived. Brenna was quick to collect hugs all around from the crew. The captives sat, sullenly, saying nothing. A few minutes later Rathbone stepped out of the gathering dusk. Keira appeared beside him, poking a gun in his ribs.

"Relax, girl, I knew you were there," grinned Rathbone. Keira grinned back at him, shaking her head. "Yes, I did, too," he laughed, as she lowered the gun and linked her arm through his. She led him to the fire and the food.

"Lady, that was impressive," he said, as he gingerly lowered himself to the ground, "watching the boys fly like that." He nodded his thanks to Kella as she handed him a plate of food.

"You took a terrible chance up there, my friend," said Lessa, as she sat beside him. "Only one other man has ever dared to get in my face like that. Why did you take that chance?"

"I had to stop you, Lady. You were out of control. With the power you wield you'd have killed her too."

"Rathbone, I'm not Gen," said Brenna, as she sat by his other side.

"I know, Brenna. The Lady gave me a shot of something up on the ridge. My mind hasn't been this clear in a long time."

"Lessa, honey, Rathbone lives with terrible pain. Can you help him?"

"Tell me of your pain, Rathbone," said Lessa. "Is it caused by the mechanical implants?"

"It is, Lady."

"But not all of it, is it? Rathbone, I can stop further damage to your body, repair some of the damage, but I cannot return your family to you."

"I know, Lady. Nothing can bring them back, just as nothing can undo what I've done over the years."

"Rathbone, I'll do what I can for you, but I want something in return."

"What's that?"

"I want you to teach me. You live with the pain, and you fought through my spell, yet you didn't lose your focus. I need to learn what you can teach."

"Lady, I'd be happy to share whatever skills I have. May I ask a favor in return?"

"What else would you have of me, Rathbone?"

"I promised to help Jorge get his family out to safety. They'll need a home."

"They'll be welcome on Nova, Rathbone. I also want something more of you."

"Lady?"

"If Micha will have you, I want you on his crew."

"I don't know, Lessa," grinned Micha, "he's a bit of an independent thinker."

"I'll try to keep it reined in," chuckled Rathbone. "It's been so long, and all I've thought about is revenge. I guess it's time to let it go. Micha, you're crew boss. I need a home and a job. I'm the best mech-tech in three sectors."

"We sure could use a good tech, Boss," grinned Gorda. "Number Two is running a bit rough."

Micha nodded, then looked at Zartah. "First man?"

"Keira trusts him; I'll take a chance on that."

"Ena?"

"He looks good to me, Micha. I'll trust him."

"Murtah?" He just nodded and went back to his meal.

"Edie?"

"Jip trusts him, my love. That works for me."

"Brenna?"

"What'll it be, Rathbone, will you behave yourself?" Brenna asked with a mischievous grin.

"Gods, you're like Gen. Yes, girl, I'll play fair, I swear it."

"Welcome to Nova Crew, Rathbone," grinned Zartah. "There's always something exciting to do on this crew." Everyone chuckled at that.

"All right," said Micha, "you're on the crew. Zartah's first man, Gorda's our specialist, Edie's our healer, Murtah's combat arts master, Brenna's dispatcher, Ena's our truth detector, and Keira there is our first warrior and weapons master. Lady Arlessa is high priestess of Nova. It's she that we serve. You'll be our tech. Everybody has their speciality, but all are combat ready at all times.

"Go ahead, Lessa, fix him. He's no good to me all messed up."

"Yes, Boss," grinned Lessa, as she slid closer to Rathbone. "Lie down here where I can reach you, Rathbone." He did as she bid him. Lessa gently ran her hands over his body, stopping here and there to spend some time at a particular spot. Finally she sang a high sweet note that lingered on the air long after her voice fell silent. She relaxed back and placed her hands flat on the ground.

Keira stepped close and offered Rathbone her hand. As he took it she easily hauled him to his feet. She smiled brightly as he tested his muscles and his range of motion. Finally, he turned his head this way and that and smiled broadly. "Lady, I'm pain free for the first time in five years. How long will this last?"

"It will last as long as you do, Rathbone," smiled Lessa. "I couldn't change your mechanical parts without destroying you, so I enhanced your human parts to accommodate them."

"I dared not dream of this day," he sighed, his eyes filling with water. His laugh was filled with emotion. He wiped away the tears of relief as he fully realized he was free of the pain. Keira grinned and punched his arm. He smiled at her. "Hey, pretty woman, aren't you ever going to speak to me?"

"She can't, brother," said Gorda. "The Arlens cut out her tongue because she liked to sing so much."

"The evil bastards," sighed Rathbone, as he shook his head sadly. "I'll teach you to sing again, girl."

Keira stepped back from him, her eyes going dark and a snarl on her lips. "No, wait, let me explain," he said hastily. "On my home planet, Urn, there's a game men and women play with their voices. They call it throat singing. It works like this, I make a sound, and then you make the harmony. Let's try it."

Rathbone made a deep note in his throat. Keira just stared at him, so he did it again. She tried a few sounds then she got it. He sang another note and this time she reached it easily. It was clear her voice was rusty from lack of use, but it was sweet, and everybody sat still to listen. After a few successes, Rathbone began to string a few notes together; Keira followed easily up and down the scale.

After a while she stopped and rubbed her throat, but there were tears in her eyes as she gazed at him. "Thank you, Keira," he smiled. "The last time I did that was with Gen before she got sick."

She stepped close, then reached up and lightly kissed his cheek. She patted his chest as she stepped away and reached for some water.

"Rathbone," said Micha, "my friend, that was a mighty gift to Keira. What can we do in return?"

"Well, Boss," grinned Rathbone, "young Jorge there needs a home and a job. Have you got room for him on your crew?"

"Sure. I'm going to need another fighter ship if the crew keeps growing like this."

Everyone laughed at that. "I've got one for you, Boss," said Rathbone. "It's not Arcalian, but she's the latest thing the Company's got. Needs a few parts, but I've got those in my hideout."

"Now, Kella, I owe you a great debt," said Lessa. "How can I repay?"

"Lady, my father is reaching the point where he'd like to retire, but finding a place of safety isn't easy for a man like him. All he wants to do is retire in comfort and tend his garden."

"His garden?"

"You know that Mama died while I was in prison on Borealis Prime; Papa hasn't been the same since. He just wants to grow flowers like he did as a child. You spoke of finding him a place on Nova. Is that a possibility?"

"I believe the temple could use a chief gardener," smiled Lessa. "He's welcome to come look the place over to see if the position might serve his needs, but what of you, Kella? What can we do for you?"

"When Papa retires I'll inherit the family business. I'm well rewarded, Lady. When I'm running the business, my network will always be available to the Temple of Nova and her crew."

"That's very generous, Kella, but poor business practice," grinned Micha.

"I owe you my life, Micha. Besides, we've been doing a brisk business with Nova since the revival. I want that connection to grow stronger."

"Done," smiled Lessa. "Micha, what do you want to do with the prisoners?"

"We were going to offer them freedom and a home, Lessa. I'd like to stick to that."

"You do what you like, dear friend, and I'll honor any promise you make to these men."

"Thank you, Lessa. All right crew, it's time to make a new plan. Pull those prisoners in closer here." The captive cyborgs were moved in closer, and then Micha spoke again.

"Prisoners, here's the deal we're offering. Any of you who want to renounce the Company and join us is welcome. I want you to consider this. Your mission failed. Lessa beat you, the crew beat you, the Black Witch destroyed those who attacked Nova Prime, and you have failed to capture Brenna.

"Now, here are the options. You can join with us; start a new life. If you do there'll be combat situations, but you'll probably end up doing more farming than anything else."

"Don't listen to him," chuckled Zartah, "there's always something exciting to do on this crew." There was a round of laughter at that.

"The second option is we turn you over to the viceroy. He'll probably interrogate you, then send you back to Elliston in disgrace. The third option is to try something with us and get killed for your trouble. Before you choose this option, think of the families you'll leave behind. What will be their fate? Think it over and give me an answer in the morning.

"Lessa, you and Brenna are on guard duty tonight. Take a ship and go into orbit directly overhead."

"Thank you," said Lessa, as she took Brenna by the hand and led her to the nearest ship. Moments later the ship lifted off and vanished into the night.

"You're not as smart as you think you are, Merc," growled the commander. "You've just sent your greatest asset away."

"They've been parted for too long," Micha replied. "The fighter's sensors will warn them of any approaching ships, they have privacy, we have a sentinel, and I've moved your objective well out of your reach should anything go amiss. Where's the bad?"

The commander didn't respond, so Micha went on. "I'm guessing that idiot who led the attack on me was the man in charge of the whole operation. Killing the witch and her crew would be the hardest task so that man would have been in charge. The second would lead the attack on Nova Prime, and that leaves you commanding the babysitting job.

"The thing is I don't follow the logic. With all of your enhancements, you would have been my natural choice for the attack on Lessa. Why would they send so many enhanced men to bring Brenna home?"

The fight seemed to go out of the commander then. His shoulders sagged as he responded. "We were to be her bodyguards. We knew she'd put up a fuss, but the plan was to toss her in the ship and take her home. The fastest fighting ship was all tricked out for a long trip so we could get her home with minimal stops."

"He's right there, Micha," put in Rathbone. "I've seen that ship. You could put the whole crew in there and still be comfortable enough."

"Good to know," grinned Micha. "Jorge, what's the maximum compliment that ship can carry?"

"She'll carry fifty fighting men and a ten man crew," he replied.

"Boss, tell me you're not thinking of going right into Elliston," sighed Gorda.

"I haven't lied to you yet, Gorda," chuckled Micha, "and I won't start now."

Just then his communicator squawked. "Micha," came Lessa's voice, "put some thought into how we can get into Elliston Prime space undetected. We need to get Jorge's family out of there, and I want an appointment with CEO O'Loran."

"I'm already working on it, Lessa. Go on radio silence now. We don't want to attract any attention."

"Understood, Boss," came the reply followed by silence.

"See, Gorda..."

"I know, Zartah, I know. There's always something exciting to do on this crew," Gorda replied, shaking his head sadly. There was another round of laughter at his expense.

"Micha, are you serious?" asked Jorge. "Are you really going to help rescue my family?"

"I have no choice," grinned Micha. "I'm Lessa's guardian. Where she goes, I go. Since we're going to be on Elliston anyway, there's no harm in picking up a few passengers, is there?"

"What about my family?" asked one of the prisoners. "You said if we join you we could have a home on Nova. I don't have any death insurance and either you kill me or the Company will when we go back without O'Loran's daughter."

"Would you truly be killed for failure?" asked Micha.

"We're not considered human anymore," sighed the commander. "We're machines; Company assets to be used or disposed of as they see fit. He's right, Merc, no matter how this plays out we die anyway. Sadly, our families die with us one way or the other."

Suddenly there was a gun at the commander's head. "The man's name is Micha," growled Zartah. "The next time you speak to him, I want to hear his name and I want to hear respect in your voice."

Micha turned to Ena and spoke. "Is he telling the truth, Ena?"

"Yes he is, Micha."

"Are these lads going to cause me any trouble?"

"I don't think so, Micha."

"They're looking a bit cramped up; Ena thinks they're willing to behave. Should we turn them loose?"

"Might as well, Boss," said Murtah. "I'm not wiping their arses and if we leave them tied up they might explode." All the others laughed and agreed.

"Turn 'em loose, Rathbone," grinned Micha.

"Yes, Boss." Rathbone stepped up to the men and slipped out his laser knife. "You all know who I am; betray Micha's trust here and I'll hunt you down, understood?" There was a round of sheepish nods as he cut them loose.

"Rathbone, you said you have the parts to fix that ship?"

"I do, Boss. I can have her ready to fly in a day, but there's a small problem."

"And that is?"

"There are two wounded men and at least two more able-bodied men there with them."

"I'll deal with that. At first light you and Keira go to your hideout and collect the spare parts. We'll go deal with the opposition. Now, back to the business at hand; which of you men are with me and who remains loyal to the Company?"

"So you want us to trade one army for another," said Dav. "Why would you trust us even if we do?"

"As I said before, you don't have a lot of options. Join us and you'll be treated as a human, not a machine. We'll do what we can to get your families out to the rim where you can keep them in safety. You'll get paid sometimes and not others, but you'll have a home you can call your own.

"I'm not going to try to talk you into this. I don't need you, and if I can't trust you to give me one hundred percent effort, then I don't want you. I can pass you off to the Borelian Guard and let the viceroy decide your future."

"If you don't need us, then why make the offer, why take the chance, Mer...Micha?" the commander caught himself as Zartah's blaster leaped to his hand.

"Someone took me in when they didn't need me, and it's happened more than once. I now offer you the same to you. Accept and one day you'll get the chance to pass it along to another. That's how we live."

"Count me in," sighed Dav. "That's the best offer I've had in a long time."

"I agree," nodded the commander. The rest of the men nodded in agreement as well.

"Any objections?" asked Micha. There were none. "Anyone want to be handed over to the viceroy?" There were no takers.

Micha tossed the commander one of his own comms units. "Contact your men at the ship. Tell them all's well and that you'll return tomorrow. You'll brief them then."

He nodded, then took up the unit, holding it close to his mouth. "Commander Darks to Onyx One, come in Onyx One."

"Onyx One here, Sir."

"Target acquired. We'll return tomorrow with a mercenary crew. Do not fire upon us. There will be a full briefing."

"Mercs, Sir?"

"Mercs, flying Arcalian fighters. Repeat, do not fire upon those ships. We'll be with them; with our objective."

"Understood. Onyx One out."

Micha sat thinking for a moment. Zartah grinned as Micha looked up and turned his gaze to the ships. "Jorge, could you find that ship in this moonlight?"

"Sure, Micha."

"Gorda, fly Jorge, Murtah, and Zartah, out close, but don't let them know you're there."

"We setting up sniper posts, Boss?"

"Yes, Zartah. Get as close as you can without being seen, but be ready when we arrive. If those boys even look suspicious, take them down."

"Got it, Boss." The four men rose and gathered up their weapons then leaped aboard the remaining ship. An hour later Gorda was back.

"All set?" asked Micha.

"All set, Boss."

"You don't take any chances, do you?" said the commander.

"No more than I have to, Commander."

"I'm relieved to hear that," he grinned, as he settled down further, squirming a bit to get more comfortable. "It means my chances of survival have just gone way up."

"Oh?"

"You're right, we were beaten. Brenna nearly drove us crazy and she got away from us. Rathbone was picking us apart and we were down to less than half of our numbers. I expected to die by your hand, get killed by Rathbone, or killed for my failure by the Company. I can see how you operate, and I think we all stand a better chance of surviving this mess if we follow you."

There was a round of chuckles at that, then everybody settled down to sleep. Keira and Rathbone took the first watch. A few hours later Micha relieved them, Edie at his side. Jip went with them and happily snuffled around while they settled down to watch.

Edie leaned against Micha and laid her head on his shoulder. "What is it, my love?"

"Edie, how do you do that?"

"I can always tell when something is bothering you. What is it?"

"I've got a lot of people depending on me to keep them alive, Honey. Lessa will want to go to Elliston Prime to face O'Loran. We'll be in the jaws of the beast, and I have to make sure we all come out again. We also have to gather up the families of these men.

"I'm just a farm slave, Edie. How did I end up like this? It scares the hell out of me when I think about it. It would be so much simpler to just take Brenna and go home to Nova."

"You carry a heavy burden, my man. People have come to depend on you because you turned their lives around. You give them purpose, direction, and you make them feel worthwhile, important.

That's how you got here. It's your practical farmer's nature that makes you so successful.

"Micha, we all know the risk we take here. We all know this could go wrong. We've always known, but that doesn't matter."

"It doesn't?"

"No, lover, it doesn't. What matters is that we belong, we stand for something, we're part of something, and if we die tomorrow it'll all have been worth it. The idea isn't to live as long as possible, my darling man, it is to live as well as possible. Folk who have a strong purpose live well. That's your gift to us, and why we all follow you without question."

Micha sighed deeply, then pulled Edie closer. "How did I get lucky enough to bond with such a wise woman?"

"You won her in battle, my fine warrior."

He chuckled as he pulled her tighter and kissed her deeply. "Micha, we're supposed to be on watch," she breathed, as he gently lowered her to the ground.

"Jip'll watch," he whispered into her ear as he began to nibble at her neck. The dog wagged his tail and settled down, his ears still canted forward alertly.

Dawn found Edie sleeping peacefully, Jip at her side. Micha was awake and on watch. Suddenly his comm unit crackled to life. "Micha, we've got incoming!"

"Skeeter! Who, Lessa? Where?"

"Looks like Arlen slave raiders. Eight ships. I'm coming to pick you up."

"Incoming!" bawled Micha as he snatched up his weapons. Everyone sprang to life, grabbing at weapons and hastily brushing the sleep from their eyes as the Arcalian fighter dropped swiftly through the atmosphere, landing almost on top of them.

"How long, Lessa?"

"An hour or less, Micha. Think fast, do we run or do we fight?"

"Rathbone!"

"Here, Boss," he grinned, shouldering his weapons.

"Take Lessa and Brenna with you. Take the cyborgs as well. I need that ship in the air and ready to fight. Commander Darks, take your men and go with Rathbone. Your mission is the same. Protect Brenna and her companion. The crew will see how long we can stall those raiders.

"Kella, get in that speeder and get as far away from here as you can as fast as you can. I don't want you caught up in the fighting." She gave him a quick hug then fled. Her speeder leaped skyward then vanished into the light of the rising sun.

"They may not be after any of us," said the Commander.

"This planet is in Nova territory," growled Micha. "There'll be no slave raiding in my backyard. Get moving. Edie, you're pilot; Keira and I'll man the guns. Gorda, you've got Ena. Let's get in the air people."

Rathbone was impressed at how swiftly the crew leaped to obey Micha. "Commander, take your men and your two charges back to your ship as fast as you can. I'll swing by the hideout and pick up the spare parts." With that he sprang away at alarming speed.

"Prepare to move out, on the double," barked the commander. "I assume you can keep up," he said as he turned to Lessa.

"She can," replied Brenna, a hard edge in her voice. "The proper way to address her is Lady."

"Forgive me, Lady. As a soldier I should be more aware of proper rank."

"Accepted, Commander. We'd better get moving; we don't want Rathbone to get there first."

"No, we don't," he agreed. "I want to keep those men alive. Move out!"

The commander set a hard pace and had to shake his head at how easily the two women were keeping up. Somehow, on that long run, he came to accept his new role in life; as a mercenary working for the Black Witch. These people could have killed them all, or turned them over to the Company in disgrace. That would have meant death anyway.

These people offered life, and treated the cyborgs like any other men. He had seen the witch's power and felt a new sense of purpose; to keep the last of his men alive. He felt the chances of that were best in the witch's employ.

They were barely halfway there when the comms crackled. "Lessa, we've entered negotiations with the enemy. I'll stall as long as I can; will lead them away if I can't."

"Understood." Lessa moved ahead to increase the pace; the others followed.

They arrived at the ship to find Rathbone working at the repairs. Two armed soldiers were watching over him, weapons at the ready. "Stand down," puffed the commander as they arrived. "He's one of ours."

"Sir?"

"What did he tell you?"

"Only that he had come to repair the ship. Sir, that's Rathbone of Urn. He's killed over half our men. He's also suspected of being the one who blew up the R.I.M. labs, killing over two hundred cyborgs."

"Sadly, that was me," grunted Rathbone, as he worked a part into place. "I was at war with R.I.M."

"So, you're not anymore?" asked Brenna.

"That depends," he replied. "I signed on with Nova Crew. If the boss says go to war then I go to war. If he says no, then I fix spaceships. Ah, there we are. All right boys, go fire her up, see if she'll fly."

"Commander?"

"Stand down and do as he says," sighed the commander.

"Sir, he had a dispatch kit with him."

"You brought my kit?"

"I thought you might want it, Brenna," grinned Rathbone.

"Commander, brief these men and explain their options. Allow them completely free choice. Now someone take me to the wounded."

"Right this way, Lady," said one of the soldiers who had felt her power the previous day. He was very respectful as he led her to the two wounded men.

Brenna and Lessa tended to the wounded while the cyborgs manned the weapons. Rathbone took the helm and guided the ship into the air.

They broke atmosphere to find the crew involved in a pitched battle. Two Arlen ships drifted aimlessly amid a field of debris, but the remaining five were taking a toll on the Arcalian fighters. Another ship exploded under the fire of the two fighter ships, and then the newcomer arrived.

"That's an R.I.M. Invader class fighter ship," squawked a comm. "We'd better join forces here, Merc or we're both in deep trouble."

"Actually, that's one of my ships," replied Micha's voice. "Last chance to surrender."

"Ha! Very funny, Merc."

"Rathbone to Micha, come in Micha." It was Rathbone's voice on the comm.

"Rathbone, is your ship battle ready?"

"Yes, she is, Boss. Shall I blow this lot out of the sky?"

"Hold fire, Rath. What'll it be, Slaver?" For an answer the Arlen ships broke and fled into space. "Let them go, crew. We have other concerns at the moment. Return to the town of Attica."

"Micha?" Lessa had taken the comm.

"We took a beating, Lessa. We need to make repairs and you've got our mech-tech on your ship."

"Lead the way," she chuckled in reply.

The three ships swept down to the space port like birds of prey. Once again a group of armed men met them. They were extremely nervous. "Seems like we always show up at supper time," grinned Micha, as he alit and stepped towards them, arms wide and hands empty.

"You find what you were looking for, Merc?" asked one man, as he cautiously lowered his weapon.

"We did."

"So why did you come back?"

"We had an encounter with Arlen slave raiders. We need repairs and supplies for a long trip."

"You payin' in Company script again?"

"Our script is running a bit low," came Rathbone's voice as he approached carrying a bag in each hand, "however, we can trade sugar."

"You've got sugar?"

"Here, see for yourself." He tossed a bag towards them. It landed in the dirt and several packets of sugar spilled out. "You get the second bag as soon as we're ready to go. We'll need a few parts and fuel."

The men looked hesitant. "We could just take the town," Rathbone said dangerously.

"That's not how we work, Rath," sighed Micha. "I'm Micha, crew boss of Nova Crew. We'll pay what script we have and pay the rest when we return if you want it that way."

"Take the damned sugar, Jesup," said another man. "We'll get more for it in the long haul than the parts and fuel are worth, and you know it. Jesup, we really don't want to mess with these folks."

"We'll accept the sugar. You folks stayin' at Murgie's again?"

"There are crew quarters on that ship. Since we're low on script we'll camp on board to keep our bill down," grinned Micha.

"That's decent of you, Merc. Bring us a list of the parts you need in the morning." The man scooped up the fallen bag of sugar and turned away.

"All right," grinned Micha, "let's all go get a tour of our new home."

The ship was huge compared to what he was used to in fighting ships. Micha gazed all around in wonder as Commander Darks gave them all the tour and doled out the crew quarters. The quarters weren't spacious, but they weren't bad. The ship was built to carry fifty fighters as well as a flight crew. Nova Crew was just twenty two humans and one dog at the moment.

Commander Darks insisted Lessa and Brenna have the captain's quarters, but they gave that to Micha and Edie, taking the first officer's quarters for themselves. As Micha continued the tour he was doubly impressed with the ship. She had extra hull plating and was armed to the teeth with the latest weaponry. There was a sick bay, a huge armory, and a full galley.

"I told you she was all tricked out for a long trip," grinned Jorge.

"I'm impressed," grinned Micha. "This is a fine piece of machinery. Did you get her all back together, Rath?"

"Good as new, Boss."

"All right then, crew, settle in for the night. Seal her up Jorge, and then you get first watch."

As Jorge sealed the hatches, Lessa turned to Micha. "Have you given any thought to my request?"

"I've been a bit busy, but I'm working on it, Lessa. I assume the idea is to go to Elliston, watch your back while you meet with the CEO, and gather up the families of these men. Once your meeting is complete we return with full complement to Nova. Is that about right?"

"Indeed so, dear friend. Can we do it?"

"I think so. I'll put some more thought into it while Rath fixes our fighters. Right now I'm too tired to think straight."

"I know, my darling," said Edie, as she took his arm. "I'll take you to those nice captain's quarters so you can rest. All that negotiating always takes the good out of you."

"You're a hard woman," sighed Micha, as he put his arm around her and walked away, Jip right on their heels, tail wagging slowly.

On the Way

The crew quarters were small, two to a room, but comfortable. Rathbone sighed as he dropped his jacket on the bottom bunk. He truly expected to be alone. No one would want to share a room with an assassin. He was wrong. A second jacket landed on the bed next to his.

Rath turned to see Keira. She took his jacket and tossed it up on the top bunk. He looked into her icy eyes for a moment then grinned. "Think carefully, girl. I weigh over a hundred and twenty kilos. Do you really want to be in the bottom bunk, asleep, if the top one collapses?"

She tried to hold the cold stare, but failed. The laughter reached her eyes first, then her voice. Scooping up her jacket, she hopped easily onto the top bunk and passed his back.

Rathbone accepted the jacket from her hand and studied her closely for a moment. He'd fully expected he would end up with Jorge if he got a roommate at all. "Why, Keira?" he asked. "You know who and what I am. Why take the chance?"

She hopped down to face him again, gazing into his eyes. Keira pointed two fingers at her own eyes, then reached around and patted his back. "You're watching my back?" she nodded. "Why?"

A knife leaped to her hand. Keira opened her mouth and made a motion at it with the blade of the knife, then reached over to tap his chest with the blade. She put it away then tapped her own chest with a finger, then his. She then pressed two of her fingers tightly together.

Rathbone sighed heavily and let his shoulders sag. "They cut out your tongue, and they cut out my heart. We're two of a kind?" She nodded. "Keira, I swear I'll give as good as I get here. I'll be watching your back too."

Keira nodded, then stepped to the lockers and began to remove her weapons and clothing. When she finished, Rathbone was staring at her, bewildered. She held her nose and crossed her eyes then pointed at him. "Are you saying I smell bad?"

Keira nodded, then bleated like a goat. "Are you saying I smell like a goat?" he was trying to sound indignant, but the merriment was clear in his eyes. She gave him a thumb's up signal, then stepped through the door. He quickly stripped off and followed. Two doors away was the shower door. Keira had obvious scouted this out before. She was already in the water when he arrived.

Rath was under the water with soap in his hair when he felt a gentle touch on his chest. She was tracing some of his scars. There were a lot of them from the cyborg implants and she was tracing those. He took her hand, gently kissed her fingertips, then released her. He could see several scars on her body, too. "We are indeed two of a kind, Keira," he said, as he pointed to hers. She nodded and went back to washing her hair.

Murtah, Ena, and Gorda had found the showers by the time Keira finished and stepped under the warm air blower. Eyes closed, she moved through a slow motion dance as the air dried her. The dance was so graceful, and she so beautiful, they all stopped to watch. She finished and left the room without a backward glance.

"My gods, she must have been amazing before they broke her," mused Rathbone.

"She was," replied Gorda. "I saw her perform once, just before her planet was overrun. It was amazing. I've never seen anything half as good before nor since. The Arlens took her two days later. I was there with my crew as part of the force that drove them back. I found her, broken and bleeding, nearly dead, and got her to the medics.

Keira healed fast and was part of my crew until we both joined up with Micha.

"Don't mess with her, Rathbone."

"I'm Rath to my friends, Gorda. The girl's been hurt enough. I won't add to it."

"Thanks, Rath. I think you'll fit into this crew just fine."

Rathbone chuckled as he stepped under the blower to dry off. He returned to the room to find Keira asleep. He moved silently into the room, but his warning senses suddenly went on full alert, something was wrong. Her breathing had changed.

"Keira, have you got a gun on me?"

She chuckled as she reset the safety and tucked the weapon back under her pillow.

"You're not going to shoot me if I snore, are you?"

Her laughter was full and rich. It warmed his heart. With a smile on his face, Rathbone settled down to sleep. For the first time in many years, he was completely relaxed, and his body was free of pain.

Rathbone awakened to find himself alone in the room. Keira had arisen, dressed, and gone, locking the door behind her. He hadn't heard a thing. That worried him, was he getting careless, or was she that good? If she was, she was more dangerous than he thought. It would not be wise to underestimate this woman.

Shaking off the mood, he rose and pulled on his tattered clothes. A quick visit to the facilities was followed by a trip to the galley. He found Jip there, going from person to person, looking for handouts. "Jip, you miserable beggar, you should work for your living like the rest of us."

The big dog turned and pounced on him. They wrestled around for a moment, then Rathbone got them some food. Once they'd eaten, he left the ship and began inspecting the damage to the two fighters. "They've taken a pounding all right, but they were built for it," he said, as Micha approached.

"Will you need any help?"

"A few extra hands would nice. Two men?"

"Two it is," smiled Micha as he reached for the comm unit riding on his shoulder. "Gorda, Jorge, acknowledge."

"Gorda here, Boss, Jorge too."

"Ship number two, you guys are tech assist."

"Understood. On our way."

———◦———

FOR THE NEXT THREE days Rathbone was back in another world, one he'd thought gone forever. He tinkered, struggled, cursed, and coaxed the two ships back into fighting form and got the engines running better than they ever had. He loved every minute of it.

While Rath fussed over the ships, the crew was also busy. Lessa and Brenna had taken Jip home and Lessa blessed the land for the farmers. Jip refused to stay, so they brought him back as part of the crew. Kella returned with her father, who helped them devise a plan of action. Supplies had been laid in, weapons replenished, fuel supply topped up, and by the fourth day they were ready to go.

The ship had come equipped with five small fighter ships. Micha had given them to the people of the town to defend themselves from the slavers. In return, their supplies and repairs were free.

The three ships rose from the ground and shot into space. They had a long journey ahead of them. As soon as they cleared the atmosphere, Commander Darks sent a report. That news would reach Elliston long before they did.

They were barely away from the planet when the Invader's cargo bay doors opened and the two Arcalian fighters landed inside. A moment later, Kella's speeder returned and joined them. She had a passenger.

———◦———

"SIR?" THE SHORT BALDING man stood nervously, awaiting the tall fellow's attention. How he hated bringing bad news to the CEO. Finally, O'Loran turned to face him, then gestured toward a chair across from his desk. The nervous man sat and waited while the CEO lowered himself into his plush chair behind the desk.

"Should I brace myself, Mr. Dax?"

"I'm so sorry, Sir, but you need to be made aware of these developments."

"Relax, Jorm, I have yet to execute a messenger. How bad is it?"

"Apron Inc. and Broadsearch have merged, Sir. Their combined military is close to matching our own. R.I.M. still holds the power, but our grip is a bit more tenuous now."

"Ah well, we were expecting that move; it's no surprise. What do they call themselves now?"

"A.S. Inc."

"How very original. You're stalling, Jorm. I knew this was coming. Give me the bad news."

"Sir, our forces have been less than successful in Sector Nine."

"How bad is it?"

"The witch's hounds destroyed the first team. She's alive."

"Five ships attacking from ambush, and they were defeated by two? I said to send our best."

"We did, Sir. We did. The second team also failed. Apparently the witch didn't fall for the ruse. She was on Nova Prime when they attacked. All ships from both teams are lost. All survivors from both teams are in the custody of the new viceroy. He was unhappy to find them operating inside his jurisdiction."

"I'm sure the puffed up buffoon will put on a merry show," sighed the CEO. "What of the third team? Did the cyborgs retrieve Brenna?"

"I have a report here, Sir. They've succeeded and are on their way back with Miss O'Loran. Sir, they've taken casualties."

"Oh, did my daughter beat up the mighty cyborgs?"

"She killed three, Sir. Somehow she met and joined forces with Rathbone of Urn."

"She what??? That damned assassin is still alive and has Brenna?"

"No, Sir, he doesn't. Commander Darks has her on his ship and is returning with her. He has only eleven men left to him, but the assassin is dead."

"Finally, Jorm, a piece of good news. At least Brenna will soon be safely home, and then we can put Sector Nine back in its place. I've had more than enough of their independent ways.

"Prepare the military, Mr. Dax. As soon as Brenna sets foot safely on Elliston, I want a full armada sent to Sector Nine."

"Sir, that might not be in the best interests of the Company."

"What do you mean?"

The smaller man began to sweat under that penetrating scowl. "Such a move could leave us vulnerable to a hostile takeover by A.S. Inc."

"Dammit all to the nine hells," roared O'Loran, surging to his feet. He hurled a paperweight against the office wall where it stuck in the wall board and hung there well above the floor. He sank slowly back into his chair, brooding. "Suggestions, Jorm?"

"Perhaps we should wait until Miss O'Loran returns, Sir. The mercenaries might know something of use."

"Mercenaries? What mercenaries?"

"It seems that Commander Darks was forced to employ some local mercenaries to help subdue Rathbone. They've been promised huge rewards and are escorting the cyborg's ship home."

"You're right, Jorm. Mercs from that sector will have plenty of useful information. As mercenaries, they should easily part with the information for a large enough sum of money. Once we have the information, throw them in prison until they rot. We can't have them going back to Sector Nine spreading tales, now can we?"

"Indeed not, Sir," chuckled the smaller man.

———◉———

KELLA ENTERED THE MESS hall with her passenger. Micha instantly rose. "Greetings, Chieftain," he grinned. "Hungry?"

"I am, Micha," smiled the tall man, as he reached for a plate.

"As Chieftain of Nara Clan and the viceroy, it's your right to take command of this mission, Sir."

"Ha, not a chance," laughed Lortax. "I'm just along for the ride, Micha. Visit with friends, meet new people, that sort of thing." There was a round of laughter at that. Micha turned to address the room.

"Folks, we have our full complement now. We're going to Elliston Prime for a three-fold purpose. First, we take Brenna home so she can visit with her family for a short time. Second, we have to retrieve your families. This'll be the task of each man, to gather his family, companion and children only, and return to this ship. Last, the viceroy and the high priestess of Nova wish to have a face to face meeting with C.E.O. O'Loran.

"Once we complete our mission we'll be returning to the rim worlds as fast as possible. Further plans and individual assignments will be worked out as we get closer to the Hub worlds.

"Rathbone, you're chief engineer. Go see how much speed we can squeeze out of this ship." Micha finished speaking and sat back down. Rath rose and disappeared from the room, Jip right at his side.

Rathbone fussed with the engines for a few minutes then settled back into a seat. Unless something went wrong, he'd have little to do over the next few weeks. There was a reading tablet lying on the bench before him and he picked it up. A quick scan turned up an acceptable novel.

Free of pain and feeling safe for the first time in years, Rathbone settled back to indulge in his favorite guilty pleasure, reading. He was completely engrossed in the story and didn't hear her approach.

A voice spoke close behind him, sending him flying through the air. He rolled to his feet several feet away in a fighting crouch, a blade in one hand and a blaster in the other.

Lessa tried to stifle her laughter, but failed. "It's not funny, woman," he growled. "You are indeed that cruel witch I've heard so much about. First you heal me then try to kill me with a heart attack." Lessa completely lost the battle to hide her giggles.

"Rathbone, I am so very sorry..."

"No, you're not. You enjoyed sneaking up on and frightening the terrifying Rathbone of Urn. You did it on purpose."

Lessa hung her head in an exaggerated pose of contrition. "You're right, Rathbone. I'm a cruel and savage woman. Can you ever forgive me?"

Rath was grinning too. "Lady, you healed my body and granted me a longer life; I'd forgive you anything."

"Thank you, Rath. I'll be sure to take full advantage of that every chance I get." He chuckled at that.

"Forgive me, Lady Arlessa. I'm not familiar with the proper way to address a high priestess. There are none on the hub worlds. Do I kneel as you enter a room, or..."

"Whoa there, big fella, relax." Lessa slid gracefully into the seat next to the one he had so hastily abandoned. "We're friends, Rath. I'm Lessa to my friends and there will be no formalities unless it is a special occasion. It's proper then to kneel until bidden to rise. I promise there'll be no formal occasions aboard this ship. I came to talk."

"About what, Lady?" asked Rathbone, as he resumed his seat.

"To start with, what were you reading?"

"Oh nothing really, just an entertainment novel."

"Really?" There was merriment in her eyes as she continued to tease him. She picked up the reading tablet and glanced at it.

Rathbone was blushing furiously. "An adventure/romance, Rath? I never would have suspected."

"You're completely merciless, you know that?" he sighed, still blushing. "Fine, I enjoy the stories. They remind me of the life I once had."

"Oh, Rath, I'm truly sorry."

"It's alright, Lady..."

"Lessa."

"Lessa. You've granted me a new life. I intend to enjoy it to the fullest."

She smiled and nodded. "Rath, out there when we were rescuing Brenna..."

"I did promise to help you if I could, Lessa. Is this why you sought me out?"

"It is."

"You really had no plans to frighten the lights out of me?"

"Not at first, but it was hard to resist."

"I'm sure it was. I truly must teach you better self-control."

She laughed heartily at that. "So, where do we begin?"

"We begin by trying to understand the nature of the problem."

"My temper is the nature of the problem. It gets the better of me and I start to lose control. The curse of it is, I'm so much more powerful when the rage takes me."

"That's true for all of us, Lessa. Can you tell me what triggers the anger?"

She relaxed back in the chair and thought about that for a long moment. Rathbone made no effort to break her train of thought. "Frustration," she announced at last. "It's usually frustration. There are things I want to do, things that must be done, and when anything at all hinders that I lose patience. The anger rises up in me like a wave and tries to claim me. It knows what I'm truly capable of and wants

126 PRUDENCE MACLEOD

me to exercise that power, use it to destroy all in my path, all who would oppose me."

"So you see that rage as a separate being, apart from your true self, something that tries to control you?"

"Yes. Yes I do."

"Good, then we are almost there already. Lessa. Tell me what this is." He passed her a screwdriver.

"A screwdriver," she replied, slightly puzzled.

"A broader definition please."

"A tool?"

"Indeed. Could you kill someone with it?"

"Yes."

"Is that its primary purpose?"

"No, but it could be used for that purpose." He nodded his approval.

"What is this?" he asked as he passed her his blaster.

"A blaster, a weapon."

"Yes. Could you use it as a tool?"

"No. Wait, yes, under certain circumstances it can be a tool. Its primary function is to kill, but it can be set to stun, or it can be used as a threat. In that sense it can be used as a tool." Rathbone was grinning with delight.

"So, the rage that takes you isn't part of you. Like the screwdriver and the blaster, it's separate from you."

"Yes."

"Excellent, Lessa. What is its purpose, its primary function?"

She thought about that for some time. He did not disturb her. "I'm not certain of its purpose. Its function is to give me access to far greater power, but when it does it tries to control me."

"All right, gaining access to greater power is a good thing, like having a blaster when you're attacked. However, the blaster is of no use if you shoot yourself in the foot. A blaster has a tendency to twist in the hand, yet you can use one with confidence, yes?"

"Yes."

"How did you gain that confidence?"

"Through practice. Are you saying that with practice I can learn to control my temper?"

"Lessa, you've given this emotion a name and accepted all that the name carries with it. Give it a new name, call it the sonic screwdriver, the ethereal blaster, or jixob; it matters not, as long as you give it a name that has no real meaning attached to you. Call it a sword, your sword of power. A tool or weapon that is there for you to use or not as you choose."

"This is interesting. I must consider all you've said, Rath. I believe you may have just given me the key." She stood and stepped toward the door. "I'll leave you to your reading. Don't worry, my teacher. Your secret is safe with me."

He was shaking his finger at her as she left, her silvery laughter lingering on the air long after she'd gone. With a sigh of contentment, Rathbone went back to his novel, only now his seat was turned to give him a clear view of the doorway. He was smiling.

A while later he heard someone and looked up. It was Micha. "Hey, Boss, what's up?" he asked as his boots hit the floor.

"Enjoying your new job, Rath?"

"Yes, I am, actually. Am I about to lose it?"

"No," laughed Micha, as he lowered himself into the other seat. "At least not for a while, and not permanently."

"You've got a task for an assassin?"

"Easy, Rath. That's not what I want. If I want somebody dead, I'll most likely do it myself. I've got something else in mind."

"Oh?"

"It's my guess you have a network of people scattered throughout the hub worlds. That's how you managed to survive for so long without getting caught. I'm also willing to bet you've got a hideout somewhere near Elliston Prime. Am I right?"

Rathbone instinctively paused, then shook his head and laughed. "Yes, you're right. What's on your mind, Micha?"

"I'm a man who always likes to have a back-up plan in place. You know, just in case things go sideways."

"As things often do," chuckled Rathbone.

"Exactly. The plan this time is to get to Elliston Prime, gather the families of these men, keep Lessa from getting us all killed or from blowing up half the hub worlds, and get back to the rim in one piece."

"Tough job. What do you need from me?"

"We need a place to fall back to, and a ship waiting that can get us all out of there. If we don't need to use it or the hideout, so much the better."

"I can arrange that, I'm sure. I should go on ahead, will you trust me to do that?"

"I will."

"Why, Micha? You haven't known me that long and you're putting the lives of your whole crew in my hands."

"Your war was with R.I.M., but you kept Brenna alive and protected her. You helped Lessa keep control when I wasn't there to do it. At every turn you've proved true to your word and my people. Will you do this for me?"

"If you'll trust me to do it, I will."

"Can you get one of our fighters souped up enough to outrun this ship?"

"Maybe, but not by much, why?"

"Skeeter. I'd like you to have the back up in place before we arrive in the hub. I could send you ahead in Kella's speeder, but it is pretty cramped even for one person. That's a long way to go in a speeder. I'd rather send you guys in a fighter."

"Guys?"

"You, Jip, and Keira."

"Keira?"

"She'll skin me alive if I send you ahead without somebody to watch your back. She's the best I've got, Rath and she likes you. You can trust her."

"I'd trust her with my life anytime, Micha. I promise I'll watch her back too."

"I thought you two seemed to have teamed up."

"I haven't..."

"It's all right, Rath, I didn't think you had, but you two seemed to have a bond and I think you have the best chances of survival if it all goes sideways. If it goes bad, keep Keira alive and get her out."

"All right, Boss. Do you want me to see if I can get to O'Loran?"

"No. If by some mischance he crosses your path, kill him, but don't go looking for that chance. I'll probably get the best opportunity."

"You?"

"We're all agreed O'Loran has to pay for what he's done. If Lessa kills him that will always be a wedge between her and Brenna. One of us will have to do it to keep that from happening. I'll probably get the best chance, so don't get off course. His days are numbered."

"Now that is a comforting thought."

"We've got some time yet, so start tomorrow and see what you can do with a fighter. If I have to, I'll hold this ship back a bit to give you the time you need."

"O'Loran will smell a rat."

"Leave that to us. We'll think of something. You just do your thing and make that fighter ship faster. Outfit her for a long trip; take whatever extra ammo or supplies you might need."

———◉———

"SIR, MR. O'LORAN, DO you have a moment?"

"That depends, Jorm, is it good news or bad?"

"Perhaps a bit of both, Sir," chuckled Jorm, as O'Loran turned from the window to face him. "I have news from one of our agents in Sector Nine."

O'Loran lowered his tall frame into the plush chair behind the desk and indicated that his assistant should sit. "Now what has that bottomless pit of bad news spawned?"

Jorm sat back and relaxed in his chair. He would enjoy bringing good news for a change. "Well, Sir. It seems that the ship carrying Miss O'Loran has stopped for repairs. They were on Paxix for three days, but just before they requested assistance, a mid-sized fighter ship of Arcalian design emerged from her cargo bay and continued on at speed. Two days later it stopped to refuel at Nyla. Our agent there recognized the pilot."

"This would interest me because? Spit it out, Jorm, I can see the delight in your eyes. Who was flying that ship? Was it Brenna or was it the witch?"

"Neither, Sir," grinned Jorm. "There were two people on that ship. A female merc who never spoke, and the pilot. Rathbone of Urn."

"Rathbone?" O'Loran surged to his feet and began pacing about the room. "That misbegotten half-robot is still alive? You see this as good news, Jorm? Are you hoping he will succeed and you'll inherit my office?"

The smaller man laughed at that. "No, Sir. I don't want your job. That's the last thing I want. No, I'm happy to be delivering your old enemy into your hands. Rathbone is headed this way, yes. However, our agent managed to place a tracer on the ship. We know where it is, and by the speed it's travelling, it's in a hurry.

"The assassin will have to refuel at Torval Seven or Mylarn. My bet is Mylarn as it is a bit more out of the main travel routes and a primitive planet. Torval Seven is a bit too civilized; an Arcalian fighter would stand out far too much there. Having said that; we can have a welcoming committee at each refueling station. Sir, he seems to care a great deal for his companion."

"Does he now? Excellent. Do it, Jorm. Get those troops in place. Kill the cyborg if possible but, at the least, I want the woman alive. Rathbone has escaped my grasp far too many times for me to be complacent. Even if he escapes, I want that woman alive."

"Sir, if you recall…"

"Yes, yes, I remember what set him on this vendetta in the first place. That's his weakness, Jorm. If he escapes and we kill her he'll be twice as dangerous. If he escapes and we have her alive we can lure him into a trap. Get those troops in place at once."

"Already on their way, Sir." Jorm tapped at the tablet in his lap for a moment. "They have their updated orders now."

"Excellent, Jorm, my old friend. Rathbone of Urn. Why in the name of the nine hells of Porapix is he still alive? His body should have torn itself apart years ago."

"I have no idea, Sir, but I'll bet the good doctor would love a chance to examine him and find out."

"He'll get that chance," declared O'Loran, his voice low and deadly. "Once we have Rathbone, the doctor will be the one I turn to for answers. If we are extremely lucky, and we have him alive, the doctor can perform the autopsy while the cyborg is awake to enjoy it."

Jorm just swallowed hard and said nothing, a shiver running up his spine.

THEY WERE TWO DAYS out from their refueling stop when Keira found the tracer signal. She was fighting the boredom of a long flight by constantly running scans, always on the lookout for danger or signs of pursuit. She brought it to Rath's attention immediately.

"Well, that throws spent fuel in the soup," he sighed. "Leave it there for now, Keira. Let's think about this first. Someone, a Company spy, recognized one of us. Probably me, as you wouldn't trigger the Company's interest enough for a tracer." She shrugged her shoulders in a question.

"We know it's a Company tracer because that's an R.I.M. military frequency; rarely used except for dark ops. You know, big hush-hush stuff. So, the Company knows I'm alive and will be setting a trap for us. Forewarned is forearmed, girl. We have time to make a plan of our own. First thing we need to do is get word back to Micha. Is there a way you can contact him with a coded message he will understand?" She nodded.

"All right, I'll turn away so you can report." He turned away, but she slapped his arm hard. She pointed to her eyes then slapped his back. She then pointed to his eyes and pointed to her own back. She looked angry. "You're here to watch my back, not spy on me, is that right?" She nodded. "Micha actually does trust me?"

Again she nodded, then made a few hand signals. She'd been teaching him the hand signs she used to communicate, so he understood. "You asked for this assignment? Why?"

"To keep you out of trouble," she signalled. He laughed and shook his head. Keira turned back to the controls and unrolled a keyboard. She pointed to the frequency she was using so he would know it if he ever needed it. Rathbone nodded his appreciation for her trust.

Her fingers flew as he watched. "Micha, the hounds are tracking the wolf."

"Code," grinned Rathbone, "in case the signal is intercepted. So Micha will know we're being tracked. He will also suspect they will put a tracer on his ship as well."

She nodded and signalled.

"You think he'll have a back-up plan for this? I know, I know, Micha always has a back-up plan. I like that young fellow more and more all the time.

"All right, Keira. We'll assume Micha can take care of himself. Now we must devise a plan of our own."

She grinned and signalled.

"Yes," he agreed, "we should have a back-up plan too. Let's put our heads together and see what we can come up with."

For the next seven days they worked on their plans. They also worked on something else Rathbone thought of; a vocal language. Keira couldn't form words, but she could sing notes. This was a language only they could understand. It was basic, but it worked. They practiced communicating in both vocal and sign languages as they sped toward their destination. The combination of these two extra means of private communication would serve them well in the days to come.

Springing the Trap

A nother week of practice passed and the fuel began to run low. Keira tapped the fuel gauge and Rathbone nodded. "All right, partner, the time has come. We'll stop at Mylarn. I know that planet. It's a cold and primitive place with a number of wild tribes and far too many big predators. There's only one refueling station there, so we know where they'll have their trap set. Are you ready?"

She grinned and hit a perfect D note. Keira settled into the pilot's seat while Rathbone checked his weapons. He filled a pack with extra ammunition and assorted throwing knives. As the small planet grew in the view screen, Rathbone strapped on a jump chute. When he was ready, he nodded.

Rathbone was ready at the airlock as Keira brought the ship in fast and low. She overshot the fueling station and disappeared behind a hill for a moment, then reappeared and landed close to the fuel docks. As she opened the lock and descended to the ground, she was swarmed by a dozen armed troops.

Two men held guns to her head while the rest searched the ship. They reported back, empty handed. "Sorry, Sir. The ship's empty. There was no one else aboard."

"Where is he?" the officer snarled in her face, as he pressed his weapon to her head. "Answer me. Where the hell is he?"

Keira shrugged her shoulders with a questioning look. The officer grabbed her collar and shook her violently. "Answer me, dammit. Speak; or I'll cut out your tongue." For an answer she opened her mouth wide and waggled the small stub of her tongue at him, fury dancing in her eyes. He released her and turned away.

"Sir?"

"Someone's already cut out her tongue. We'll get no answers from this one."

"So what now, Sir?"

"We were ordered to bring her back alive. Take her to our ship and confine her in the brig. O'Loran will learn nothing from her, but that's not our problem. Rathbone isn't here so we've done what we can. Let's go."

They marched Keira away towards the huge hanger nearby. It was the only place big enough to hide a ship from incoming crafts. At a signal from the officer, the doors were opened and an auto-hauler pulled the ship out to the refueling docks.

While the ship was refueled, Keira was locked in a secure room. As soon as the ship was fueled, the pilot began ignition sequencing. Three switches into the process, he received a negative contact alert. Hair stood stiff on his arms as he punched in the code for a full diagnostic. His eyes widened in fear as the screen showed numerous error messages.

"Sir, the engines have been sabotaged and the ship's crew hasn't returned from the hangar."

"What? Why? How? When?"

"Sir, it must have happened while we were securing the prisoner and searching her ship."

"Rathbone. That bastard was on that ship with her. That's why she missed the first approach. She was dropping him behind us. Dammit, they knew we'd be here. They must have discovered the tracking device."

"Sir, what do we do now?"

"Can you make repairs?"

"I might find the necessary parts back in the hangar, Sir..."

"But?"

"Sir, I don't fancy my chances if Rathbone of Urn is in that hangar."

"We can't just sit here. Comms, signal base for assistance. Tell them we have the woman and Rathbone is trapped on this planet."

"Negative, Sir. The comms panel has been disabled."

"What? Skeeter! Can you repair it? I know, I know, maybe there are parts in the hangar. Well, one thing we can count on for certain. Rathbone will be in that hangar."

"Sir?"

"We have no choice, do we? The woman is safely locked up in the brig, so we leave her there and go after the assassin. I just hope the ship's crew is still alive. Post two men to guard her and assemble the rest at the air lock."

"Yes, Sir." The soldier hurried away. He soon returned and reported that all was in readiness. The commander led his men down to the air lock, where they paused to check their weapons. They were about to face the most deadly threat any of them had ever faced, a man who refused to die. A man who could not be killed.

———◦———

KEIRA SWUNG LOW OVER the hill and Rathbone bailed out as she banked for the turn. He waited until the last second before he fired the chute to slow his fall. It was a hard landing, one that would have killed a normal man, but Rathbone was far from normal. He rolled a couple of times then leaped to his feet and raced toward the hangar, praying he wouldn't encounter any big predators. He didn't.

There was a high, electrified, fence protecting the refueling station from predators. Rathbone leaped it with ease and raced to the hangar; the back door was open.

Slipping silently inside he made his way to the big ship that took up much of the hangar. There were several men in the lunchroom, and he listened for a moment. Grinning, he secured the door from the outside. He'd heard them talking about the soldiers and how they were supposed to stay out of the way until it was all over. All five of the workers from the refueling station were there, as were the ship's crew. Some days it was just better to be lucky than good.

Once he had the men locked in the lunchroom, he ran to the ship and slipped inside. It was an easy task to disable the comm panel and then the engines. He had barely enough time to vacate the ship before the big doors opened and the remote-controlled auto hauler began to pull the ship out into the open.

Rathbone double checked to make certain the workers were still trapped, then he leaped to the catwalk, high in the hangar. He took up a position with a clear view of the big doors and the open space beyond then settled down to wait. A little while later, he broke into a huge grin as the soldiers exited the crippled ship and began to march toward the hangar.

The soldiers were well out in the open, with no hope of close cover, when a shot from a projectile weapon rang out, the bullet bouncing off the pavement at their feet. "That's far enough," bellowed Rathbone. "I don't want to kill any of you, but I have no problem doing just that if you force me to it. Lay down your weapons and step away. Live to fight another day."

"Not a chance, Traitor," replied the commander, "besides, your woman is trapped inside the ship with my men. Kill one of us and she dies. Drop your weapons and come out peacefully. She'll live another day."

"You don't fully understand the situation, Commander," called Rathbone. "Keira isn't trapped in the ship with your men. Your men are trapped inside with her. They're probably dead already."

The commander laughed at that. "Nice try, Traitor, but my men are the best. Your woman is securely locked up, with two heavily armed men at her cell door."

"If you say so, Commander, but I'm afraid we must ruin you day."

As his words died on the air, there was a shot from behind and one soldier's weapon leaped from his hands. They all spun around to see Keira standing in the fighter bay door. She made one hand signal, then disappeared from sight.

"Last chance, Commander. Lay down your weapons. Keep your men alive one more day."

It didn't happen. The commander barked an order and the men scattered for cover. Three fell almost instantly and two more were badly wounded before they reached shelter behind the smaller buildings. The commander swiftly directed his men to lay down covering fire, while three were sent to the back door of the hangar.

Rathbone was already outside by the time they arrived. These men were well trained, but they were only human and they hadn't seen much actual combat. They were no match for the big cyborg. He leaped from behind a bush and felled the first man with a single blow. The second man went down with a knife in his chest. The third got off a shot, but he hit the body of his companion as Rathbone used the dying man as a shield. Rathbone put three shots into the soldier, then raced back inside the hangar.

The remaining six soldiers were just entering the hangar through the big open doors. Seeing Rathbone, they took cover behind work benches and equipment. A hail of bullets and the sizzle of blaster fire followed him as he raced through the hangar. He zigzagged across the open area and ducked behind a small ship that was in for repairs.

They concentrated their fire on that ship, but somehow he managed to get around it. The commander was horrified as, in spite of all their efforts, Rathbone made his way to the first man's hiding place and killed him. A few moments later he had found and dispatched another, and then another. In terror the last three men tried to flee, but they met Keira coming the other way.

It was over in an instant. The commander's last thought was to wonder at how any woman could possibly move that fast. He died without knowing the answer.

"Are you alright, Keira?" Rathbone asked, as he walked out to meet her.

She nodded as she slung her rifle back over her shoulder.

"Any alive in the ship?"

She shook her head then signalled, a grin spreading across her face. "I love it when a plan works out."

"So do I," he grinned. "Well, Micha wanted us to find a ship big enough to carry everybody out if the mission goes awry. Looks like we have our ship. You put the Arcalian ship into the fighter bay and I'll go put the engine back together.

She nodded and stepped away. Keira had barely taken two strides before a shot rang out. Blood spurted from her chest and she fell to the ground. The wounded soldier who had fired had no time for a second shot as Rathbone was on him. A big boot crushed the man's skull, then Rath was back at Keira's side.

She groaned and held her hand over the wound, trying to staunch the blood flow. "Keira, thanks be to the gods, you're alive." She gave him a weak smile as he swept her up and carried her onto the ship. He found the infirmary and laid her gently on a bed.

"Now let's have a look at that wound." He opened her shirt to see the hole in her shoulder. "Damn, girl, you are one lucky soldier. Your rifle strap slowed it down a bunch and it missed the bone. I have to dig it out of there, but it should heal up fine in time. I'll see if I can find something to knock you out with."

Keira shook her head and indicated he should do what he had to do. She took the thick part of her collar between her teeth and bit down. The hard look in her eyes told him to get to work.

"All right, if you're sure; but I'm no medic," he cautioned her, as he searched for and found the sterile instruments. "This will hurt like the nine hells. Be as still as you can."

She nodded and bit down harder on the cloth, the muscles of her jaw rippling from the effort. She flinched several times and groaned twice as he probed for the bullet, but she didn't move. Finally, he found it and began to pull it out. She screamed and fainted as he extracted the jagged bullet from her body. Rathbone stitched up and bandaged her wound, then made her as comfortable as possible.

Keira awakened to find herself covered with a blanket, her wound bandaged, and an assortment of pain killers on the table beside the bed. She selected one and gave herself the injection. She was so terribly weak. Collapsing back on the bed, Keira was soon asleep again. As she slept, the witch's magic worked its wonders.

Keira awakened twice and each time she found food, water, and pain killers on the table beside her. The thrum of the big engines in the hull told her they were in space again. She ate, then went back to sleep.

On the third day, she awakened refreshed and restless. Keira pulled away the bandage to find the wound sealed and a fresh new scar on her upper chest. Carefully she tested the range of motion in her arm. She knew Rathbone had been afraid she wouldn't regain the use of that arm. Keira smiled as she began to move gracefully through a series of combat arts moves. She had full use of her body again.

After prowling the ship for a while, Keira finally found Rathbone in the engine room. Grinning, she slipped silently in behind him and slapped his shoulder. He exploded into action, striking out as he launched himself away from his seat.

Rathbone rolled to his feet in a fighting stance to see her grinning at him. "Keira!" With a shout of delight, he leaped at her and swept her into a bear hug, holding her tightly to him. "Oh gods girl, I was afraid I'd lose you."

Keira returned his embrace. It felt good to be held by this man. For some reason she'd wanted this. He seemed to be in no hurry to release her and she was in no hurry to go. She had watched the play between Micha and Edie and it reminded her of her parents.

She'd thought such things were out of her reach after the Arlens had tortured her, but now...perhaps...

"Who and what are you, Keira?" he asked softly, as he gently released his hold on her. "I struck at you. A normal person would be dead, but you batted aside my blows. I'm so very sorry. It would destroy me if I hurt you. Promise you'll never do that again."

"Forget that," she signalled, a smile on her lips. She gazed into his eyes for a long moment then stepped back. Her face sobered as she spoke using both sign and voice. "You ask who I am. I'm Keira of Nova. I'm a warrior of Nova Crew. I have no mate or living kin.

"You ask what I am." She paused for a moment, fear and hesitation easy to read of her face. "I'm your woman if you want me."

Stunned, Rathbone just stared at her, slack jawed. When he neither moved nor spoke, her eyes hardened with tears and pain. Keira spun on her heel and ran.

Rathbone started from his trance and ran after her. The full depth of what she'd said penetrating his mind and heart. Hearing him behind her she sped away. He ran as fast as he could, but her speed was equal to his own, and he couldn't catch her.

Eventually she ran out of ship and turned to face him; a wounded soul prepared, once again, to fight for her place. The pain and anger were easy to read by the tears that streamed down her face. A blaster leaped to her hand as she began to signal to him. "Don't touch me. I will shoot you. I can see you don't want me. I'm not a real woman. My body and mind are broken. Perhaps you can find a soft woman more to your liking on Elliston."

Rathbone let his posture completely relax, offering her an easy target. "Of course I want you, woman. You have no idea at all of your beauty. Any man with a pulse would want you. I know some of what was done to you, Keira; that's why I held back from declaring my feelings for you. I ,too, am broken. Perhaps together we can become whole again.

"I am Rathbone of Urn, warrior of Nova Crew. My mate passed into the mystery many years ago. I have no living kin that I am aware of. If the offer is still open, I would be honored to have you as my mate. I warn you; I'm no prize, girl. You'll surely have your hands full trying to keep me out of trouble."

The blaster fell to the floor with a soft clang. "You truly want me?" she signed through her tears.

Rathbone stepped closer and gathered her into his arms. "Of course I want you, silly woman," he whispered into her hair, as he held her gently. "What man wouldn't? Keira, I was so afraid to show my desires because of what was done to you. When you declared, I was stunned at my good fortune and didn't respond quickly enough. I hurt you and that was never my intent."

She pushed back and gazed into his eyes. Tears still wet her cheeks, but she was smiling through them now. He pulled her close and kissed her. Keira flinched slightly then responded. His tongue probed at her lips and she jerked away, turning her face away from him, her hand over her mouth.

The big man pulled her back into his arms. Gently, he moved her hand away from her mouth and tipped up her chin with a forefinger. "Oh, no, you don't woman. I want all of you." Gently he kissed her again. As he probed at her lips she stiffened, but opened her mouth and gave herself to him. She moaned with pleasure as he explored her with his tongue.

Rathbone's hands caressed her arms and back carefully, gently, seeking the limits of her courage. As his huge paw closed on her buttock, she flinched again. Gently he took her shoulders and held her away from him.

Fear and confusion were clear in her eyes and expression. "So it's going to be like that, is it?" he asked, a grin of pure mischief on his face. "All right then; if you want me, you'll have to catch me first." With that, he sprang away.

Keira was startled for a second, then she gave chase. Rathbone could easily outrun the fastest man, but he could hear her gaining on him. Laughing, he fled through the ship with Keira closing in on him. He reached the captain's cabin and leaped through the door only to be tackled from behind. He fell forward onto the bed with her on his back. With a groan of protest, the bed succumbed to the assault and collapsed.

Rathbone was on his back with Keira astride him, gazing at him with mock ferocity. With a jerk she ripped the shirt from her body and tossed it aside. She then tore open his shirt and placed her hands flat on his broad chest. Her expression turned serious as she began to trace his scars with her delicate fingers.

Tentatively he reached up to lightly trace some of the scars on her chest. She gave a small gasp as his fingers brushed the new scar just above her breast. The look in her eye was no longer fear or uncertainty, it was lust. She took his hand and moved it onto her breast, moaning with pleasure as he gently kneaded her firm flesh and lightly tweaked the nipple.

Keira gasped and ground her hips against his growing erection. With a growl of lust she leaned over and thrust her breast into his mouth while frantically fighting to release the catch that held his pants together.

———◉———

"SIR, THERE'S BAD NEWS I am afraid."

"Sit down, Jorm. I assume it has to do with Rathbone. It's always bad news where that accursed assassin is concerned. Go ahead, let me have it."

"Well, Sir, we were right about his fuel stop. The military sent out their men on the Star Wolf."

"The Star Wolf... the new intruder class ship?"

"Yes, Sir. It was to be an easy run, so most of the crew was given leave on Elliston. They took a small crew out and dropped off half the soldiers on Torval Seven, then proceeded on to Mylarn. That's the last we have heard from them until today."

"That figures. What happened?"

"The condensed version, Sir, is Rathbone locked the ship's crew in the hangar, killed all the soldiers, and stole the ship. We believe he may be headed for Urn."

"That's a ploy, and we both know it. Rathbone's coming here. He wants to kill me and probably is near death. He wants to take me out before he dies."

"What should we do, Sir?"

"Prepare a reception committee for him, Jorm. I have another appointment. It may be a few days before I return. Is there any word from Brenna?"

"They're well on the way, Sir. They should be arriving in less than two weeks."

"Excellent. Send word to my companion that I want a gala ball arranged to welcome my daughter home."

"Yes, Sir. Should I release Lady O'Loran from custody?"

"Yes. Give her freedom of movement, but keep guards with her. Get busy, Jorm. I'll be back in a few days."

"AH, MR. O'LORAN, YOU'RE a month early. What brings you to the lab today?"

"I have news, Doctor. Your Frankenstein's Monster is returning."

"Sir?"

"Rathbone of Urn is still alive and he's coming here."

"What???" The man in the white coat paled until his face matched the coat.

"Yes, Doctor, that monster is still alive and coming here. I'll try to bring him to you alive for study, but no promises. However, this does speed up our timetable. I want you to finish the upgrades now."

"Now? Sir, that could be dangerous. We've been going slowly so we can..."

"We're out of time, Doctor. That assassin is coming for me, and I want to be ready. We have to finish it and we have very little time left. Prepare your operating room."

"Yes, Sir. Right away, Mr. O'Loran."

As the man scurried away, O'Loran picked up a heavy metal bowl and crushed it in his hands. "You will not find me easy prey, Assassin, this I promise you," he muttered as he gazed out the window.

Entering the Hub

Rathbone started awake, surging to his feet and grabbing for a weapon. He was alone in the captain's quarters. Once again, Keira had awakened, dressed and left without disturbing him. Relaxing, Rathbone yawned and stretched, then stepped into the facility to wash the sleep from his eyes.

Keira was on the bridge, busy working, first one console then the other. She looked up and smiled brightly as he entered. She sang a sweet note of greeting then returned her attention to the console.

"Keira, how the hell do you keep disappearing from the room without me knowing? It's starting to make me a little crazy." He pulled her into a hug and lightly kissed her cheek.

"It's because I belong to you; I'm a part of you. That's why my movements don't disturb you," she sang and signed in reply.

"I think you do it to torment me," he grumbled. She laughed and pushed him toward the captain's chair. "Oh no, girl, this is your bridge. I'm going down to the engine room, then I'm going to check those fighters in the bay. I knocked things about a bit to get our ship in there."

"Hurry back to me," she signed, then returned her attention to the panel on the wall.

"I will," he sang, as he left and trotted down the corridor. He knew it took more than two people to operate a ship this size, but by using their super speed and reflexes they could manage until he could recruit some help.

Rathbone found the engines purring away as he knew he would. He continued on to the fighter bay to sort out some of the chaos there. It took a good while of fiddling around, but he managed to get every fighter, plus their Arcalian ship, straightened out for a fast exit if needed.

Smiling with satisfaction he headed back to the bridge, stopping by the galley for some food on the way. He walked onto the bridge and passed Keira a plate of food. She smiled with delight and sank back into the captain's chair to enjoy her meal.

"I think we're about close enough to send out a call," said Rathbone, as he checked a few dials then sat at the comms station.

Keira stepped up behind him and laid her hand on his broad shoulder. She sang a few notes and he nodded. "Yeah, I know the military will be monitoring everything. I've disabled the tracking devices on this ship as well as the fighters in the hangar bay. Now I need to get us a bit of help to run this ship and to get Micha's backup plan in place.

"Here's how it works:" He grinned as he worked the controls. "This frequency is only used for machine to machine comms. Our ship is asking for permission to drop refuse on a small moon outside Zora 5. The signal will appear to be from an old freighter that used to haul garbage off Elliston prime. If any of my friends are still there we'll soon get a response."

Even as he spoke the response came in. "Okay, it looks good. With luck, by tomorrow I can show you off to my friends."

"You want to show me off?" she signed.

"Indeed I do," he grinned in reply as he pulled her down onto his lap. She melted into his arms and kissed him deeply, but the kiss was interrupted by a signal from the refuse moon. They were to dock at bay three.

"Skeeter," growled Rath, as he leaped up and moved to the pilot's station. He made a course correction then slammed his huge fist against the arm of the chair, nearly breaking it.

"What?" sang Keira.

"Bay three is the code to run," he explained. "When I escaped from the death lab years ago, it was a garbage hauler that took me out from bay three. We'll have to go to the backup location. There are a lot of old ships and other space junk orbiting a gas giant in the next system. That's our port of call."

Seven hours later they approached the gas giant with its rings of dust, ice, rocks, and space junk. They settled into orbit right at the fringe of the debris field. A few moments later they felt a soft bump as something locked onto their airlock.

The air lock opened, but there was no one there, just a chair. Rathbone started to laugh and stepped into the lock. He opened the door to the other ship and called out. "Come on over, Deke, I won't shoot you."

"Well, that's good news," laughed a voice, as the doors opened and the man walked through to give Rathbone a hug. "Rath, who has a gun in my back?" he asked, as he released Rathbone.

"Deke, turn around and meet the missus. Honey, this is Deke. Deke, this is Keira."

Keira gazed into the man's eyes for a long moment before lowering her weapon. Finally, she smiled and reached for his hand.

"It's a pleasure to meet you, Keira. Old Rath is looking fat and sassy; I expect that's your doing. It looks good all over him." Keira smiled and winked, as she gave his shoulder a squeeze; then turned and headed back towards the bridge. "She's not a big talker, is she?"

"She can't, Deke. An enemy took her years ago. They cut out her tongue."

"Out in Sector Nine? Sounds like something the Arlen military would do."

"Yeah, it was."

"The Arlen military is run by a dictator and a field marshal. He's one cruel bastard and expects the same of his men. She must be tougher than she looks."

"She is; I sure wouldn't want to face her in a battle."

"That doesn't bode well for your future then, does it?"

"Shut up, Deke," chuckled Rathbone. "Come on, we'll find her on the bridge then you can bring me up to speed on why you're here."

"That's an easy one. I got word from Gramps that you were still alive and headed for Elliston Prime."

"You're still in contact with Poppa?"

"Oh yeah, we all are. His spy in O'Loran's office sent word you'd captured a ship and were headed towards the Hub. It wasn't too hard to figure out where you'd probably make your stops."

"It was that easy to figure out, was it?"

"Well, Gramps did the figuring," said Deke. "Nice ship," he said, as they walked onto the bridge, "how many on your crew?"

"Just the three of us," replied Rath. "Anybody with you?"

"Nope, just me and that old broken down speeder."

"Break the seal and cut it loose. We have to keep moving."

Keira gave Rath a questioning look. "It's all right, Honey. Deke is a friend. You can trust him." She nodded and turned to Deke, gazing into his eyes as if judging the worth of his soul. Finally, she smiled and made a wide gesture at the whole bridge.

"She wants to know if anything here is familiar."

Deke glanced around then back to Keira. "It's all familiar. It's a lot newer and fancier, but it is familiar. I used to fly warships years ago. I can fly her. So where are we going? There's a big welcoming committee waiting for you on Elliston Prime. They'll spot this ship long before we break atmo."

"We're not going to Elliston," grinned Rathbone. "We're going to Refuse."

"That should be a lot easier to reach in one piece. Ready for orders, Captain Keira."

Keira laughed then took his arm and steered him toward the captain's chair. She made several swift hand signals to Rathbone, then turned away to the pilot's station. Deke looked at Rathbone, puzzled.

"She says you need to be captain. She can hear your directions and respond quickly. You can't understand her, so it is better if you command the bridge.

"I'm no captain, Rath. I'm a pilot. You be the Captain. Keira and I will be the crew." She looked over at Deke, smiled and nodded. She stepped away from the pilot's station and moved to check external sensors. The area was clear and she signalled Rathbone.

"Fine," chuckled Rathbone, as he settled into the captain's chair. "All right, crew, set course for Refuse and see if you can get us in there unseen."

Deke set the course then took the ship out of the scrap field and headed her out into open space. "We should let them know we're coming, Rath. They'll need time to gather supplies and weapons. They'll also need time to locate O'Loran and get his schedule."

"We're not going after O'Loran, Deke."

"We're not?"

"A lot has changed in the past couple of years."

"Like you found a way to stop the pain?"

"I encountered O'Loran's daughter and the crew of mercs she runs with. Keira was on that crew. They're called Nova Crew, and they have a witch with them. She healed my injuries and fixed the problems. I'm part of that crew now. The crew boss, Micha, told Keira and I to find a ship big enough to carry a number of families out to the rim worlds.

"So that's why we're going to Refuse. We need to disguise this ship and get her ready to haul in a hurry. We're just the backup plan. The gods only know what Micha is really up to."

"You serious Rath? You're working for somebody else and he sent you here?"

"He serves the Black Witch, Deke. She's got a hate on for O'Loran as big as mine. She wants to talk to him and Micha will make that happen. We're the backup plan. With any luck you'll never meet the witch."

"Oh?"

"She survived Nova, Deke. She's cleaned out the atmosphere and is rebuilding the planet."

"Oh skeeter." Deke saw the look Keira was giving him, so he decided to confess. "I flew the ship that poisoned Nova Prime all those years ago. I was a young pilot, on my first big mission. I had no idea what I was really carrying and just followed orders to drop the payload from space.

"Maybe I should meet her, Rath. Maybe I should face somebody who survived that."

"I'll want to talk to her long before you meet face to face, Deke."

"Ah well, that's for another day. Today you have some studying to do." Deke tossed an information stick to Rathbone. "That's the new codes and frequencies. You know Gramps; always keep changing things up so they can't track you."

"Thanks, Deke. You got them memorized? All right, as soon as we get close let them know we're coming in."

———◉———

THE SHIP DIPPED LOW and rocked back and forth as she approached the refuse planet. Anyone watching scans would think her a near derelict, headed for her last resting place. She settled down between two large piles of salvage and junk. The sun was just beginning to break over the horizon.

They were met by an old man in a long robe as they opened the hatch and descended to the ground, weapons at the ready. A wide grin of delight appeared on the old man's face as he saw Rathbone. He leaped at Rath and seized him in a bear hug.

"Poppa, it is good to see you again."

"It is good to see you still alive, Rath. What has happened? I sense no pain in you at all."

"There is none," grinned Rathbone. "I have lots to tell, but what about you? You're pretty spry for a man with ruined knees."

"All that payroll script you gave me came in handy. There's this med-tech out in Sector Four who can work wonders with knee replacements, if you've got the money. Now, who is this?" The old fellow had stepped past Rathbone to go nose to nose with Keira.

"Careful, Poppa. This is my companion, Keira of Nova Crew."

The old fellow looked Keira over carefully, stepping back slightly as she shifted her stance. She was taking his measure as well. "You've chosen a very dangerous companion, boy."

"Far more dangerous than you know, Poppa. Don't make her angry. Bad things happen when she's angry." Rath was grinning with pride now as he watched the two people he loved most size each other up.

The old man's eyes met hers, then he spoke softly. "You've been hurt, probably tortured. You've taken wounds and you kill without hesitation in combat. You've trained harder than most and that's kept you intact, but not whole. You've yet to speak so I'm guessing someone cut out your tongue."

She nodded slightly, never taking her eyes off the old man.

"Are the bastards all dead?"

Keira signalled to Rath with hand and voice. "She says it's a work in progress, Poppa."

At that, the old fellow's face split into a wide grin. "You're a perfect companion for him, Keira. He needs someone to watch his back and I'm getting too old for the task." He offered his hand and she took it in the warriors grip, then pulled him close and hugged him. "Welcome to the family, Keira," he whispered, as he returned her embrace.

"Enough of this," chuckled the old man, as he stepped back from her. He reached for the comm at his shoulder. "Come out and get some shrouding over this ship." Several men soon appeared with equipment. Lines were shot over the ship and loose shrouding was pulled over her to hide her from sight.

"All right, come inside and tell me what we're up to," grinned the elder Rathbone. "I've located O'Loran, but he won't be easy to get to."

"We're not after him anyway, Poppa," said Rathbone, as he and Keira fell into step with the old man.

"Oh? Well then, let's find the kitchens and you can fill me in."

Making Plans

"I don't like it, Boss, we should have heard from Keira by now. I hope... Hold on, incoming message. Huh, speak of the missing."

"What's she say, Gorda?" Micha rose from the captain's chair and approached the comm station where Gorda was decoding the message.

"She says, 'The den is warm.' Does that make sense?"

"It means they were successful and our backup plan is in place. All right, you've got the bridge, Zartah. It's time to gather the brains of the outfit and make a plan."

"Good luck with that," he grinned, as he took the captain's chair.

Micha found Lessa, Brenna, and the viceroy in the mess hall with Edie and Jip. "I'm sure glad you didn't send this guy off with Rathbone and Keira," laughed Edie, as she wrestled with the dog.

"I tried to, but he wouldn't go," grinned Micha. "Lessa, Chieftain, Miss O'Loran, we just heard from Keira. They're all set, so we have a fallback. Now it's time for you to tell me what's up so I can get organized. We're only a few days from Elliston now."

"Well it's about time you put some thought into this, Micha," teased Lessa, knowing full well he had thought of little else. "You should probably call in Kella and Siemon Darks; they'll be able to advise us on this."

Micha squeezed the common his shoulder. "Kella and Commander Darks to the mess hall." He poured himself a protein drink and sat with Lessa, Brenna, Edie, and Lortax. They were soon joined by Kella and Siemon Darks.

"Okay, we're all here, Chieftain. What's the plan?"

"Lessa and I have objectives, Micha. The planning part is your job," chuckled Lortax. "Lessa and I want a meeting with a certain CEO of a new super company before we take Brenna home. Once that's been accomplished, then we want a meeting with CEO O'Loran. Your task is to make it happen and get us all back out alive."

"There's the families of the cyborgs too, Micha, don't forget them," said Lessa, mischief dancing in her eyes.

"I haven't forgotten, Lessa. Commander Darks, how's that family extraction plan going?"

"I'll have to personally escort Miss O'Loran into her father's presence and you'll want to be with me then. Jorge's been working on the extraction plan and he seems to be ready."

"Fair enough, we'll let that go for now. Kella, have you been in touch with your networks?"

"I have, Micha."

"What can you tell me about this new super company?"

"It's called A.S. Inc., and it is a merger of the last two companies not absorbed by R.I.M. Their combined military is strong, but not quite equal to R.I.M., although they'd present a strong opposition to a hostile takeover attempt."

"So, you two are planning to throw in with this new A.S.Inc, is that right?" asked Micha as he turned back to Lessa and Lortax.

"If we can hammer out a mutual agreement," replied Lortax, "it could restore balance to the galaxy."

"It would also keep R.I.M. forces out of Sector Nine," grinned Micha. "I like it, but it'll mean bringing the Arlen Alliance under control."

"It will, but one thing at a time, Micha."

"Kella..."

"Working, Micha," she replied, as her fingers flew over a small device in her hand. "Not too sure how quick I can do anything, but I've got people on it now."

"That's all I can ask," smiled Micha.

"Brenna, tell me what you want to have happen?"

"Micha, I would like to see my father again, if only to express my horror at the things he's done. Would it also be possible for me to visit my mother?"

"Actually, I think that is a good idea," grinned Micha. "It'll give you time to prepare her to meet your companion." Lessa shook a warning finger at him, but he pretended not to notice.

"All right, as I see it we have to stall for time a bit. Brenna, we're close enough now; see if you can contact you mother. A few days' visit would give Lessa and the viceroy time to have their meeting and get back. It'll also give Jorge time to start gathering the families.

"Lessa, if you get your meeting with the A.S. Inc. CEO you should take Murtah and Ena with you. You'll have to take the Arcalian ship. Kella's speeder is far too small."

"I'll still have to go, Micha."

"I know, Kella. You'll want to arrange some mutual trade agreements I'm sure."

"Well, it would be an opportunity to good to pass up," she grinned in reply.

"All right, so far, so good. Now I need to know what kind of fire power we're likely to face. Commander Darks, can you shed any light on this?"

"I really hope we don't have to shoot our way out," sighed Siemon Darks, as he relaxed back in his chair, "because if we do, our chances are less than zero. The CEO's office is in a secure, heavily armored building. He'll have a hundred armed men, all specially trained, in that building. Miss Brenna may be able to get you in to see him, Micha, but he'll never let you out alive unless he has no other choice."

"Then he'll have no other choice," said Lessa, a cold dangerous note in her voice.

"Hmm, that could prove interesting," said Micha. "I imagine we'll have to leave our weapons behind, but I expect his security forces will have plenty of those. We can borrow some of theirs." This brought chuckles from the others. Micha reached for his comm. "Jorge to the mess hall."

He arrived a moment later. "What's up, Boss?"

"How's the plan for evacuating the families going?"

"I think I have it worked out, but I want to run it past you first."

"Talk to me, Jorge," grinned Micha.

"I see it like this. Every man goes home and gets his family. We all gather at the spaceport and board a small excursion ship. You know, a holiday for the soldiers after a combat mission. Once they're off Elliston the ship just cruises away, nobody the wiser for weeks until it doesn't return, and by then it'll be too late. Everybody will be well out in Sector Nine."

"I like it, Jorge. Can you get a ship?"

"I can probably arrange that," said Kella. "I can get a ship and get them out to Sector Nine, but you'll have to rendezvous with them before they get to Nova. I wouldn't want Lady Norlene to blast them before they set foot on their new home."

"All right, Kella," chuckled Micha, "Set it up. You've got a go, Jorge. If it goes sideways on you, Rath has a backup already in place."

Suddenly Zartah's voice sounded over the ship wide comm. "Battle stations. Battle stations. Micha to the bridge. This could get exciting folks."

"Skeeter," exclaimed Micha, as he leaped over the table and raced out the door. The others were right behind him. Once through the door Jorge broke off, Edie and Jip headed for the medical bay, while Micha, Lessa, Darks, and Lortax raced to the bridge. They arrived to find a fleet of Company ships bearing down on them.

Micha grabbed the ship-wide comm. "Power down the weapons, now." He sighed and strode to the center of the bridge where the visual comms could easily find him, and waited. He didn't have long to wait. The comms soon leaped to life and a man in an impressive uniform began barking orders at him.

"Intruder, stand down your ship and prepare to be boarded, acknowledge."

"Understood and refused."

"Why you insolent pup, I'll blow you out of the sky."

"You will not," replied Micha. "I have Brenna O'Loran aboard this ship."

"Yes, and I'm here to escort her to her father."

"Refused. Commander Darks and I will provide that escort."

"Darks has been declared unfit and will be replaced."

"No, he won't," said Brenna, as she stepped into the field of vision with Commander Darks on her arm. "I like this man and I trust him. You, I don't know or trust. Commander Darks will continue to be my escort. You may inform my father of my decision."

The man's face was turning purple with rage and Brenna had to suppress a giggle. The Admiral was still sputtering as the fleet surrounded the ship. Finally he turned his attention to Commander Darks. "Darks, report. Why the hells are you not in command of your own ship?"

"It is no longer my ship, Admiral. The ship now belongs to Micha."

"Explain."

"We picked up Miss O'Loran, but before we could get under way we encountered Rathbone of Urn. He disabled the ship and killed over half my men before we joined forces with this crew. Micha's crew eliminated the Rathbone threat, but there was a price to be paid. The ship was half the payment; the rest will be in script."

"Just who the hell authorized you to give away a Company intruder class ship?"

"CEO O'Loran himself," replied Darks, keeping a completely neutral expression. "He gave me strict orders to use whatever means necessary to bring Miss O'Loran home safe and sound. With Rathbone on the warpath, I had no other choice."

"So there you have it, Admiral," smiled Micha. "This is my ship, I have a passenger who prefers our company to yours, and that's all there is to it. However, since you're here, it would be nice if you could escort us to Elliston Prime. I hear there are lots of pirates in this sector."

"Very well," replied the admiral, his voice going all oily. "Would you folks care to join me for dinner in the Admiral's mess this evening?"

"Nice try, Admiral," chuckled Micha, "but I'm not going onto your ship and I'm not letting you aboard mine. We'll stay here, you stay there, and we'll get along just fine."

The admiral began to sputter again, but Micha interrupted him. "Nice talking to you Admiral, but I've got work to do now. Micha out." He gestured with his hand and Gorda cut the comms.

"What do you think, Boss? Will he try to board us?" asked Gorda.

"He doesn't dare risk Brenna," grinned Micha, "but he's going to be a serious pain in the buttocks. This is truly going to cramp our style."

"So what do we do, Boss?"

"You tell me, Gorda. This is your kind of action. We need to get this fleet off our back in a day or two. Suggestions?"

"We need a diversion, Boss. Something to call him away."

"Okay, sounds good. Viceroy."

"Yes, Micha?"

"What would happen if the Admiral suddenly got the idea that A.S. Inc. was massing forces on their borders?"

"Well, that would surely call him away."

"What else?"

"Well, once A.S. Inc. realized he had his fleet headed for the border they'd respond. That could get seriously tense."

"Yes, indeed. Would that help your negotiations any?"

"Micha, you're a thoroughly bad man and I'm glad you're on our side. Yes, my friend, it would indeed help me. Just don't start a bloody war."

"Kella, do you think some of your people might be able to start a rumor?" Micha asked into his comm.

"Sure. What do you need, Micha?" He told her. "I love it. I'll contact my people."

"We're being monitored."

"All messages are in code and the code changes with each message. They'll never figure it out, except for the one we want them to."

"Make it happen, Kella."

"Yes, Boss," she chuckled.

"Now we wait, folks," sighed Micha. "Now we wait."

Later that day, messages were sent home by the men, informing their loved ones of their impending return and of the excursion they planned as a grand holiday. Commander Darks sent word to his companion to join the excursion. He promised to meet up with them as soon as he'd delivered Brenna to her father.

The Admiral snorted in disgust as he read the messages. "I don't care about this crap, are you making any headway with those coded messages?"

"I don't believe they are code, Sir," replied the ensign. "If they are, it is a code we can't seem to break."

They were a day out of Elliston Prime when the ensign raced onto the bridge. "Admiral, we've cracked some of their code. These people have some very strange connections, Sir."

"Well, speak up man," barked the admiral.

"Sir, they received a message saying that A.S. Inc. forces are massing on the border of Sectors Five and Six. Sir, the message came from CEO O'Loran's office building."

"Blast. Signal the fleet. To the border of Sectors Five and Six. All possible speed."

"Aye Sir!"

———◉———

"LOOKS LIKE THEY BOUGHT it, Boss," chuckled Gorda, "They lit out like their buttocks were on fire."

"I love it when it works," grinned Micha. He gripped his comm unit. "They went for it, Kella. Your speeder is too small, take the Arcalian ship."

"Understood."

"Lessa, you're clear to go."

"We're on our way, Micha."

A few moments later, the Arcalian fighter dropped out of the launch bay and shot away. Micha gave them a few minutes to get some distance, then called Brenna to the bridge.

"Miss O'Loran, I think it is time for you to arrange a visit with your mother. I'd like to stall for a day or two before we have that meeting with your father."

"Micha, are you planning to kill my father?"

He sighed and let his shoulders slump. "I haven't decided on that yet."

"But you have been thinking about it."

"Yes, I have. Sadly, I expect that, even if I do, the man who takes over his position will be no better. I'm wondering if we're not better off as we are. You know the old saying, better the demon you know than the one you don't."

Brenna reached out to gently squeeze his arm. "My father has done unforgivable things, Micha. I swear, I will not think less of you;

no matter what you decide to do. However, I would like to face him first."

Micha just nodded, but didn't speak. Brenna patted his shoulder, once again marvelling at his youth and the weight he bore on his shoulders. In spite of everything, Micha was still barely more than a boy in his years. It was too much responsibility for one so young. She vowed not to add to his load.

Stepping over to the comm station, Brenna began the search for her mother. It took a while, but she eventually tracked her down on a ship headed to Elliston Prime. They decided to rendezvous in space for a visit. Commander Darks then signalled the delay to the surface.

A few hours later a military ship approached carrying Landy O'Loran. The ships locked up and Brenna's mother stepped through the air lock and into her daughter's arms. She had been accompanied by her guards, but Commander Darks pulled rank and sent them back, taking full responsibility for her himself.

Brenna took her back to the mess hall and introduced her to Micha. They settled into chairs and Micha brought them tea, asked if there was anything else, and then left them alone.

"Oh, Brenna, it is so good to see you well after all these years. We've heard the most awful things."

"Oh? What have you heard?" smiled Brenna, as she patted her mother's hand.

"Well, that you had become a dispatcher, for one thing. Brenna, how could you ever do such a task?"

"I was in the middle of a battlefield, Momma. No one else would help those poor people, so I did what I could. I still do."

"Still? You're still a dispatcher?"

"Yes, Momma, I am. Life is very different out on the rim."

"I can see that by the way you're dressed in that ragged uniform. Have you no decent clothing, Brenna?"

"None at all. In truth I wouldn't mind a chance to get tidied up a bit."

"I will certainly arrange that for you. We also heard you'd chosen a woman as companion, a witch from that plague planet? However did she survive? Brenna, I can't say I approve of your choice."

"Wait until you meet her, Momma, before you pass judgement."

"Is she here?"

"No, Lessa isn't on this ship. Momma, since when do you have military guards?"

"Since that evil assassin began hunting your father. Thank the gods you were out on the rim out of that one's reach. I'll admit I've been a virtual prisoner these past few years. It's such a relief to have a conversation without those soldiers listening in."

"Well, no one's listening in here, so tell me what you are up to these days."

"Well, your father let me out of prison..."

"Prison?"

"The summer house, he has it fortified to protect me from that awful assassin."

"Oh..."

"As I was saying, dear, I'm free as a bird and on my way to Elliston to plan a gala to celebrate your return. It's to be in three days and I have so much to do..."

Landy continued to rattle on, but Brenna was only half listening. She was a bit startled at how much her life and her ideals had changed since she was that naive girl who had left for the galactic rim to save the children orphaned by the trade wars.

"Brenna, Brenna, are you listening to me?"

"Huh? Oh yes, Momma, of course I am. Yes, I'll be delighted to attend the gala."

"*And I will be bringing Lessa with me,*" she vowed silently. "*Lessa can face Daddy, but Micha won't start a firefight with all those innocent people around. I just might be able to get this done and keep everybody alive. Micha said it best, better the demon you know and the one you don't. I know this one all too well."*

———◦———

AS BRENNA SAT CHATTING with her mother, Rathbone and Keira were putting the final touches on their ship's disguise. The shiny new warship now looked like a battered old explorer. Her surface had been recolored and a few unnecessary bits and pieces had been welded onto the sides.

The disguise wouldn't hold up to close scrutiny, but it would do at a glance. Under the façade she was still a warship and battle ready. The new name, Far Seeker showed dully in the fading daylight. "I think she's ready as can be, Keira, my love," sang Rathbone.

"Just in time, Rath," said the elder Rathbone, as he approached and handed Rath a reading tablet. "Here's a message from Jorge."

Rathbone glanced at the message then passed it to Keira. She read it and hit the delete button. "Looks like we're going to Elliston after all," he smiled.

"You'll need a crew who knows their way around down there."

"Yes, I will Poppa, you know anybody looking for dangerous work?" There was a round of laughter from the men gathering around. "We'll be taking on passengers and crew, and we won't be coming back, men. If you sign on you'll end up out on the rim or dead in battle. Think it over. We leave in two hours."

———◦———

"LEAVE YOUR WEAPONS here," snarled the huge soldier. Lessa, Lortax, Ena, and Murtah had just stepped off the ship. They were in the docking bay of a huge cruiser.

"I'm Viceroy Lortax and this is Lady Arlessa, high priestess of Nova. These people are her personal guards, they keep their weapons."

A man came hurrying towards them. "Greetings, visitors, please forgive my tardiness. I'm Enos, personal assistant to CEO Borga. I'll escort you to the visitor's lounge."

"They must leave their weapons," repeated the soldier.

"These people are our guests, not our prisoners, Sergeant."

"It's all right," grinned Murtah, as he unstrapped his weapons belt and tossed it back onto the ship. Ena did the same.

The big soldier scowled as they walked away, following Enos. He led them to an elevator and a swift ride later they emerged into a luxurious lounge. A small severe looking woman rose to greet them.

"Welcome," she said, as she stepped forward and offered her hand. "I'm CEO Borga. Please forgive the opulence of this place, it belonged to my predecessor."

"Viceroy Lortax." He smiled as he took her hand briefly. "This is Lady Arlessa, high priestess of Nova."

"Ah, the Black Witch of Sector Nine. Forgive me, Arlessa, but I don't believe in your mumbo-jumbo religious foolishness, nor do I care for trickery, but I do deeply admire the way you have driven O'Loran to the brink of madness. It is for that reason alone I've agreed to this meeting.

"Please be seated." Once they were sitting she spoke again. "Now what favour have you come to beg of me?"

Before Lessa could speak, Ena laid a hand gently on her shoulder. Lessa patted that hand and remained silent. Ena's warning had told her much. "We come to offer an exchange." She smiled as she relaxed back into the huge chair. "We're traders by nature."

"What business would I have with traders?"

"None," replied Arlessa, "but your people may have. However, that isn't the issue. Lortax."

"Here's the situation, CEO Borga. You have the reigns of a new super company, but R.I.M. is still bigger. Right now you're starting to look like a threat to them. If they attempt a hostile takeover, they will most likely succeed.

"As viceroy, I command a sizable military force. Not on the scale that you do, or that of R.I.M., but if mine were added to yours, the scales of power would be balanced. We come to offer a treaty of mutual protection."

"A treaty? You mean you've declared your independence and you want me to keep R.I.M. off your back so you can play the king."

"Call it whatever you want," replied Lortax, relaxing his body posture, "it'll keep them off your back too. At least it'll buy us both some time, time that we don't have right now."

CEO Borga didn't respond immediately, but took a moment to reflect before speaking. "Enos?"

"The Viceroy has a valid point, Ma'am."

"Indeed so. I wish there was another way. Any other way, but I cannot see one. R.I.M. is already amassing forces along my borders. All right, Viceroy, you have your recognition and treaty. Enos, draw it up."

"Yes Ma'am." He scurried to a computer and began working.

CEO Borga offered refreshments and poured the drinks herself while Enos worked feverishly. She asked about the possibilities of minerals trade with an independent Sector Nine.

At one point, when she was deep in discussion with Lortax, Ena leaned close to whisper in Lessa's ear. "Lady, she is lying about something. I sense a trap."

"As do I," replied Lessa. She made eye contact with Murtah who nodded slightly and mouthed the word *trap*. Lessa winked and relaxed back in her chair.

At length, Enos was finished and brought the document to them for signatures. They read the highlights then signed, and afterwards toasted mutual success with drinks.

"I must now return to my home offices," said CEO Borga. "Enos will see you back to your ship. It's been a pleasure doing business with you, Viceroy. Lady Arlessa."

"And you as well, CEO Borga," smiled Lessa. "Lead on, Enos, my friend."

Enos ushered them out of the lounge and onto the elevator. He turned to select the destination then turned back, but he was alone. Sweeping his arms wildly about, he searched the small space but he found no one. In a panic he returned to the lounge, but they weren't there either. A further search turned up nothing. Apparently, their ship had departed mere moments after it arrived.

As they stepped into the elevator, Lessa waved her hand and Enos froze as still as a statue. They filed out of the elevator and Lessa waved her hand through the air again. They felt a strong tingle this time, but she smiled. "Let's take this elevator to the docking bay."

They rode down in silence then headed back to their ship. "So, the CEO was too busy to see you today?" grinned the big soldier.

"Apparently so," Lessa replied easily. "We shall return another time. Please clear us for launch." He chuckled as he turned to his station.

"Did you get what you needed?" asked Kella, as their ship slipped out into space and shot away.

"We did, Kella."

"Sure didn't take long."

"It took bloody hours," grumbled Lortax. "Lessa, what the nine hells did you do back there?"

"Just a small time shift into the past," she grinned. "By the time she gets wise we'll be back on Micha's ship."

"Sometimes you scare me, Lessa," sighed Lortax. "Ah well, perhaps this'll make her think differently about your mumbo-jumbo."

"So, you got your treaty agreement," mused Kella. "This could bode well for business."

"Kella."

"Sorry, Viceroy, you're not supposed to know about that," giggled Kella.

"Kella, as Viceroy of the newly independent state of the Borelian Alliance, I intend to put a stop to your illegal activities."

Kella went deadly quiet and Murtah shifted to a fighting stance. They owed Kella far too much for this to be happening. What the hell was Lortax thinking?

"Kella, since the Borelian Alliance owes no allegiance to any of the companies, then no company of any stripe has exclusive trade rights in the Alliance territory. Also, since I'm the law there, I intend to grant you a free trader's license to operate anywhere within our borders."

Kella turned to Lortax, her mouth open, but no sound coming out. Murtah grinned and relaxed, sinking back into his seat. "Say something, free trader," chuckled Lortax.

"Sir, are you serious?"

"You've earned this and more, Kella. You'll still have to walk softly outside our borders, but as of right now you have the right to ply your trade within our borders legally."

"I don't know what to say..."

"Just say you'll get us back on Micha's ship before the fireworks start."

"Yes sir, Viceroy Lortax." Kella was smiling through happy tears as she opened up the ship's engines.

"Well, now that you're all legal and such, Kella, what are you going to do for fun?" asked Ena.

"I'll stay close to Zartah. He's always got something exciting going on." There was a round of laughter at that. "Perhaps I'll speak to Father about moving our head office to Nova, now that we're all above board and legal."

"There's plenty of room there, Kella," smiled Lessa. "There are lots of salvageable materials as well. You're welcome to come if that's your desire."

"It is, Lady."

"Nova grows strong again," sighed Lessa, as she relaxed back in her seat. "There were times when I despaired of this day ever coming."

"Well, don't get too excited yet," said Lortax. "We still have to deal with O'Loran and drive the R.I.M. troops out of our space."

"I know, old friend, I know, but I grow more hopeful by the day. We will succeed, Lortax. We'll see our people free within our lifetime."

Preparing for the Ball

"Well, Doctor?" asked CEO O'Loran. "Am I going to live?"

"Yes, and a lot longer than most of us," replied the man in the white coat. "You, Sir, are my greatest creation."

"Is it finished?"

"I believe so, unless you can think of something else you want to add, but I wouldn't be in a hurry to do more. Give your body time to adjust to this much first."

"As you say, Doctor. I do feel fine, however. It's amazing to me that I do actually feel the same as I always have.

"Come, Doctor, I want you to accompany me back to headquarters. I have a new lab established there for your use. We'll soon have our hands on that monster of yours, and I want to be present when you examine him in minute detail. I want to know how he has survived so long. Perhaps there is much to be learned from the assassin yet."

A small luxury ship with full military escort carried them back to headquarters on the other side of the planet. Upon arrival, the doctor left to inspect the new lab while O'Loran went straight to his office. His assistant was waiting for him.

"Welcome back, Sir."

"Thank you, Jorm. Have you been on top of things while I was away?"

"I've done my best, Sir, but things have been hopping."

"Come inside and relax, Jorm. Bring me up to speed." Jorm followed the tall man inside. He sank into the chair that faced the massive desk as O'Loran eased himself into his own chair.

"I'm still a bit stiff from the surgery," muttered O'Loran, as he relaxed into the plush chair.

"Surgery, Sir?"

"Yes, emergency surgery. Relax, Jorm; it was successful and I'm good as new. Now what's been happening in my absence?"

"Well, Sir, first we lost track of Rathbone."

"That's no surprise. What else?"

"Lady O'Loran arrived on Elliston this morning and she has now been joined by Miss Brenna."

"Brenna's here?"

"She's at the apartments with her mother, Sir. They have their military escorts with them, and the place is well fortified. I believe them to be completely safe."

"Brenna hasn't tried to escape?"

"No, Sir, she actually appears to be excited about the gala planned to celebrate her return."

"Well, that's the best news I've had in a while. What else?"

"We sent a small fleet out to escort them in, Sir, but it was called away to the border of Sectors Five and Six. There was word that A.S.Inc was amassing forces there. Our people arrived and found no one, but soon after that the enemy appeared. They're in a standoff situation as of now, but I doubt we have anything to worry about there. I believe it's all bluff and bluster."

"You're probably right, but best not to get complacent. Mobilize the rest of our forces, pull everything back to the hub and stand by on full alert until further notice."

"Yes, Sir."

"What else?"

"Well, Sir, it appears that Commander Darks traded his ship, plus a promise of money for the services of the mercs."

"His ship???"

"Yes, Sir."

"That man is a complete incompetent."

"Sir, if I may ask, how did Darks become commander-in-chief of the cyborgs?"

O'Loran sighed and gazed out the window for a moment. "That damned assassin killed the rest. When the dust settled from Rathbone's rampage, Darks was the only officer left alive. He was actually quite effective at first, or so his file says, but as he rose higher..."

"I see."

"Yes, well, I plan to dismantle that program, let the good doctor learn what he can, then start fresh."

"Dismantle, Sir?"

"Yes. Rathbone has destroyed most of the cyborgs anyway. We'll dismantle the rest. Have Darks report to me immediately then give them all two weeks leave. Keep this between the two of us for now."

"Yes Sir. Right away, Mr. O'Loran." Jorm rose and hurried from the office.

Later that day, Commander Darks was ushered into the CEO's office. "Report, Commander."

"Yes, Sir. We arrived in Sector Nine without incident. My troops were assigned to retrieve Miss Brenna, so we set about the task. We managed to separate her from the witch and take her into custody."

"She didn't come willingly?"

"No, Sir. She killed three of my men instantly before we could restrain her. At that time, Rathbone attacked. He disabled our ship, killed several men, and captured Miss O'Loran. We hunted him and he killed half of the men who were left, but Miss O'Loran got away from him and rejoined us. We joined forces with a mercenary crew, and they managed to eliminate the Rathbone threat. We then repaired our ship and returned to Elliston with Miss O'Loran."

"Just what did you have to pay the mercs for their assistance, Commander?"

"You gave me clear instructions to do whatever was necessary to return Miss O'Loran safe and sound, Sir. The mercs demanded our ship plus a million each in script. I felt I had no other option."

"I see. Did it ever occur to you to that the mercs might be working with Rathbone?"

"No, Sir."

"Did it occur to you to eliminate the mercs as soon as you were free of the assassin?"

"The mercs performed in good faith, Sir. So did I." Siemon Darks fought to keep his face impassive. After the way he and his men had been treated by Micha's crew, this was hard to take. It did, however, reinforce his decision to join the crew and make Nova his new home.

O'Loran didn't try to hide his disgust. "Very well, Commander. You and your men have two weeks leave, then report to headquarters for reassignment."

"Sir."

The commander snapped to attention, then turned and marched out of O'Loran's office. He was in a dark mood as he rode the elevator to the ground floor. As he left the building, he bumped into a woman who gave him a sneer as she hurried away.

He stepped through the door and reached into his pocket for the control key for his ground transport. Something else was in that pocket. A note. Settling into the seat of the transport, he unfolded and read the message. "Cyborg program to be terminated. Cyborgs to be dismantled for further study." Keeping his face impassive he refolded the note and replaced it in his pocket.

⸺⬤⸺

IT HAD BEEN A BIT OF a shock to Landy's guards when Commander Darks arrived with Brenna O'Loran and a crew of mercenaries. Landy herself had nearly fainted at what happened and how fast it happened.

It began as they approached the building, but Commander Darks got them inside without incident. It was different when they stepped into the luxury apartment.

"Halt! Drop your weapons! Now!" Six heavily armed guardsmen were pointing weapons at them.

"Stand down," barked Commander Darks, "these people are cleared. They're with me."

"Drop your weapons and get on your knees," snarled one man, as he shoved his weapon in Edie's face. That did it. Landy screamed as Micha moved. All six of her guards were unconscious on the floor before her scream died.

Landy was staring at Micha in horror. Micha was standing by Edie, gently caressing her face. "I could have done that," Edie smiled, as she gave Micha a saucy wink.

"I know," he replied, his face still showing concern, "but I don't like angry men threatening you. I never have."

"That's one of the things I love best about you, my man," she murmured, as she kissed his cheek. "Shall I wake them up?" He nodded and she opened her med kit then set to work.

A few moments later the six men were awake and under guard. Landy was in Brenna's arms, being comforted. "It's all right, Momma. It's all right, they won't hurt you. These folks are very professional, but they mean business."

"I can see that," gulped her mother. "Are these the people who brought you home and defeated that awful assassin?"

"Yes, Momma, these folks brought me home."

"Are they cyborgs too?"

"No, Momma, I don't think so, but they are quite capable." She winked at Micha as he hauled the man who'd threatened Edie to his feet.

Micha shoved the man over to his companions. "Who are you people, and why did you threaten us?"

"We're Landy O'Loran's personal guards," muttered one man, as he gazed at the floor.

"Not very good at it are you?" said Micha. This brought a snicker from his crew. "Hear me well; I will speak of this only once. The next time one of you threatens my companion there will be six new widows on Elliston. Do you understand?"

"Understood," came a series of soft grudging replies.

"Pick up your weapons, keep them at rest, and stay out of our way. Gorda."

"Boss?"

"Keep an eye on them, if you see something you don't like, deal with it first and ask questions later."

"Understood, Boss," grinned Gorda. "It's best not to annoy the boss," he said to the six men as they gathered their weapons, being careful to point them at the floor. "Bad things happen when he's angry."

"Understood," grumbled one of the six.

"Zartah, secure the place."

"Boss." Zartah moved like a stalking cat through the huge apartment. He was back in a few moments. "Secure, Boss. The place is heavily fortified. Looks good."

"Good," said Micha. "Miss O'Loran, we'll do our best to stay out of your way until we're ready to leave. We'll see to your protection."

"Thank you, Micha. Come, Momma, all is well. We're perfectly safe and we have some shopping to do, don't we?"

"What? Oh, yes, of course. We have arrangements to make." Landy was fanning herself with her hand. Micha and crew seemed to fade into the background as Landy took over and began giving directions over her comm. If there was one thing she was good at, it was hosting a ball.

Soon the place was buzzing with people and goods. At Brenna's insistence, Edie tried on some of the gowns. The seamstress soon had one that fit her perfectly. Brenna brushed out her hair and smiled at her friend.

"Brenna, I've never even dreamed of wearing something so fine. I've seen vids of the women, but I never..."

"Hush, Edie, you're so beautiful. Wait until Micha sees you; he's going to faint."

"Oh, he will not," blushed Edie.

"He will so. Come on." She grabbed Edie's hand and dragged her out into the main living room.

Micha's mouth fell open as he saw Edie. Grinning wickedly, Brenna sent her fingers flying across a wall panel and the room was filled with soft romantic waltz music. Micha closed his mouth and swallowed hard as Edie fairly floated across the floor to him, her bare feet hidden in the sweep of the gown.

"Well, hello there, handsome warrior," purred Edie, as she reached him. "What's your name?"

Micha drew a deep breath to break the spell, then tossed his weapon to Zartah. "Hello, beautiful princess." He smiled as he reached for her hand. "My name's Lucky. Dance with me." He swept her into a graceful waltz. It was now Edie's turn to be enchanted. She fairly floated along as he swept her about the room. As the music stopped he stepped back and gave her a deep bow.

Edie was blushing furiously as the people in the room began to applaud. Landy approached and took Micha by the arm. "Who are you, young sir? No soldier I've ever known could dance like that. Are you of the upper classes?"

"I was born a slave, son of a slave," he smiled gently. "My mother was a high-born lady, captured in a slave raid. She taught me the speech and ways of her people in case I ever managed to escape. She taught me the dance. My father taught me the speech and the ways of the farm slave."

"Then you're far better educated than most men are," she said kindly. "Bring this man a proper suit, he and his companion are going to the gala as my guests."

"Now wait...," began Micha, but he saw the look on Edie's face and relented. He sighed and nodded. "Yes, ma'am. We'd be delighted to attend." Edie's bright smile made his heart soar.

"Thank you, Mamma," Brenna whispered to her mother a few moments later.

"These people aren't just random mercenaries, are they Brenna?"

"No, Momma, they're dear friends. They've saved my life many times and Edie has been like a sister to me through my darkest days. Please don't tell anyone."

"I won't Brenna. You're going back with them, aren't you?"

"Yes. You could come with us. There would be no guards where we're going. You could come and go as you please."

"I fear I'm not cut out for life on the rim, my darling daughter. I'll do what I can to help you, but I'll remain here with your father."

Micha spent the rest of the day wishing he had stayed on the ship with Murtah while Edie spent the day in a magical world she had only heard of in stories.

———◦———

WHILE MICHA WAS BEING fitted for a suit, a battered looking old explorer settled to the ground at the far end of the spaceport. Security seemed to be extra tight everywhere and as soon as the ship touched the ground there were soldiers waiting. The hatch opened and an old man in a grey uniform descended to meet them.

"Identification," demanded the commander of the squad. The old man passed over his ident card and the soldier stuck it in a card reader.

"Erkin of Saggit, what's your business on Elliston?"

"We're here to pick up a group for a cruise around the hub worlds. Normally we don't work out of Elliston, but this job was too sweet to pass up. Why all the extra security people? Has a war started or something?"

"Rathbone of Urn is headed this way, Gramps. We're on the lookout for him. You can pick up your passengers and drop them off when you return. None of your people are to leave that ship."

"Understood. I alone will arrange for fuel and pick my passengers at the main terminal. I can hire a shuttle for that purpose, can't I?"

"Yes, you can hire one at the terminal. There's a regular scheduled shuttle due by in twenty minutes. You could catch that one. I'll station a man to see that your people comply with the lock-down order."

"Thank you, Officer. I'll speak with them myself." He went back aboard for a few moments then reappeared and went to the office to order fuel. He then caught the shuttle to the main terminal. From there he took a taxi into the city. A few errands, a few packages, and some calls later he picked up a passenger then they returned to the spaceport.

The passenger was dropped off at the main terminal where he found a familiar face. "Jorge, good to see you in one piece. Got your folks all together?"

"We're all here except Commander Darks, Gorda. Oh look, there he is now. All right, we're set. Let's go."

A hired shuttle appeared, and all the families were loaded aboard. Gorda, now dressed in the old man's uniform, gave the location of the ship and the shuttle set out. It pulled up by the ship and Gorda waved at the soldier on guard as he opened the hatch.

The families and their luggage were loaded on board with the help of two more people in uniforms of baggage handlers. The soldier was too bored to notice they'd appeared from inside the ship, not outside. Once everything was on the ship, the two baggage handlers left on the empty shuttle. They soon appeared at another ship closer to the main terminal.

Gorda climbed to the bridge and settled into the pilot's chair. He signalled the tower with a request for lift off. An hour later he got the clearance. Everyone had settled in and were excited as the ship lifted off smoothly and headed out into space. Once they were clear of the atmosphere, Commander Darks took the ship wide comm.

"Attention, attention, this is Commander Siemon Darks. Actually, I'm the former Commander Darks. I have in my hand an order just issued by CEO O'Loran. I quote, 'Cyborg program to be terminated. Cyborgs to be dismantled for further study."

"What that means people, is your providers and companions were to be killed and dissected. You'd all have been left without resource. However, we won't let that happen. This isn't a cruise ship, as you may have noticed. It is a well-armed warship. We're taking you all out to new homes on the rim worlds where you'll be safe.

"I now pass you to our new captain."

"Hi folks, my name is Gorda. I'll be your captain for the next month or so. I've got a quick message for you from Viceroy Lortax. I'll just read that to you now."

"Greetings new citizens of the Independent Borelian Free Alliance. I welcome you on behalf of my people. I've sent messages with Gorda to inform my people that you're to be well cared for and protected until such time as we can have you all settled in your new homes. I wish you fair journey and good speed."

"That's it, folks, settle in and relax. Gorda out."

"You might want to give me back my station and go sit over there," a man said to Gorda. He was indicating the captain's chair.

"You're Deke, Rath's friend," grinned Gorda, as he slipped out of the pilot's chair and offered his hand. He shook the man's hand warmly. "She's all yours, Deke. Once we get well away we'll take opposite shifts so we can both get some sleep."

"That works just fine for me," Deke replied with a grin, "at my age I need all the beauty sleep I can get."

------◆------

AS THE TWO BAGGAGE handlers boarded the ship, Lessa pounced on the smaller of the two. "Keira," she laughed with delight as she hugged the warrior woman in greeting. Keira smiled brightly as she returned the hug. As the hug ended Keira stepped back and began to signal.

"Lady Arlessa, Viceroy, I present to you my bonded companion, Rathbone of Urn."

"I've heard you two decided to swear a bond," grinned Lessa. "Keira, are you certain?" Keira nodded solemnly and hooked her arm through Rath's. "In that case, I, Arlessa, high priestess of Nova, do bless your bond. Lortax."

Grinning, he stepped forward. "I, Lortax, Viceroy of the Borelian Free Alliance and chieftain of Nara Clan, do bear witness to this bond. Congratulations."

"Well, now that the pleasantries are over, can we get on with making a plan to kill O'Loran," grumbled the old man who had first appeared from the other ship.

"Relax Poppa," chuckled Rathbone, "I'm sure Micha has a plan."

"I'm sure he does," grumbled the old fellow, as he jerked his head in the general direction of the galley and walked away. The others followed and relaxed back into chairs. "Show them the message he sent you. He said we didn't have a lot of time to get this organized."

Lessa pulled a device from her pocket and thumbed the on switch. Micha's image appeared and his voice spoke from the small device. "With luck the families are on their way by this time. There is a gala celebration in Brenna's honor tonight. Lessa and Lortax, stay out of sight until the last moment, then join the party. Rathbone, there are two extra invitations for you and Keira. Come to the party, but stay out of sight until I need you."

Lessa shut it off then tossed it in the air and vaporized it with a gesture. "There you go, Rath, you get to take your new bride dancing."

"You won't be able to take weapons to the gala; everyone will be double checked. You'll have to improvise," said the elder Rathbone. Keira just grinned and made a few hand signals. "What did she say?"

"She said there will be security people there; we'll borrow their weapons if we need them." The old fellow just grinned as Keira winked at him.

"Rathbone, I want you to hold back tonight," said Lessa.

"Lady?"

"My issues with O'Loran are ..."

"I know, Lady. Micha told me not to go hunting for O'Loran and I won't."

"What else did Micha tell you?"

"Lady?"

"Don't forget you're talking to a witch. I know you're holding back. What else did he tell you?"

Rathbone sighed and let his huge shoulders slump. "He said to kill O'Loran if he crossed my path."

"Did he say why?"

"If you kill Brenna's father, that'll always lie between you. Brenna may fully understand why you did it, but it would come between you. However, if one of us does it, your bond with your companion will remain intact. As for me, I'd love to be the one, but it really doesn't matter as long as he's dead."

"Damn that boy," sighed Lessa, as she slumped back in her chair. "He's determined to protect me no matter if I want it or not. Very well then, Rathbone, when the time comes, I'll create the diversion."

"Lady?"

"I've been practicing, Master. Observe."

Suddenly a snarl of rage curled her lip and her eyes blazed. She leaped from her chair, knocking it over as she fairly trembled with the force of the emotion that surged through her. "Behold," she said as she snapped her arms straight out from her sides. A flaming sword leaped to each hand, the blades dancing with a malevolent fire, seeking prey, seeking anything to destroy. "Behold the Swords of Nova."

The room crackled with the fury and violence constrained in the two blades. Lessa snapped her fingers and the blades disappeared. She shook off the mood and smiled brightly. "Well, how did I do, my master."

"Lady, that was brilliant," said Rathbone. "But can you do it under stress? For that's where it will count."

"We shall soon find out, my friend," she sighed, as she picked up her chair and sat back down. "I believe I can, Rath."

"There's no room for uncertainty," growled the elder Rathbone. "Hesitation kills. If you can't control the weapon don't pick it up. If you pick it up, control it." Lessa spun to go nose to nose with the old fellow, but he didn't flinch.

For a moment they stared each other down, but it was Lessa who cracked first. It was just a hint of a smile at the edges of her mouth and the corners of her eyes, but it was there. "You need to work on that control," he grinned.

"Being around you two is like being a novice again back at the temple," she smiled. "I have it under control. I know what's at stake here, I know full well how wrong things can go, and I will not fail. Rath, if you even suspect I'm losing it, kill O'Loran."

"Count on it, Lady," said the younger Rathbone.

"All right, people," sighed Lortax, "the day's wearing on. It's time for us to get ready for the ball. Our new pilot is quite resourceful. He's brought us clothes that'll help us blend in."

"If you all don't mind, I think I'll sit this one out," grinned Kella. "I'd prefer not to show my face on Elliston if I could. Besides, somebody has to stay with the ship."

———◉———

CEO O'LORAN LEANED back in his chair and gazed thoughtfully out the window. "Are you certain, Jorm?"

"Yes, Sir, there's no doubt. Here's the visual from the security cameras at the space port. It's Rathbone and his woman in porter's uniforms. He's here on Elliston."

"Then we can assume the gala tonight will afford him the opportunity he seeks. I want every human entering this building carefully scrutinized. Find him, mark him, but take no action until I give the signal."

"Yes, Sir."

"Are the other security arrangements in place?"

"They are, CEO. Fifty of the invited guests are in fact our security people. They'll pass for guests, but they'll be close to you and they will be armed."

"Excellent. Landy has informed me that all is in readiness and that Brenna is anxious to see me. I wonder what she's up to?"

"Sir?"

"Why did it take this latest sortie to bring her home, and why, in the end, did she change her mind? I expected her to fight and kick up a fuss. I fully expected her to try and escape every chance she got. Why did she change her mind about leaving her witch behind and returning home?"

"I'm sure I have no idea, Sir."

"I think we need to be doubly alert tonight, Jorm. I suspect that the mercenaries Darks hired are actually the witch and her bloodhounds."

"Mr. O'Loran, do you really think so?"

"It's the only answer, Jorm. Ah, this could all work out so well, but we'll have to be on our guard. We've got the witch, her dogs, and Rathbone, all within our grasp. Assign another hundred guards to the building. Have them stay out of sight until everyone has arrived, then I want the building locked down."

"Yes, Sir, I'm on it." Jorm stood and hurried from Mr. O'Loran's office.

"So you've all come for me, have you? I welcome you to the last party you will ever attend. This night will see the end of you all. Brenna will be safely home with her mother, Sector Nine will then be brought to heel once the witch is dead. As soon as that's done, this A.S.Inc upstart will be crushed. I will be emperor of the galaxy, and I'll rule for generations of men."

O'Loran banged his fist down on the desk as he voiced his dream, and the heavy metal desk buckled slightly. Thoughtfully he gazed at the dent for a moment then pulled his keyboard closer to hide the blemish on the metal. "Not just yet," he mused with a cruel smile. "Perhaps later this evening, but not right now. For now, no one must know."

Later that evening O'Loran and Jorm sat watching the security feed as the guests arrived. They weren't happy. Most of the guests were already inside and there was no sign of their prey. "Jorm, could they have gotten wind of our plans?"

"I doubt that, Sir. We've been extremely careful."

"Then where the blazes are they?" The CEO began to brood and Jorm was getting nervous.

"Sir, isn't it time for you to make your entrance?"

"Yes, I suppose it is. Landy's been greeting all the guests and making excuses for me as usual, but I suppose I must go be sociable. Keep your eyes peeled, Jorm. I'm depending on you."

"Yes , Sir." Jorm breathed a sigh of relief as the CEO straightened the brightly colored sash at his waist then left for the great room and the ball. As he watched his boss leave the office, Jorm didn't see two faces that should have been familiar to him, pass the cameras.

———————◉———————

"LANDY, WHERE'S BRENNA?" asked an elderly woman, as Landy swept past.

"Waiting to make a grand entrance," smiled Landy, as she continued on her way. As usual her husband had left her alone to greet the guests, many of whom he had invited himself and she didn't know. She personally greeted the more important people that she knew, but wished Brenna would make her entrance. She hoped the girl hadn't used this opportunity to run off again.

Outside, Brenna was starting to fuss when she saw a familiar figure approaching. "Ah, there you are, my beloved. I was just beginning to worry you might stand me up."

"Perish the thought, dear heart. I'm looking forward to this evening." Brenna took her arm and steered her toward the entry.

There was a man there, announcing the arrival of the more important people. He gulped and stared as Brenna, resplendent in a royal blue gown approached with a companion. The companion was a woman like none he had ever seen before. She was a striking woman, tall with hair that shone golden in the lights. Brenna passed him a card and he gulped again as he read it. Before he could speak, a tall man joined the two women.

"Go on," smiled Brenna. "Introduce us, just like it says on that card."

"Ma'am, are you..."

"Just do it, now."

"Yes, ma'am." He reached for his mike and in a shaky voice, read the card. "Announcing Miss Brenna O'Loran of Nova and her bonded companion, Arlessa, high priestess of Nova. Also introducing their guest, His Excellency, Lortax, viceroy of the Borelian Free Alliance.

A hush fell over the assembled guests and all eyes followed as the two women led Lortax into the room. Brenna led them to Landy and introduced them. "Brenna," hissed Landy, "you told me she wasn't here."

"Mother, I said she wasn't on the ship, and indeed she was not at that time. Will you not at least acknowledge her and my introduction?"

"What? Oh, yes, forgive me. Arlessa, is it? Please Arlessa, do excuse my bad manners. It's a pleasure to meet you and welcome you to Elliston."

"It's all right, Landy," Lessa said softly as she took the woman's hand and gazed into her eyes. She sent a wave of healing energy to the upset woman and felt Landy instantly relax. "I do understand we've taken you by surprise. Please forgive our little drama, but we did want to a grand entrance tonight."

"Well you've certainly managed that," she smiled, completely relaxed. "Arlessa, what did you do to me?"

"It was just a little healing energy, Landy. I could sense your distress and thought it might help."

"It has helped immensely, Arlessa, thank you."

"Come dance with me, Lessa," laughed Brenna, as she dragged Lessa out onto the dance floor.

"So, your Excellency, you're the viceroy of the Free Alliance?" asked Landy.

"I am, but I prefer to be called Lortax."

"I know someone who won't be amused to hear about your Alliance, Sir," she said with a soft smile.

"Then shall we annoy him further?" smiled Lortax, as he held out his hand. "Come, dance with me." She accepted his hand and he swept her out onto the dance floor.

While all eyes were on Lessa and Brenna or Lortax and Landy, two men spoke softly at the bar. "They knew we were coming, Zartah," Rathbone said softly as he stirred his drink. "There's far too much security here. We should withdraw."

"Not possible, the place is locked down," said another man who had just approached.

"Who're you?" asked Zartah.

"This is my grandfather, Zartah," said Rath. "He's here to help. All right then, we're trapped in here. You're first man, what's our play?"

"We ask the boss," grinned Zartah, as he turned and offered his hand to Keira. "Dance my lady?" She smiled brightly and took his hand.

Rathbone watched as Zartah swept Keira out into the dancing throng and slowly worked their way towards Micha and Edie. With a skillful move Keira was suddenly dancing with Micha while Zartah was whirling Edie about the floor. As the music stopped and everyone applauded he could see that Keira was actually using hand signals to talk to Micha.

The music began again and soon Zartah was waltzing with Keira once more. By the time the music stopped again they had made their way back to the bar. Keira gave a few swift signals and Zartah made his way casually towards the exit to the washrooms. The elder Rathbone looked puzzled.

"Micha says to spread out and make sure no one can get behind us."

"Smart man," approved the old fellow.

"He also said that if we can, slip away to cause as much mischief as possible on his signal."

"Smart man indeed. You two love birds go find a corner to cuddle in while this old man finds a wall to hold up."

All eyes of the massive security team were on Lessa and Brenna. They paid no heed to giggling couples who looked for quiet places to be alone. A tall man who seemed to be a bit drunk swayed toward the restrooms and was also ignored.

The elder Rathbone smiled to himself as he saw Micha and Edie trade partners for a moment then back together again. The other couple slowly faded to the side then disappeared deeper into the building. As CEO O'Loran was announced and entered the room, the old man vanished towards the kitchens.

The Meeting

The sound of his name was still in the air as O'Loran strode into the room. He went straight to his companion and gave her a perfunctory kiss on the cheek. She returned it then pointed out Brenna and Lessa on the dance floor. He waited with her until the music stopped. Brenna had seen him, surely. She had.

Brenna and Lessa moved toward Lessa's arch enemy. Micha whispered to Edie who look as though she might protest, but she moved away, headed toward the washrooms. Micha moved in closer to Lessa, but was instantly surrounded by a dozen or more armed men. They had no idea why he was smiling.

"Brenna, my darling, it's so good to see you again," her father said as he took her in his arms and hugged her. Her return hug was stiff. "Why did you stay away so long?"

"I was busy, Father."

"So I've heard. A dispatcher, Brenna? I'm surprised, and I'll confess, somewhat pleased to find you have some steel in you after all."

"Yes, well, apparently I'm my father's daughter. Father, allow me to present my bonded companion, Arlessa, high priestess of Nova. Lessa, this is my father."

"So, we meet at last, witch. Have you come to zap me into oblivion with your trickery and magic?"

"I've come to meet the man who could order the destruction of an entire planet and feel no remorse from the act."

"That little adventure was the making of my career," he said with an oily smile. "I learned that day that true power comes to those who are willing to wield it."

"Yes, I know," she replied, the rage starting to flow through her like a fire. She blinked her eyes and forced it back. This wasn't the time, nor the place. That would come soon enough. "Actually, I came to accompany the viceroy on another matter. It brought us near Elliston, so it was natural Brenna would want to visit her family."

O'Loran had actually missed the announcement at their arrival. "Your little viceroy is here, is he? Wonderful, please introduce me."

"I'd be delighted. Lortax." She held out her hand and O'Loran nodded to his people to let the man through. "CEO O'Loran, this is His Excellency, viceroy Lortax, of the Borelian Free Alliance."

"CEO," smiled Lortax, as he extended his hand.

O'Loran ignored the offered handshake. "The Borelian Free Alliance? You've declared independence then?"

"We have. That's why I've come. To ask for your official recognition and a signed non-aggression treaty."

"Have you now," sneered O'Loran. "What you'll get, you simpering buffoon, is the same treatment the Novans got."

"I thought you might see it that way," replied Lortax, his smile never wavering, "that's why I brought you a small gift." He pulled a reading tablet from his pocket and passed it to O'Loran. "Go ahead, read it. I'll wait."

The entire ballroom was silent now, everyone straining to see and hear. Even the music had stopped. O'Loran read then, with a snarl on his face, he crushed the device in his hand. There were gasps of surprise from the press of people nearby.

"So, A.S. Inc. has recognized your little nation, have they? That won't help you, I'm afraid."

"Actually, it will," replied Lortax. "You should have read it all, Mr. O'Loran. There was a mutual defense treaty in there as well. If you attack Borealis, A.S. Inc. will come to our aid. If R.I.M. attacks A.S. Inc. then, of course, Borealis will come to their aid."

"What??? O'Loran, how could you have allowed this to happen," demanded a balding man with an impressive moustache.

"Not now, Fonis," snarled O'Loran.

"Don't you try to brush me aside, Sir," puffed the older fellow. "I'm chairman of the board, and I'm calling an emergency meeting of the board first thing tomorrow to discuss this. You will be present, Sir, and you'll bring this man with you." He turned on his heel and huffed away.

"I must agree, CEO," smiled Lortax. "Tomorrow's time enough to talk business. This is supposed to be a party. Another dance, Landy?" He offered his hand and she took it. The music resumed at once and they danced away.

O'Loran jerked his head and the security men stepped back from Micha. "Keep your dog on a tight leash, Witch," he snarled. "I wouldn't want him to come to harm."

"Nor would I," smiled Lessa. "Come, Micha, a dance with an old friend." He took her hand and led her into the crowd.

"Father," said Brenna, as she took his hand and tugged him onto the dance floor.

"Brenna, why her? Of all people possible?" he asked sadly as they danced.

"She saved my life, Father, and she loved me, she made me strong. Father I'll do all in my power to keep you alive, but you must stop trying to antagonize Lessa."

"I'm not cowed by a bunch of religious mumbo-jumbo, Brenna. Her parlour tricks won't frighten me."

"Then you're a complete fool, Father. An angry Lessa is that last thing you want to see, trust me. If you can just stay calm and behave for a few days I can get her off planet and back home without incident."

"Really?"

"She came to kill you, Father. This last attack on Nova was the final straw. She's done holding back on my account unless you cooperate. Agree to leave us in peace and I'm sure I can get her to withdraw peacefully."

"Of course."

"You don't believe me. You're mocking me and my desires as usual." She sighed as he twirled her around. "Father, why did you order this last attack on Nova?"

"I could care two clips for Nova."

"Then why? What was the point?"

"It's what this rebuilding of Nova stands for. It's complete defiance of Company policy. See what this woman has done, Brenna? She's destroyed a stable government, installed her own puppet, and began the destruction of the Company I've worked so hard to make great. She is trying to destroy me, and I won't let that happen.

"Brenna, please stay here on Elliston with your mother where you'll be safe. This woman is dangerous. She and her minions won't last long and I don't want you getting in the line of fire."

"So, you're still going to try to kill her?"

"The witch and her hounds must be removed for the good of the Company. I'll destroy them and bring Sector Nine back into line, and then I'll absorb A.S. Inc. for helping them. They will all pay dearly for plotting against me."

"Father, will you not relent? Even for me?"

"No, child, I cannot, will not. Not even for you."

"Is there nothing left of my father in there at all?" pleaded Brenna, tears in her eyes.

"I am your father, Brenna, and I want what's best for you."

"No," she sighed, as she stopped dancing and stepped away from him, "my father is gone." Her eyes went hard, and he saw a stone cold warrior looking back at him. "You've chosen your own path and the fate that goes with it. I can do nothing to help you now, nor will I try further." She turned and walked away.

As Brenna walked away from her father, Rathbone and Keira slipped through the lower levels of the giant complex. They had relieved two maintenance men of their uniforms and stuffed the bodies in the air shafts. Suddenly Rath held up his hand. He'd heard a familiar voice.

He made a few hand signals and Keira's eyes opened wide. She nodded and they silently approached one wide doorway. The door was locked, but Rath hurled himself against it and he crashed inwards. "Hello, Doc," growled Rathbone, "remember me?"

The two lab assistants slunk back against the wall, but the doctor didn't seem to be frightened. "Ah, yes. Rathbone, isn't it? Why are you still alive?"

"I take my vitamins," replied Rath, as he slowly advanced on the smaller man. As the doctor saw him move, he pressed a button. There was a crackle of energy in the room. Rathbone lunged at him but was caught in an energy field and knocked unconscious. Keira tried to reach him and met the same fate.

The doctor smirked as he turned off the defense shield. "Help me get them onto the tables and restrain them. We'll need heavy restraints for him. He's one of the cyborgs."

None of them saw the woman watching through the door. She quietly moved away unseen. "Bloody fools," muttered Edie, as she slipped away to report to Micha. "They've got Rath strapped down hard, but Keira will be out of that in a heartbeat, and she's going to be mad. Now let's see what else I can find around here that might be useful."

While Edie explored the lower levels, Zartah had gone up. What he found was mostly a maze of offices, floor after floor of them. Finally he gave up and rode the elevator to the top floor, at least he tried to. It stopped two floors short of the top. He grinned as he sent it back to the ground floor without him. Zartah headed for the stairs. The instant he touched the handle of the heavy door the alarms sounded.

Without hesitation he turned and fled into the maze of offices. More alarms sounded as he tried doors. Zartah grinned as he suddenly started pounding on doors as he raced along the corridor. Another bank of elevators appeared and he pushed all the buttons then fled onwards, setting off as many alarms as he could.

Back at the gala, Micha casually approached the elder Rathbone. "Are you Rath's grandfather?" he asked, as he sauntered past on the way to the bar.

"I am."

"Can you get out of this building?"

"Yes."

Micha continued on to the bar and got a drink. Returning, he stopped near the old man leaning against the wall. "Go to the ship," he said, as he spoke into his glass. "We may need to make a fast retreat."

"Understood."

Micha continued on his way back to Lessa. A moment later the alarms began to sound and military troops began pouring into the building. In the confusion the old man slipped away. He could hear O'Loran bawling orders as he exited the building.

At the sound of the alarms, all of the security people suddenly surrounded CEO O'Loran to protect him. Furious, he began shouting orders. "Not me, you idiots, round up the witch and her mercs. Get them, get them now! Seal off the building! Search every floor and bring everyone you find here to this room."

Lessa leaned over to whisper in Brenna's ear. "Get your mother out of here. Take her to the ship."

"Understood, my love. Do what you must."

Brenna stepped close to O'Loran. "Father, I should take Mother home. Give us two men to escort us there."

"Of course," he muttered, signalling two security men to accompany them. Brenna took her mother's arm and led her toward the door, followed closely by the two security guards.

Once through the press of soldiers who had the building sealed off, one of the men hailed a taxi for them. As it pulled up, Brenna opened the door and helped her mother into the seat. With a swift move she took a step back between the two men. She swung her arms up wide, grabbed each man by the back of his head then slammed their heads into the side of the vehicle. Both fell to the ground, unconscious.

Landy stared at her daughter in horror as Brenna got into the cab. "Spaceport, please," she said pleasantly.

"Yes, Ma'am," gulped the driver. Brenna smiled as the taxi pulled out into traffic. Not one soldier had seen what she did; all eyes were on the entrance to the building.

"Brenna, how did you...?"

"I've been training, Mamma."

"Where are you taking me?"

"I can take you back where you'll be a prisoner in your own home, or I can take you out to the rim with me. There you will be free to come and go as you please."

Landy's shoulders slumped and she relaxed back into the seat. "Your father has become obsessed in the past number of years. It's that assassin that has driven him mad, Brenna. "That horrible Rathbone of Urn. How can we protect ourselves from him?"

"There's no need, Mamma. Rathbone is a personal friend and no threat to us at all."

"A personal friend???"

"It's a long story, Mamma. I'll tell you all about it on the journey home. First we have to get back to the ship."

The taxi dropped them at the main terminal. They took a shuttle from there to the docking station of their ship. As they approached the hatch opened then closed again behind them. They found an old man on the bridge, in the pilot's chair. "Hello, you must be Brenna of Nova, Dispatcher."

"I am," she replied. "Identify yourself."

"I'm Rathbone of Urn," he smiled.

"Rath is a friend and he is a lot younger, try again."

"I'm Rath's grandfather and I'm your new pilot."

Brenna laughed and stepped into his arms. She hugged him then stepped back. "Poppa of Urn, I have heard all about you."

"I've heard about you too, Brenna. I spent some time with Rath and Keira."

"Poppa, this is my mother, Landy O'Loran of Elliston. Mamma, this is Rathbone of Urn, the Elder."

"I saw you at the gala, did I not?" asked Landy, as she accepted his offered hand.

"You have a good eye, dear lady." He smiled as he bent over her hand. "Few people ever notice me, and I like it that way. Ladies, I suggest you find more appropriate clothing. Micha gave me the impression we may have to leave in a bit of a rush."

"Come on, Mamma, we'll find you something in our quarters."

—————⊙—————

ZARTAH CROUCHED BESIDE a large cabinet, trembling as the armed soldiers burst into the office, pointing weapons at him. "Who are you?" demanded one man.

"Orza of Gonar Three. This is my office," stammered Zartah. "See, look there." He pointed to the name on the desk and the door.

"What are you doing here?"

"I have a deadline. I was trying to get caught up."

"Did you see anyone?"

"A man with a large blaster kicked in my door. He said he'd shoot me then he ran down the hall, kicking at the other doors. He's a madman."

"Describe him."

"He's shorter than you, wide shoulders, balding, and he has a huge blaster."

"Stay here and don't come out until we sound the all-clear, understand?"

"Understood."

The soldier led his companions back into the corridor. "Clear!" he shouted then stepped to the next office.

Zartah stood and stretched then settled himself comfortably in the big office chair. He put his feet up on the desk and crossed them at the ankles. "Morons," he chuckled. "That was exciting. I wonder how the boss is making out."

Micha wasn't having as much success. He'd moved closer to Lessa and Brenna to protect them, but had been swarmed by armed security guards. He dare not start a fight with all these innocent party goers around. Micha decided to bide his time and hope the rest of the crew was having better luck. As soon as Brenna left, he was herded together with Lessa and Lortax under heavy guard.

"Where are the rest of the mercs?" demanded O'Loran.

"Unknown, Sir," reported a guard. "We're searching the entire building room by room. They're in here somewhere, and we'll find them. We have the building sealed off."

"Find them all. If they try to run or fight, kill them."

"Understood, Sir."

"Some of you people start escorting the guests out of the building. Check every identity thoroughly before you release anyone."

Slowly the huge room began to empty out. The search went on, but no mercs were found. As the last of the guests left, O'Loran turned to his three prisoners. "It's nearly dawn now. You will be held here until I've finished this annoying board meeting, and then I'll deal with you."

"No need to rush away on our account, CEO," smiled Lortax.

"Take them to the board room and lock them inside," snarled O'Loran. "Place triple guards, I don't want them escaping. Find the rest of them and put them in there as well. When I return I expect to find them all waiting for me, do I make myself clear?"

"Very clear Sir."

O'Loran stalked away then rode the elevator to his office on the top floor. There was a small but elegant apartment, heavily fortified at the back. He retired there to get some sleep.

The crew was herded into the boardroom. There were two guards with them then the door was secured from the outside. A moment later Micha saw a slight flicker in the overhead air duct. He began to cough and clutch his chest. The guards pointed their weapons at him, but Edie dropped out of the vent, chopping down with her hands as she landed between them. Both men fell to the floor unconscious.

"I think it's time we left the party," said Micha, as he gathered up the guards' weapons.

"I agree, Boss," said Zartah, as he dropped into the room as well.

"No, we can't go yet," said Lortax.

"Not until O'Loran is dead," said Lessa, fury dancing in her eyes.

"No, Lessa, don't kill him, at least not yet," said Lortax. "You saw what happened down there. He's being called on the carpet tomorrow. It could be our only chance to force them to recognize our independence. We may still be able to salvage a peace treaty with the board of directors, if not O'Loran. We need to be at that meeting."

Lessa fumed for a moment then turned to Micha. "Advise me, Micha. What do you suggest?"

"Personally I'd like to hunt him down, kill him, then head for home at full burn, Lessa, but our clan chieftain has made a different request. Do we now declare our independence from Borealis?"

"No, Micha, we don't. You're right, we're Nara Clan, we will obey the chieftain." Lessa sighed deeply and sank into one of the plush chairs.

"Thank you, Lessa, Micha," Lortax said softly. "Micha, it wouldn't hurt to have a back-up escape plan in case the diplomacy fails."

"Understood, Chieftain." Micha crouched and retrieved the communicators from the two fallen guards. He passed one to Edie. "You two gather up more of these and some weapons. Find Murtah and Ena then make a hole to the roof."

"They're two floors down near the elevators, Boss," said Zartah. "We can't get to the top with the elevators without the security codes."

"See if you can get the codes, if not, we take the stairs."

"That will set off a lot of alarms."

"That won't matter. Have you seen Rath and Keira?"

"They're in the lower levels," said Edie. "They've been captured and strapped to tables in a lab."

"You'd better get them out of there."

"The fools strapped Rath down hard, but not Keira," chuckled Edie. "She's just a weak female, after all. It shouldn't take much to hold her, right?"

Micha just shook his head. "Oh man, she is going to raise holy hell when she comes to. All right, we'll assume Keira and Rath can deal with that little problem. Go get some equipment and then rest as long as you can."

"Understood," said Edie as she kissed his cheek, then made an impressive leap back to the ceiling vent. She pulled herself inside easily and Zartah followed.

"We might as well get some rest until the excitement starts," grinned Micha, as he sank into one of the executive chairs and leaned his head on the back. He closed his eyes and was instantly asleep.

"I wish I could do that," sighed Lortax, as he, too, settled back and closed his eyes.

"He's always been like that," chuckled Lessa. "He calls it a slave's trick. You sleep while you can." She settled down as well. They wouldn't get a lot of rest; it was nearly dawn already.

⎯⎯⎯◉⎯⎯⎯

"GOOD MORNING, SIR," said Jorm, as he hurried into the office. He looked sleep deprived and was in no rush to make his report to the CEO. He was about to get a short reprieve.

"Good morning, Jorm. Has the board arrived?"

"Yes, Sir. They're gathering in the board room as we speak. Sir, may I ask what you are going to do? I've heard rumblings of removing you from office."

"I know, Jorm, old friend, but it's the board that will be removed. Today we dispense with this charade and take full control of the Company."

"Sir?"

"You've known this was coming, Jorm. Today is the day."

"Very good, Sir. Congratulations."

"Save that for after I throw out the lot of them. Let's go deliver the bad news."

"Yes, Sir. Oh, I do have one more bit of good news."

"You do?"

"Yes. In all the confusion last night, Rathbone penetrated the building, but the doctor trapped him and the woman with him. He has them sedated and strapped to tables in the lab as we speak."

"Oh, that is wonderful news indeed, Jorm. Today will be a day of days; I can feel it. Onward to savor our victory." He strode from the room with Jorm hard on his heels.

———◆———

"WHAT'S GOING ON HERE? Who are these people?" demanded a loud voice. Lessa and Lortax were instantly awake. Micha didn't stir, but Lessa caught the grin on his face. He'd been aware of these men long before they entered the room.

"Ah, Good morning, Chairman. Mr. Fonis, isn't it?" smiled Lortax. "Yes, well, CEO O'Loran thought it more convenient to hold us prisoner here until you arrived."

"I'm sorry to hear that, Viceroy. As soon as this meeting is concluded I shall instruct CEO O'Loran to make proper amends. Now, if you'd be so kind as to tell me; who are these men tied up and lying on the floor?"

"Oh, those men? They're the security men assigned to watch us and make sure we didn't escape," said Micha, finally opening his eyes and lowering his feet to the floor. "They were annoying me."

"I see. Perhaps you could release them, so we can get this meeting started."

"Of course," said Micha, as he reached down and cut one man's bonds. He released the other then pointed to the door. Both men left the room. Micha spun his chair around and smiled.

"Thank you," huffed Fonis, as he took his seat at the head of the long table. "Ladies and gentlemen, please be seated. This meeting will now come to order. We are here to discuss the declaration of independence by the Borelian Alliance and their mutual protection treaty with A.S. Inc. Where is CEO O'Loran? He has much to answer for."

"I'm right here, Chairman," smiled O'Loran, as he strode into the room. Five security men followed him in. "What would you have me speak to?"

"CEO O'Loran, we would have you speak to the following situation. A.S. Inc. is amassing troops along our borders. They've signed a mutual protection pact with the Borelian Alliance, which has declared its independence."

"There's also the matter of reparations for the genocide of Nova Prime which you ordered many years ago," said Lessa, as she rose to face him. "Do you deny you gave that order?"

"Not at all," he replied easily. "I came up with the plan, made the arrangements, and gave the order to eradicate that rebellious scum on Nova Prime. It was the making of this Company and of my career."

"Outrageous," sputtered one man partway down the table.

"Unacceptable," declared another.

"CEO O'Loran, what have you got to say for yourself?" demanded Chairman Fonis.

"Only this," replied O'Loran, as he paced slowly around the huge table, making all the board members extremely nervous, "when I joined the management team of R.I.M. there were seven companies squabbling over territory and resources. Under my guidance R.I.M. has grown to be the largest and has absorbed all but one other. That will soon happen. My methods may be harsh, but they are effective."

Micha put his hand to his ear and spoke softly into the communicator he'd taken from the security guards. "Edie?"

She came on instantly. "Here lover."

"Is everybody ready?"

"Yes."

"Can you contact Kella, at the ship?"

"Yes."

"Tell her to warm it up, this is going to get ugly, and fast."

"Understood."

Micha smiled and turned his attention back to the Chairman, who was speaking again.

"This has gone too far," declared the chairman. "This board has been too tolerant of you for too long. By the consensus of the board, achieved at a secret meeting last night, you are hereby stripped of your title of CEO. Please leave this room and clear out your desk."

The entire room was silent, watching for his reaction. O'Loran's smile only broadened. People began to sweat. "So I've lost my title, have I? Very well, I shall have a new one. Ladies and gentlemen, I now disband this board as redundant and useless. I declare myself, Emperor Loran the First of the Galactic Empire. R.I.M. Company's assets are hereby confiscated by the state. As Emperor, I claim all resources in this galaxy.

"Now for you, witch. I have a treat for you too." He picked up a remote and lit up a huge wall screen. A laboratory room came into view with three men in lab coats standing over two naked people strapped to tables. It was Rath and Keira.

"Doctor, can you hear me?"

"Loud and clear, CEO."

"That's Emperor now, Doctor."

"Ah, congratulations, Majesty. Please consider these two as my coronation gift."

"Thank you, Doctor. You may proceed."

Rathbone had awakened again to find himself still on the slab, confined in heavy restraints. He tested the bonds, but was unable to break them. He let his gaze wander around the lab, looking for something, anything, he could use to escape. Eventually his gaze met the doctor who smirked and nodded to another table. Keira was there and strapped down as well, her pale body gleaming in the harsh lights. Rath fought his restraints, but it was a futile effort.

Realizing he couldn't break free, he relaxed and the restraints eased a bit. His heart ached as he gazed at his beloved Keira. At least they were fated to die together. He wouldn't be left behind again. Keira slowly opened her eyes.

Keira didn't move or give any other sign that she was awake. Rathbone watched her intently as she surveyed as much of the room as possible without giving away the fact she was no longer unconscious.

Carefully she tested the straps that restrained her. Rath saw just a hint of a smile reach her lips. It was there for only a fleeting moment then it was gone, but his heart leaped with hope. This was no ordinary woman the fools had strapped down. This woman was a hardened warrior who had been enhanced by the most powerful witch in history.

The doctor picked up a scalpel and approached Keira. Rath struggled against the heavy restraints, but Keira wasn't moving. Rathbone fought his bonds and cursed wildly, threatening the doctor in a dozen vile ways. He was trying to keep the man distracted as much as possible.

"I swear, you bastard, if you touch her I'll tear off your head and spit down the hole. I'll erase your seed from the galaxy," he railed. This only served to make the doctor chuckle with delight.

The doctor's voice could be heard clearly in the board room. "Pay close attention, Rathbone, this will be interesting for you. I'm going to perform an autopsy on your female friend here. She may scream a bit at first, but she'll quiet down soon enough."

The board room was frozen in horror as he advanced on Keira with the blade. Rathbone roared another protest, but Keira didn't move. "I will now make the first incision." The doctor bent over Keira and reached toward her chest.

Suddenly Keira's muscles bunched and her restraints parted. She caught the doctor's wrist in her hand and snapped it. Her other hand snatched up a tray and crushed his skull with it. The doctor's dead body lay across her lap, twitching. She thrust it aside and pulled her legs free just as the other two lab attendants threw themselves at her. One died with the doctor's scalpel in his throat as her strong hands snapped the other's neck. Keira was free.

Pushing aside the bodies, she leaped to Rath's side and released his restraints. As he surged from the table, Rathbone pointed at the camera. "O'Loran, you're next."

"I'm in the board room," replied the newly declared emperor. "I'll make sure you have a clear path to me." He was talking to an empty room; Rathbone was already on the way. "Attention all security personnel, Rathbone of Urn is in the lower levels. He is headed for the boardroom. Kill him, and his companion, on sight."

Meeting Adjourned

The Chairman rose to his feet and addressed the security detail. "You there, as Chairman of the Board, I command you to take this madman into custody."

The head of the detail turned to Emperor Loran. "Sire?"

"Kill him."

The man whipped out a pistol and shot the Chairman, who crumpled to the floor. The rest of the board members were horrified. They shrank into their seats and began to study their hands very intently.

"I assume the meeting is adjourned," said Lortax, as he rose to his feet. Before the new emperor could respond, Micha sprang into action. His stolen blaster fired several times and the security detail all lay on the floor, unconscious.

Micha pressed his hand to his ear to activate the comm unit. "Crew, this is Micha. Rath and Keira are coming up to the board room. Clear a path for them, then make a hole all the way to the roof. Edie, tell Kella to move it. Time's up." He leaped at Emperor Loran and got a shock.

As Micha leaped at him, Loran swung a huge fist. Micha was knocked across the board room and hard against the wall. A normal man could not have survived that blow. However, Micha was far from ordinary. He shook off the blow and came back in at terrifying speed. Loran's next blow missed; Micha was behind him, driving sledgehammer blows into the backs of his knees.

The emperor didn't go down as expected. Instead he turned and batted Micha away again. "Did you think it would be that easy to defeat me?" he roared.

Micha rolled to his feet and opened fire, with the blaster driving the emperor back against the wall hard enough to kill a man. Loran groaned as he sank to the floor. "Plan B worked," grinned Micha, as he tossed away the drained weapon. He scooped up another from one of the fallen security guards.

"It's not going to be that easy, boy," said a harsh voice behind him. Micha turned to see Loran rising from the floor. He shot out his arm and a blast of energy erupted from the palm of his hand, knocking Micha back into the wall hard.

Fury and madness blazing in her eyes, Lessa rose from her chair as Micha sank slowly to the floor. The emperor shot a beam at her too, but it had no effect. She thrust out her hand and Loran was driven back through the wall to land amid a pile of rubble. He didn't move. Lessa, her hair blown back by a wind no one else could feel, stepped through the hole until she was standing over the self-proclaimed emperor. Again she thrust out her hand, and the emperor was driven through the floor to land in the office below, falling rubble burying him there.

"I consider Nova avenged," declared Lessa, as she turned to the members of the board. "Behold, the Sword of Borealis." A flaming sword appeared in her hands. She swung it against the long table and it split down the middle, falling onto the laps of the people sitting around it. "Stay out of Borealis territory in future, or I will be angry." With that, the sword vanished. She strode out of the room with Lortax close behind.

"She means it folks," grinned Micha as he followed them. "Bad things happen when Lessa gets angry."

"What are we supposed to do now?" asked one of the trembling board members.

"The CEO is dead," replied another, "and so is the Chair. We need to elect a new Chair then we have to appoint a new CEO."

"Yes, yes," said a third. "I nominate Tsora for Board Chair."

Ignoring the board members completely, Jorm Dax roused the security detail. Taking one man by the arm, he led him to the hole in the floor and pointed to the rubble below. "The emperor's body is in that mess. Find him and bring him to the first aid station on level three. Watch out for Rathbone of Urn, he's trying to get to the board room."

"Yes, Sir." The five men hurried out to go to the next floor down. Jorm turned to see the newly elected Board Chair puff himself up and make a nomination for CEO. "Morons," he muttered, as he followed the security men from the room.

———— ◉ ————

RATHBONE CHARGED INTO the corridor; Keira close behind. They ran straight into half a dozen soldiers. By the time the men realized two naked people were attacking them, it was too late. Rathbone waded into them with deadly efficiency. He killed three, but there were no more opponents. Keira had finished the rest. Swiftly, they dragged the bodies into the lab and dressed themselves in the uniforms of the victims. They re-emerged into the hallway fully clothed and heavily armed.

They made their way to the elevators, the uniforms giving them precious seconds each time they encountered troops or security personnel. The elevators were locked down so they took the stairs. Two floors later, they took to the air shafts, leaving a trail of broken, unconscious, or dead bodies behind on the stairs.

They had emerged from the air shafts and resumed the battle on the stairs, when suddenly there was another round of weapons fire in the distance. All went silent then. They reached the next floor, and Keira kicked open the door. Rathbone bolted through, his weapon at the ready, but all he found was an empty corridor. There was a communicator lying in plain sight.

"It's probably a trap," he whispered softly to Keira, "but maybe not. There's only one way to find out for certain." She covered the corridor with watchful eyes, nodding her agreement. He reached for it gingerly, but nothing happened. "Hello?" he said, as he picked up the comm unit.

"Rath, it's Zartah. We've got the way cleared for you. The boardroom is five floors up, but O'Loran's not there. Lady Arlessa punched him through the floor to the next one down."

"Then he's dead. What's our next move?"

"Take the stairs to the roof. It's time to go home."

"Understood. We're coming." They didn't make it.

———————— ◉ ————————

KELLA FIRED UP THE engines, but the ship was immediately grabbed in a restraining beam. Dozens of heavily armed soldiers began to converge on them. "Ship, switch off your engines and open the hatch," demanded a voice on the comms. Kella's eyes opened wide, but the elder Rathbone took the comms station.

Winking at Kella, he spoke. "Tower, this is CEO O'Loran's personal ship. I have his companion and daughter already aboard. The CEO is under attack by an assassin at his offices. I'm to land on the roof to carry him to safety while the military neutralizes the threat. Release the restraining beam immediately."

"I don't believe a word of this foolish story," replied the voice.

"Then you damn well should, you young fool," said a woman's voice right behind Old Rathbone. "Give me a visual; I want to see the face of the man I'm going to have executed." It was Landy. She patted Rathbone's shoulder then stepped out to be seen. Brenna stepped up beside her.

"Lady O'Loran, I beg forgiveness, Ma'am. We weren't informed that the CEO had commissioned a new ship. We'll release you at once."

"Do so, and quickly." She turned away and the elder Rathbone switched off the comms.

"Nicely done," he smiled.

"Yes, well, if there is one thing I am good at, it's dealing with pompous servants," she sighed as her shoulders slumped. "Now get us out of here alive."

"Yes, Ma'am, I work as we speak," chuckled Kella. "Grab onto something. This could be a rough ride."

The soldiers outside backed off as the ship rose swiftly into the air. The tower was clearing the traffic away from the route to the offices of R.I.M. Inc. which made it a bit easier. They landed on the roof to find most of the crew there waiting for them and engaged in a fire fight with soldiers. Most of the crew, but not all.

———⊙———

THE ELEVATORS CAME back to life and started moving. Soon armed soldiers began pouring from the doors and up the stairs. Rathbone and Keira fled into the air shafts again. They had time for a single message before the smoke grenades were launched into the shafts. "Zartah, we're cut off. Run!"

Even as Rathbone spoke, Keira was aware of the smoke grenades exploding in the shaft above them. She grabbed Rath's arm and motioned downwards. Together they beat a hasty retreat back down the air shafts. They'd been lucky; the soldiers had all gone for the floor two above them. They were able to reach the lower levels again before the smoke overcame them.

"Rath, Rath, can you hear me?"

"Micha?"

"Get up here, we're under fire."

"We're cut off. Go."

"We'll come back for you."

"Just go. Your pilot knows where. Keira and I'll find you. Go." Rathbone threw the comm unit away.

"Which way now?" signalled Keira.

"We go down; all the way down. They'll be expecting us to go up."

Suddenly the whole massive building shook and threatened to collapse. Catching his balance, Rathbone steadied Keira then led the way to the stairwell.

———◉———

"RATH SAYS GO," SHOUTED Micha, as he retreated back into the hatchway and closed it. The outside of the ship continued to take fire, but there were no heavy weapons for the soldiers to bring to bear. They hadn't expected to face a combat ship. The ship raked the rooftop with weapon's fire, then blasted off at near full burn. That move launched them high into the atmosphere and destroyed the top two floors of the building.

Micha charged onto the bridge. "Pilot, Rath says you know where to go."

"I do have a few ideas," grinned the old fellow.

"Pick one and hit it," said Micha, as he flopped into the captain's chair which Kella had just vacated. "Are we being followed?"

"Three ships, but we can outrun them," replied Kella.

"I'd rather hide," said Micha. "We had to leave Keira and Rath back there. I don't like it and I want to go back for them as soon as reasonable."

"That will never be reasonable," said Landy, as she and Brenna arrived on the bridge. "We've come to be your hostages should you need them."

"Thank you ma'am, but I'd rather not go that route, at least not yet. Pilot, can you shake them off our tail?"

"Working. See that gas giant ahead? The atmosphere is quite flammable when you mix it with standard fuel."

"What's the plan?"

"I'll lead them into the atmosphere and jettison half our fuel. As we burst out of atmo I'll fire a shot back at them. It'll make one hell of a firestorm and will fry all their external sensors. By the time they make repairs we'll be safe in harbour. Is that acceptable to you, Captain?" The old man was grinning and Micha returned the grin, relaxing at last.

"Make it happen, Pilot."

"Aye, Sir."

The ship made a few course corrections then dove into the atmosphere of the gas giant. The three armed ships followed, closing the gap between them. As the ship broke out of the atmosphere a single shot was fired back into the maelstrom of gasses. The swirling ball of flame that erupted engulfed a large portion of the gigantic globe's atmosphere. The three gunships drifted out into open space, helpless.

"Sweet," sighed Micha, as he watched on the sensor screen. "Nicely done, Pilot. Now take us to the hideout."

"Aye, Captain. You might as well relax folks, we've got a couple of hours to kill."

"In that case," said Micha, as he rose from the chair, "I'll go take inventory of the crew. I need to know what kind of shape we're in."

———— ◉ ————

AS THE SOLDIERS CAME pouring out of the elevators, Jorm began issuing orders. "Assassins are making for the roof, do not let them escape. I need six men as guards here with me. The rest of you help these men get that rubble off him."

The men set to with a will until they found the body of the self-proclaimed emperor. "Be careful with him," demanded Jorm.

"Take him to the infirmary on the third floor. You men accompany them as guards. You six, come with me. We need to get up to my office."

Jorm's six guards led the way to the elevators and then inside. He used his special codes and the lift carried them to the top floor. They could hear the battle raging out on the stairwell and up to the roof. Jorm went to a secret panel, opened it and the safe behind it. He extracted a locked box, then turned away. "Right, now back to the infirmary." He peeked out the office door, saw the way was clear, then raced back to the elevator.

Jorm and his guards rode down to the third floor in silence. As the doors finally slid open, the guards led the way, making doubly certain the corridors were clear. When they reached the infirmary, they found the soldiers and security guards surrounding the body of the emperor. "I'm afraid he's dead, Sir," said one of the security men.

"He's not dead yet, just injured. Everybody out of the room."

With puzzled looks, they left. Jorm shut the door tightly behind them and locked it. He then rolled the body onto its side. Taking out a first aid kit he carefully sealed the many wounds he found on the body, and then he pressed firmly at the base of the skull. A small panel appeared and slid aside.

Jorm studied the circuitry inside for a long moment, then reached in with tweezers and removed a chip the size of a fingernail. He then opened the box he'd retrieved from the office safe. Gingerly he chose a replacement chip and inserted it into the slot in the emperor's skull. Taking a small probe, he reached in and pushed gently on a small red button, the reset button. Jorm closed the service port at the base of Loran's skull then settled back to wait.

A few moments later the body jerked twice, then Loran's eyes opened and he surged to his feet. "Where are we?"

"We're in the third floor infirmary, Sir."

"So I was injured. What happened, Jorm?"

"You fought the hound and beat him, Sir. You then battled the witch and lost. She destroyed the boardroom table with a flaming sword. The woman is terrifying. She warned everyone to stay out of Borealis space. I got busy finding your body and bringing you back. While that was happening the rebels escaped and blew off the top two floors of the building in the process. At least, that's what the comm chatter is saying.

"Oh, the board of directors is still in the boardroom. They have elected a new board chair and appointed a new CEO by now, I suspect." Jorm was grinning.

"Damned idiots," sighed Loran. "Send someone to throw a grenade into that room. I'm sick of the lot of them."

Jorm spoke briefly into his comm unit then nodded. "Tell me, Mr. Dax, why did you resurrect me? I was down and the board ready to appoint a new CEO. You could have had it all, Jorm. Why?"

"I've told you before, Sir," he smiled. "I don't want your job. As your assistant I wield a great deal of power, but the assassins will always come for you, not me. Besides all that, you're a lot more adept at the political games than I am. I wouldn't last a week as emperor."

"Jorm, my old friend, I have always admired your survival instincts. Are the rebels being pursued?"

"Only a few ships, Sir. The bulk of our forces, those that were within reach, are amassed along the border with those of A.S. Inc. Three were all we had on Elliston. Perhaps they will get in a lucky shot and bring down the rebels."

"Highly unlikely. I have seriously underestimated these rebels and the witch. Sadly, right now, we have to regroup, rebuild, and make a new plan."

"Are you still going to announce the monarchy?"

"Yes, but in light of this treaty between A.S. Inc. and the Borelian rebels, I think I will hold off on claiming the whole galaxy. At least for the time being. First we must sow the seeds of mistrust between those smug new allies. Once we are certain A.S. Inc. won't interfere, we'll crush the Borelians."

"And then A.S. Inc.?"

"Of course."

"Well, then," smiled Jorm, as he pressed the button on a small device in his pocket. The emperor froze in place like a statue. Jorm's grin broadened. "The first thing you must do is declare me Lord Dax and grant me property. The combined property of the remaining board members will do nicely."

Wiping the smirk from his face, Jorm pressed the button again and the emperor came back to life as though nothing had happened. "Jorm, my old friend, your devotion and hard work need to be properly recognized. I will proclaim you Lord Dax and grant you vast and profitable territory. The combined property of the board of directors should do nicely. Come along, we have work to do."

⸻⸻◉⸻⸻

RATHBONE AND KEIRA made their way down to the lowest sections of the building, well below ground level. They encountered first one and then another man in janitorial uniforms. They borrowed the uniforms and left the unconscious bodies in a storage room, bound and gagged. The weapons were left behind as janitors don't carry such things.

They found three others pushing a full container of garbage up to a small, unmanned, hauler and commandeered the machine.

"You there," demanded one man, "give us a hand here." They helped the men attach the cart to the hauler. Suddenly the man who had spoken looked at their ID badges. "Wait a minute, you're not Zander. You're a woman. Who the hells are you people?" He got no further as Rathbone attacked. The three men were unconscious in a heartbeat. They put them in an empty office, then mounted the hauler.

"Keira, if we get stopped on the way out," said Rathbone, "let me do the talking. I'm a better liar than you are." She laughed and punched him on the shoulder. He so loved to hear her laugh.

They entered the big service elevator and rode it to the surface. Rath backed the hauler up to one of the big bins and dumped the load from the cart, then he parked the hauler to the side. He and Keira began walking toward the exit to the back streets. "Halt! Stand and identify," demanded a detail of soldiers, their weapons pointed at the two. Keira stiffened slightly, but Rath stopped and raised his hands.

"Easy, lads," he said in a thick accent, "be easy now. It just old Zander and Mic headin' home after a long shift." He waved his janitorial badge in their general direction.

"You're janitorial? You can't leave yet. No one is allowed to leave until further notice."

"Aw now, lads, we've been cleaning up the mess them rich toffs made for over ten hours now. We're half killed, we are. All I wants is home, a beer, and me vid screen, then ten hours sleep. Come on now, we've no weapons or none such."

"Let them go, men," sighed the sergeant.

"But, Sarge..."

"The man's dead on his feet; he's no threat to anybody. Let them go. That's two more we won't have to process."

"All right, buddy, go on, but keep quiet about this."

"Not a word," grinned Rathbone. "I'll toast ye with a cold one soon's I get 'ome." He and Keira walked slowly, tiredly out of the area and down the street to catch a shuttle deeper into the city.

They took two more shuttles until they were in a far rougher part of town. Rath led her into a battered old café and ordered coffee. He winked at the man behind the counter. The fellow nodded toward a booth at the back and they gratefully sat down.

He brought them coffee then looked all around, they were his only customers. He hit the button on a remote carried on his belt. The booth slid smoothly into the wall and another identical booth slid out to take its place.

Rathbone and Keira were in a large room, tastefully decorated and lit with soft lights. A large woman squealed with delight and threw herself into Rath's arms. "Oh, dear gods. Rath, you're still alive." She squeezed him again, then stepped back. "In fact, you look better than I've seen you in years. Did something magical happen?"

"It did, Serena. First I met a witch who fixed me, then a goddess who married me. This is my bonded companion, Keira of Nova."

"Bonded companion? Truly?" The woman turned to Keira with a bright smile. Keira liked her instantly. "I can see you're a warrior like Rath. That's good; he needs a woman to keep watch over him. I'm Serenadisaen of Urn, but you may call me Serena." Keira matched her bright smile and gave her a nod. Serena's face began to darken.

"Keira was taken by an enemy who tortured her and cut out her tongue, Serena. She can't speak, but she uses hand signs and musical tones. Wait until you hear her at throat song."

Keira was enfolded in another motherly hug. "My gods, girl. Point out this enemy and I'll have his heart served up on a platter." Keira gently returned the embrace then released Serena. She gestured and signed with her hands, then Rathbone translated.

"Keira says thank you, but the man is well marked and one day she'll kill him herself."

"I believe you will," said Serena. She gave Keira another motherly smile then turned away. "Not today, however. You're both half-starved and sleep deprived. First I'll feed you, then you will sleep for days. After that we will discuss what needs to be done."

She walked away towards a large table and they followed her. She pulled a cord and a few moments later the man from the front appeared through a doorway carrying a huge platter of food. "Serena," said Rathbone, as he and Keira tucked into the food, "can you get a message to Refuse?"

"Of course. What shall I say and to whom?"

"Grandfather is there. Tell him we're alive and safe. We'll join him as soon as we can."

"Consider it done. Rath, was it you who set this city ablaze this night past? R.I.M. headquarters has been crawling with security for days and last night the military were called in. This morning the top was blown off the building as a ship launched at full burn. They could have set the whole damn atmosphere on fire. Are you behind this?"

Keira sang and signalled causing Selena to first look at her then back to Rathbone for a translation. "Keira wants to know how you and I met," grinned Rath.

Serena turned to give Keira that warm smile once again. "In other words, mind my own damn business," she chuckled. "All right, Keira, I really don't need to know; I'm just curious.

"To answer your question, I used to babysit this fine fellow when his grandfather was off world. Rath is like a son to me."

The man from the front stuck his head through the door and spoke. "Vid screen. Now." Serena grabbed a remote and flicked on the screen.

"Now to repeat this item for those of you just tuning in. The former CEO of R.I.M. has just disbanded the Company and seized its assets. He has declared himself Emperor Loran the First, of the Galactic Empire. At the time of his official announcement there were a number of assassinations throughout R.I.M. territory. Many people who could have opposed this move have been removed by order of the emperor. The new monarchy has begun.

"Earlier today a band of rebels from Sector Nine made an attempt on the emperor's life, but they were unsuccessful. With the rebels defeated, the military has now begun the task of reorganizing all society. Martial Law has been declared. Rebels will be dealt with harshly. Any opposition will be crushed without mercy. These are the words of the emperor."

The commentator continued to rattle on, but Serena turned it off. "Rathbone, what in the name of the nine hells have you done this time?"

"Me? It wasn't me? I tried to kill the bastard, as you may recall."

"Too bad you hadn't succeeded," she sighed. "This is going to make it a lot harder to get you off world. You may have to lay low here for a while."

"Don't worry, Serena, a lot of this is just O'Loran blustering and bluffing. The truth is, A.S. Inc. has made a mutual defense pact with the Borelian tribes of Sector Nine. A.S. Inc has troops lined up at your borders now. The new emperor knows he dare not turn his back at this point. If he tries to come down hard on his own people he'll be taken over by A.S. Inc. and he doesn't want that to happen. It's all bluff and bluster. The only thing that has really changed is his title."

"I do hope you're right," sighed Serena. "It is hard enough for a smuggler to make an honest living these days." Keira snorted and tried to hide her giggles. She failed and burst out laughing. "Stop it, Keira," giggled Serena, "you know very well what I mean."

"He's gone completely mad now," sighed Rathbone.

"Maybe he just got tired of making all that profit for the shareholders," grinned Serena. She sat back and shook her head. "It really doesn't matter, I guess. He was a right bastard anyway. Maybe if a lot of people turn on him you'll be able to get close enough."

Keira sang and signalled. "There's something else, Serena. Lady Arlessa tried to kill him. Apparently she failed. If she couldn't do it, my chances aren't very good. We need to get back to our people and make a new plan."

"Fine," sighed Serena, "but first you rest. You're in no shape to do anything right now, and your lady is looking seriously neglected. Take her to one of the back rooms and make her happy while I go see what we're up against. I'll also get word to Poppa Rathbone. Get some rest, kiddies." She smiled and headed out to the front of the old café.

Rath took Keira by the hand and led her to a room at the back. It was small, but nicely appointed with a bed just big enough for the two of them. Rath kicked off his boots and collapsed back on the platform to rest, smiling as he patted the space beside him. Keira stepped out of her boots and cuddled into his arms. He kissed her forehead and whispered, "Thanks for saving my life today, Sweetheart."

She rolled back slightly to sign to him. "How am I supposed to keep you out of trouble? That man was too confident; he knew he had a defense."

"So how did you get caught?" He was grinning and she playfully punched his arm.

"I saw you fall and ran to you. Next time, I'll just run away."

He gave a soft deep chuckle at that. "You're a wise woman, my Keira. Cuddle over here and go to sleep now. When we wake, we will figure out how to get back to our own people.

On the Run

Rathbone awakened, fully alert. He was alone in the bed. Dammit, how did she keep doing that? It was driving him crazy. What had awakened him? Listening intently, he heard water splashing in the distance. She was in the showers. He'd sensed her arise, that's what had awakened him.

He rose and stretched, then noticed fresh clothing on the chair beside the bed. He smiled. They would blend in perfectly with the average person on the street. Serena thought of everything.

Keira's eyes were closed as the water ran down over her face, but she didn't flinch as hands reached past her waist to cup her breasts. She had glimpsed Rath's reflection in the mirror as he entered the water room. She fairly purred as she turned in his arms and locked her lips on his.

Rathbone felt her nipples harden as he kissed her. His body swiftly responded to her touch. Keira deepened the kiss and rubbed her belly hard against his swelling member. She hooked her leg around his hips to pull him closer. Rathbone growled softly as he grasped her buttocks and lifted her up to impale her. He sucked in his breath as the heat and silk of her body engulfed him.

Keira locked her legs tightly around him as he began to move within her. Their lovemaking was swift and urgent, a response to the dangers and battles of the day before. She felt him explode within her just as her world dissolved in waves of stardust and ecstasy. He fought his shaking knees and held her gently as the spasms of delight slowly diminished and she went limp in his arms.

A short while later they emerged from the bedroom, dressed in the new disguises. Serena was waiting for them at the table. It was laden with food once again. "Eat quickly, my children; we have little time. I have two items of interest for you. I'll talk while you eat.

"First, it appears the word in the pipeline was true. O'Loran was dying of tumors in his heart and lungs. They couldn't be removed. Word is that he had his body completely rebuilt in a secret lab somewhere. Apparently he's more machine than human now. That's why the witch couldn't kill him.

"Second, the emperor has brokered a deal with A.S. Inc.; they've withdrawn their troops from the borders. This allows our troops to return and clamp down on Elliston. They're doing a house by house search to find criminals and dissidents. They'll be here within the hour."

"Huh, that didn't take him long," muttered Rathbone. "So he's a machine now. I wonder if he's shielded against an EMP."

"Wouldn't you be?"

"Yes, I would. So, why're they searching house to house? That seems a bit extreme."

"Word has it that someone kidnapped the emperor's companion and daughter during the madness yesterday. Do you know anything about that?"

Keira sang and signalled. Serena looked to Rath and he translated. "She says Brenna must have taken her mother with her. Serena, the high priestess of Nova is a woman of incredible power. She and Brenna O'Loran have bonded. There's a crew of mercs dedicated to the protection of the Black Witch. Brenna is a member of that crew, so are Keira and I. We serve a man named Micha who in turn, serves the Lady Arlessa."

"Good gods, Rathbone. You signed on with mercs?"

"She fixed me, Serena. I was dying and she fixed me. The price was I give up the hunt for O'Loran and join her merry band. I've had not one single moment of regret. I know it's only a matter of time until Lady Arlessa or one of her crew brings down that man and makes an end of him. I'm content with that."

Suddenly there was a great deal of noise out front. "Out the back, quickly now. Make for the space port, pad three oh seven. You should be able to hop a garbage scow out to Refuse." Serena gave each of them a quick hug, then shooed them out the back way.

They emerged into an alley that was closed over; more of a tunnel than an alley. Rathbone seemed familiar with the route, so Keira was content to let him lead while she watched for danger. Rath loved the way she was always on alert. Keira wasn't one to let her guard down.

Eventually they found themselves back on the street, a block or more away from the soldier's path. They had enough coins for shuttle fare to get them near the outer ring of the spaceport. They walked the last mile or so to reach the Refuse launch pad. It was crawling with military. They took shelter in a small tool shed and watched.

Hours passed and still there seemed to be no way to reach the pad without being seen. Worse yet, every load of garbage was being thoroughly searched. It wasn't looking good.

Eventually one ship was given clearance and lifted off. It was barely off the ground when another landed and the loading process began all over again. A tired looking pilot waved at the soldiers as he sauntered away. He passed very close to the shed where Rath and Keira were hiding.

Listening carefully, they heard the soldiers talking to the loaders. "So where's he going?"

"Home," replied one of the workers. "He's off for the next two days. There'll be another pilot along soon enough. Jake? Who's on next?"

"Not sure," replied another voice. "Think it's the new guy. You know, the big fella. He only shows up half the time."

"Well he'd damn well better show up this time," growled one of the guards, as he poked away at the load of garbage. "Why in the name of Draka are we poking at loads of refuse anyway, Sarge?"

"I agree it's a waste of time, Jaks. Back off, you're getting that slop all over your uniform."

A while later and Rath saw a huge man walking sulkily towards the shack; he stank of intoxicants. As the man passed a big arm encircled his neck. Moments later he was unconscious on the floor of the shack. He had barely struggled.

Two people then strode towards the refuse hauler. "Halt, stand and identify."

"Orcan," growled Rath. "I'm piloting that scow to train this one. That damned user is being replaced." He pushed Keira, whose head was down and shoulders slumped, towards the nearly loaded ship. "Go on, you; get in the pilot's chair. I'll be right there."

"Hey, I want to see some ID," said one of the soldiers. Keira did not stop.

"Bloody hell, man," said Rathbone. "What the nine hells do you think we're smuggling here? Garbage? The ship is almost fully auto. We go up to Refuse, dump the load, and then come back. Any deviation and a law enforcement ship comes and shoots it down.

"Look, with you lot holding things up around here, we're well behind schedule. Keep this up and there'll be garbage backed up all the way to the new emperor's office."

"All right, all right," growled the Sergeant, "just get that damn ship in the air and shut up."

Rathbone obliged by climbing aboard the ship. He winked at Keira who was in the pilot's chair. She tapped her finger on the ship's call sign and Rath grinned as he took the comm. "Tower, this is Refuse Scow Eight-Seven-Three, requesting clearance for lift off."

"It's about time," growled the voice over the comm. We're getting some stink up here. What's the big hold up?"

"Soldiers afraid we're smuggling rebels off planet."

"Right, and ferrying them to their hideout on Refuse," laughed the voice. "Clearance granted Eight-Seven-Three, you're good to go."

"Obliged," chuckled Rath, as he switched off the comm and slid to the floor to make himself comfortable.

Keira took the controls and lifted off smoothly. As soon as they cleared the atmosphere, she put the ship on auto. "There we are," she signed. "How long until Refuse?"

"We have a couple of hours to kill." He grinned as he looked her over and smiled.

"What will we do to pass the time?" she sang.

"Come on down here and I'll show you." Her silvery laughter gave him a thrill as she slid out of the chair and onto his lap.

Keira was asleep in his arms when the alarm sounded. She leaped to her feet, landing in a fighting stance, eyes darting everywhere seeking an enemy. Rathbone's heart swelled to see her, so beautiful, dishevelled and half dressed, and shaking a finger at him. He grinned as he rose and began to straighten out his clothing. She did the same.

They brought the ship in over the pre-programmed coordinates and dumped the load then Rath switched to manual control. He flew a few grid lines across the surface then landed. They were met by armed men. "Don't shoot," he laughed as the hatch opened, "it's only us."

As Rathbone descended the ramp, Jip bounded out of hiding and pounced on him. They wrestled around for a few moments while Keira hugged everyone in the crew. Finally Jip let him up and Rath joined the rest. "We'd better send that ship back with a load of explosives. It should blow up before it hits atmo."

Micha shook his hand and nodded to Zartah. A few moments later the ship lifted off again, fully on auto pilot. There would be a drive-core breach causing a massive explosion about half way back to Elliston. It would be assumed the pilots died in the disaster.

They were gathered in the common eating area of the hidden village. The crew was there, plus Rathbone the Elder, Lortax, and Landy, as well as a few of the local folk. "So you folks got off Elliston all right?" asked Rathbone.

"No problem at all," grinned Micha. "Our new pilot's pretty good at his job."

"Poppa, you've signed on with the crew?"

"Only until we get to Nova, then I'm retiring again." Keira chuckled and poked him in the ribs. "I am," he protested. "Tell her I mean it, Rath." Everyone was laughing now.

"Speaking of Nova," said Lessa, "I'd like to go home now. We did what we came to do."

"Not quite," sighed Rath.

"What do you mean?" asked Micha.

"O'Loran, I mean Emperor Loran, is still alive."

"What? Impossible," said Lessa. "I punched him through half a meter of concrete and steel. How could any man survive that?"

"He's not a man anymore," said Rath. "Apparently he became terminally ill a year or two ago. He went to that magic doctor of his, the one who made us cyborgs, and had himself rebuilt. He's more machine than man now."

"So that's it," mused Landy. "I knew he'd become ill, but he was always so distant. He would never tell me what was going on. The distance between us has grown into an impassable gulf over the last year."

"So what now, Lessa?" asked Micha. "Do we go back and finish the job, or do we go home?"

"We go home, Micha," she replied, as she patted Brenna's hand. "The man we came to face was already gone before we arrived. We've declared our independence and been acknowledged by one of the companies, and we've rescued the families of our people. It's done and time to go home."

"What is it mother?" asked Brenna, as she noticed the look of concern on Landy's countenance.

"What is to become of me, Brenna? Whatever will I do out on the primitive world of yours? I've lived on Elliston all my life. I'm not as brave as you are, my beautiful daughter."

"Actually, Landy, I have a proposal that might prove of interest to you in this situation," said Lortax.

Landy looked at him with pure mischief in her eyes. "Forgive me, Sir, but, as wonderful a dancer as you are, I'm still officially wed to that man/machine, or whatever he may be now."

Lortax blushed to his roots and started to sputter, and then he saw the merriment in her eyes. He shook his head in embarrassment as the others had a good laugh.

"That's going to cost you, woman," he chuckled. "Listen to me now. As chieftain of Nara Clan my duties were fairly simple. There wasn't a lot of politics involved. Life has changed and these days I often find myself embroiled in things I would rather avoid."

"Oh, but you dance so divinely, Lortax," she smiled.

"Thank you, Ma'am. I quite enjoy a dance, but it is of the arrangements that I speak. I loathe the task of arranging the events I have to host, and there seem to be plenty of them these days. I need a social secretary, someone who would make all the arrangements and be the hostess. Would you be interested in the position?"

"Tell me more." She smiled as she leaned back in the chair.

"I inherited a palace from my predecessor. It is on Borealis Prime, near the temple. You would have you own apartments within the palace, servants to carry out your wishes, and whatever funds you might need. I would inform you of when a gala was needed and who would be the guest of honor. The rest would be up to you. I'd show up on cue, charm the ladies while you charm the men."

"Tell me of Borealis Prime."

"It's not Elliston, Mamma," said Brenna, "but the temple is in the heart of a fair-sized city. Oh Mother, you would be so perfect for this."

"Well then, Excellency, I accept your generous offer of employment."

Wonderful," grinned Lortax. "Now, your first task is to stop teasing the poor old viceroy. Blushing is bad for his health." A round of laughter followed.

"All right," said Micha, "it's settled, we go home. Rath, Gorda's gone on ahead with the other ship. You're the specialist as well as chief engineer until we get home."

"Yes, Boss," grinned Rathbone. This crew was something new in his life, something he had never truly experienced before. They had no fear of him, they fully accepted him as one of their own, and now he had Keira. It felt beyond good to actually belong. "What do you need?"

"Options, suggestions."

"We have a ship that's one of the best. She's heavily armed, and we have the two Arcalian fighters in the launch bay. We can disguise her as a freighter then slip away when the planet is turned away from Elliston. If we just wander away like we know what we're doing, no one is likely to bother us."

"All right, what's our back up plan?"

"We've used this route before," replied Rathbone. "We'll make a few stops along the way, top up our fuel, check on the activities of the enemy, and if necessary we can change ships several times until we are outside the Hub. Once we're beyond the Hub Worlds, this ship can probably outrun anything that could come at us. I know a few worlds along the way where we could make a stand if we had to. That's the best I've got, Boss."

"Works for me," grinned Micha. "When do we leave?"

"We should load up now," said Rathbone the Elder. "The best time would be in about an hour."

"Done then," said Micha, as he rose to his feet. "Mount up people. So you're signing on?"

The elder Rathbone met his gaze for a long moment. Finally he spoke. "Rath told me about you, Micha. I didn't believe him at first. After these past couple of days, I can see it. I'm old, but I've got a few good years in me. I can still fight, and I have a lifetime of training and experience. Will you have me?"

"In a heartbeat," laughed Micha, "but you've got to teach me." He offered his hand and the old man grasped it in the warrior's grip.

"I'll do my best for you, Boss."

"All right, Pilot, go warm her up and lay in your course. Rath, you're in the engine room, Zartah, you and Murtah check the weapons, Edie and Ena, you've got the infirmary, and Kella, you're on co-pilot. The rest of you settle in, relax, and start figuring out what you're going to want to do next. I have a feeling this isn't over. Jip, you're with me." The big dog hopped to his feet and trotted along beside Micha. A short while later the disguised ship lifted off. Seemingly unhurried, she made her way towards the Hub worlds facing Sector Nine.

The first two weeks were uneventful. They made a few stops, topped up their fuel, replenished the weapons on the Arcalian Fighter in the hold and all was ready. The crew settled into a twelve hour work rotation and all appeared to be well. They passed beyond the Hub Worlds and into Sector Nine before the first sign of trouble.

Micha and Edie were just arriving at the mess hall for breakfast when the klaxon sounded throughout the ship. Zartah was on the bridge. It was his voice that came over the ship-wide comms. "Battle stations. Battle stations. Captain to the bridge."

"Skeeter," swore Micha, as he raced away towards the bridge, Jip loping along beside him, tail wagging.

"What, where?" demanded Micha as he burst onto the bridge.

"Seven ships inbound, Arlen design, probably pirates," said Zartah, as he vacated the captain's chair.

"Take a crew and man the Arcalian Fighter, Zartah," growled Micha, as he slid into the captain's chair.

"I'll take Old Rath, Rath, and Keira," said Zartah, as he bolted towards the exit. Rathbone the Elder followed close behind.

"Chieftain, the ship is yours," said Micha, as Lortax, Lessa, and Brenna came pouring through the doorway.

"Keep it," barked Lortax. "Where do you want me?"

"Comms," replied Micha as he resumed his seat. "Lessa, Brenna, side rail guns, Murtah, forward cannon. Now, let's see what these fools want. Zartah, you ready?"

"Ready, Boss."

"Launch, just don't let Keira start shooting until I say."

"Aye, Boss," chuckled Zartah. "Launching fighter."

The fighter bay doors opened and the Arcalian ship slipped out and took up a position on the right. They were ready.

"They're coming in fast, Micha," said Kella, who was now at the pilot's station.

"Bring us about to face them, Kella. Power up all weapons."

"I'm getting a signal, Captain," said Lortax.

"On speaker."

Lortax flipped a switch and the voice came through loud and clear. "You have trespassed on Arlen territory, prepare to be boarded."

"Denied." Lessa grinned. She loved the way Micha became a man of few words when things got tense.

"By order of President Garad of the Arlen Alliance, I command you to stand down and prepare to be boarded."

"Denied. Move away and let us pass."

"You bloody fool; I'll blow you out of the sky. Now stand down and..."

"All ships fire," barked Micha. A pulse of light lanced out from the nose cone and the lead Arlen ship exploded. A hail of projectiles followed and another ship crumpled. The Arcalian fighter was suddenly among them, destroying two more ships before bursting through their line and racing away. One ship gave chase, but the fighter made a near impossible turn and came back in.

All the Arlen ships had opened fire on Micha's ship. It took several hits and the façade of an old freighter was blown off into space, bits and pieces of the disguise floating away in all directions. The gleaming hull of the Intruder Class ship gleamed in the starlight. Another ship broke up under Zartah's attack then the remaining two attackers signalled surrender.

"Who is in command over there?" demanded Micha.

"He's dead," came a static riddled reply.

"Who else then?"

"Me, I guess, First Man, detached, Tozer."

"Go back to the Arlen Alliance and tell them that R.I.M. Company is no more. It's become an empire ruled by Emperor Loran. Borealis has declared independence and has claimed Sector Nine. We are now the Borealian Free Alliance and we claim this territory. Tell Garad he must present himself at the temple on Borealis Prime to swear allegiance to the viceroy. Go now or die."

They went, leaving the wounded and destroyed ships behind. "Well, that's that," sighed Micha, as he settled back into the captain's chair. "Zartah, you there?"

"Here Boss."

"Come back in, we've got to get out of here."

"Coming in, Boss."

"Looks like we're out of time folks. No more stealth, it's time to run. Kella, set course for Borealis Prime."

"Borealis Prime, aye, aye, boss."

"Zartah?"

"Fighter Ship Two aboard, Boss. All go."

"All right, hit it, Kella. Full burn."

"Aye, Sir. Borealis Prime, full burn." Even with the latest in inertial dampeners, they still felt the surge of acceleration as the ship leaped forward.

Three days later, they were in a long stretch of empty space that had to be crossed. The ship was on auto pilot, scans of the area had shown nothing, so they were all gathered in the mess hall. "Now is the time for a new plan, folks," said Micha, as he passed another hot drink to Edie, then sat beside her. "I have a strong feeling that we're not just going home, am I right Chieftain? Lessa?"

"You can all go home, Micha," sighed Lortax. "You've done more than enough already."

"War's coming, Micha," said Lessa. "You know that as well as any of us. We need to be prepared. Give us your thoughts."

"Folks, I'm a man who likes to face one problem at a time. You give me an objective and I'll do my best to accomplish that. 'War's coming, prepare', is way too broad a concept for my little brain to understand. Tell me what you want to have happen next."

"It looks like this, Micha," said Lortax. "The new emperor will come at us, we know this, but first he has to consolidate his power. That'll buy us a little time to strengthen our own defenses. Our first order of business will be to bring the Arlens into line. We have the power to defeat them, but it won't be easy or swift, and it'll leave the whole sector weakened. If the Arlens put up a fight we're doomed."

"You believe they'll fight?"

"Garad will fight. He knows that he and his two sons would be tried and executed for war crimes if they're taken alive. He'll fight."

"What is it, Keira?" asked Edie, as she placed a gentle hand on Keira's arm. "That name made you flinch. Is Garad the man who maimed you?"

Keira nodded and made a swift signal. "It was Garad and his two sons. He will pay, my sister-in-arms. He will pay and his time is coming."

Micha reached over and patted Keira's shoulder. "It appears we have an issue with Garad as well, Chieftain. Are you suggesting we send a professional assassin after him?"

"I can't ask that, Micha," replied Lortax.

"But it would make your life easier. It would also help you ward off the coming war at best, and at least make it easier for you to defend the territory, including Nova, correct?"

"Correct, Micha."

Micha turned to Lessa and grinned. "Lady?"

"I'm sorry, Micha, but Lortax is right. As dearly as I would like to go home right now, this is the best way to defend Nova. We failed to take out the emperor. We dare not fail this time. I will go after Garad myself."

"Where you go, I go, Lessa."

"Where the boss goes, the crew goes," grinned Zartah. "This will be exciting; too bad Gorda will miss it."

"We can't all go," sighed Micha. "The chieftain has to get back and assemble the armada. He also has to ensure the safety of his new social secretary."

"Micha's right," said Rathbone. "A small crew will stand a better chance."

"I can't ask you to do this, Rath," said Micha. "I'll go."

"Bad plan, Boss; I'm the professional assassin here."

Micha sighed and leaned back in his chair. "Understood. All right, Rath, this is your mission. Who and what do you need?"

"First, I need someone who can identify the targets; that will be Keira. Forgive me, Lady Arlessa, but you're rather too well known for a stealth mission."

Lessa just nodded at the wisdom of that and said nothing. "Just you and Keira?" asked Micha. "What's your back-up plan?"

"I am," said the elder Rathbone. "I've been the most successful assassin in the galaxy for longer than you've been breathing air, Micha. I go too."

"Makes sense to me," grinned Micha. "I'll come along and see what I can learn from you guys."

"You'll need fighters if it goes sideways," said Zartah. "That me and Murtah."

"You'll need a medic," smiled Edie, "that means I go."

"A dispatcher could be handy," said Brenna.

"Perhaps a witch might prove useful after all," grinned Lessa.

"You will need a truth detector," said Ena.

Rathbone was taken aback and didn't know what to say. These people seemed to be eager to do this, almost like a picnic. "People, I'm not sure you..."

"We fully understand the danger, Rath," said Micha. "This is your task. You have assets here, use them. The fate of millions may depend on your success. Who and what do you need to assure success of your mission?"

Rathbone sighed and sat back. "All right, Boss. Two teams of three go in. Me, Keira, and Ena are first team, Poppa, Micha, and Murtah are back up."

"I'll go in Murtah's place," said Edie.

"Edie..."

"No, Micha, you're not going anywhere without me." She was on her feet going nose to nose with Micha, fire dancing in her eyes. "I belong at your side and that's exactly where I'll be. Tell him, Murtah."

"Not my call," chuckled Murtah, "it's Rath's. Better let her go Rath or you'll be needing the medic sooner than you think." There was a great round of laughter at that.

"Look," laughed Rathbone, "you can't all go. The smaller the group, the better the chances of success. We're not going to fight a war here, we're trying to slip in unnoticed, take out the targets, and escape undetected. One or two people stand a far better chance of success than the whole group. That's assassination, lesson one, right Poppa?"

"He's right folks. You people are amazing, but Rath's right. Keira, and Rath, with me as back up. That's the best chance of success."

All eyes were on Micha now. It was clear he didn't like it, but he could listen to reason. That was one of Micha's great strengths as a leader; he could take advice from more experienced people. Finally he nodded. "All right, Rath, what do you need?"

"I need Keira with me to identify them, and Poppa for back up. We'll take our own weapons and we'll need a ship they won't shoot down on sight as well as a map to get us to their planet."

"I've got a few connections," said Kella. "I can get you right to the palace doors if you want."

"That would be a real time saver," grinned Rath.

"Kella, you never cease to amaze me," said Micha. "What do we need to do?"

"The next planet we're likely to see is Praxis Two," replied Kella. "I can signal ahead and have a ship waiting for us there. I have connections, so I'll pilot them right to Arla Four. I can conduct a bit of free trading while Rath and company do their business, then I can arrange shelter for them until you can come for us."

"I'll send messages ahead as well," said Lortax. I'll have the armada meet us on the way. As soon as we meet up with them we will make for Arla Four at full burn. You will be alone no longer than necessary."

"What else do you need, Rath?" asked Micha.

"I'll need a few supplies from the infirmary."

"The infirmary?"

"Micha, these men will die by my hand, but before they do they will also know why. I need something to knock them down but leave them awake while I explain the facts to them."

"Actually, I know just the thing," grinned Rathbone the Elder. "I just need a few ingredients."

"Make me a list," said Kella, "I'll have it waiting for us."

———— ◉ ————

IT WAS MANY DAYS LATER that they made planet fall. During that time Kella had shared what she could of the city layout on Arla Four, the palace and grounds, as well as the numbers of guards. The planet was under martial law; everything coming or going was searched and tested.

"So how do we get into that city?" Rathbone had asked her.

"We use a few of my contacts," replied Kella. "Grease the right palms with good Company script and we'll get in all right. The tighter you close your fist, the more sand slips through your fingers."

"I like this woman," chuckled Rathbone the Elder. "Are you single, Kella?"

"Sorry," she smiled wickedly, "but I'm wed to my job."

"Pity that," he grinned. "What do you think, Rath?"

"Well, judging by Kella's mock up, I could pick at least one off from the roof or one of the upper floors of this building here," he replied, "but that would stir them up and make the rest hard to get to."

"Maybe not; it might be the best way."

"Explain, Poppa."

"Give me a couple of days to penetrate the inner sanctum and then peg one off. While everybody runs out to chase the sniper I'll drop the other two from behind. We go to ground and wait for the viceroy to come dig us out."

"How about you give us time to penetrate and you peg one off?" muttered Rath.

"Rath, my dear grandson, you're built like a battle cruiser; there's no way for you to penetrate without being seen. I'm an old man with bad knees. They'll ignore me completely."

"Poppa, these are the men who maimed Keira. I want them to know why they're being killed."

"They'll know, Keira," said Rathbone the Elder. "I swear they will know. Let me get close to them, then at my signal, kill one. I'll dispatch the other two. They'll know who sent me and why they are dying."

"Poppa..."

"Dammit all, boy, I'm Rathbone of Urn and I haven't failed to complete a contract in fifty years." The old fellow settled back into his seat. "Besides, you're a far better shot than I am, especially with that long range projectile weapon of yours. I've always liked things up close and personal."

As he finished speaking Keira sang and signalled. Rath didn't like it. He shook his head no, but she surged to her feet and glared at him. She gestured to her mouth as she opened it to show her lack of a tongue. Rath sighed and nodded assent. "Keira will penetrate the mansion with you, Poppa," he said as she resumed her seat, somewhat mollified.

The Elder Rathbone met her gaze for a long moment before he spoke. "Understood." It was set; they had a plan.

While the main ship fuelled up, Kella took the three assassins to another part of the small spaceport. They arrived at the offices of a run-down freighter service. As they entered the office the girl behind the desk rose and walked to the door. She locked it then turned back to them. "Right this way, folks," she smiled, as she led them deeper into the old building.

They walked along a corridor then into a cleaner's storage closet. The shelves at the back moved aside at the touch of a button, revealing a large and very modern office. They stepped inside and the girl closed the door behind them.

"Kella, welcome, it's been far too long since you've graced us with a visit."

"Frank, it's good to see you. Have you a ship for me?"

"There's a special load coming on a small ship that should be exactly what you need, Kella. Are you certain you want to visit Arla Four now? There are rumors that O'Loran has declared himself emperor of the galaxy or something like that. It's said the Borelian Clans have risen up against him. If any of this is true, you know the Arlen Alliance will back the Company, I mean the emperor."

"The rumors are true, Frank," she smiled as she strolled to the chairs before the huge desk and sat down. Her companions spoke not a word, but they followed her example.

"The rumors are true? This is very bad for business. It's bad enough as it is, trying to get goods moved in and out of Arlen territory without this."

"I believe that's about to get easier," she smiled. "Soon the viceroy will come with his armada, including the Borelian Clans. The high priestess and the Black Witch will be on that flag ship with him. Arla will fall, old friend, and we'll be free to conduct business out in the open."

"What do you mean?"

"The viceroy, himself, has granted me a free trader's license, Frank. We're free to conduct business anywhere in Sector Nine without fear."

"That's a nice dream, Kella," he chuckled, "but you won't mind if I wait until the viceroy has brought Arla to heel. Garad will fight, and the Company will back him with ships and weapons."

"Garad will be dead, as will his sons before the armada arrives," she replied, meeting his gaze squarely.

"What? Is that what you're taking to Arla? Assassins? Forget it people, you'll never get close to him. Are you mad?"

"Frank, you must trust me on this. Keep this to yourself, but you'll know when it is done. Allow me to introduce you to my companions. This is Rathbone of Urn, the elder, this man is Rathbone of Urn the younger, and this woman is Keira the Avenger."

"Keira the Avenger, dear gods, woman," said Frank as he stared at Keira. "I well know who Rathbone of Urn is, although I never expected to meet him. However, Keira the Avenger of Nova Crew. Every Arlen soldier knows and fears that name. Arlen mothers frighten their children with threats of Keira the Avenger, she who was tortured to death by Garad and his sons, but who returned from the dead to avenge herself against all Arlens.

"Kella, tell me you haven't contracted with these people."

"I am a business woman, Frank, you know that. My contract with them is to get them to Arla in one piece. What they do then is their own business. You know how we operate, Frank."

"Yes, I know; honor the contract and stay out of politics. So who holds our contract."

"Keira. I owe her my life twice over; this is what she asked of me. She's hired assassins to avenge her, and she's come along to witness the execution. We take them in, and then we bring them back out. This'll pay my debt. Your percentage will be as it would for a normal contract of this nature."

"Forget it, Kella. If they succeed then things should greatly improve for us. If they fail I want no way for them to be connected to me. A friend has asked me for a ride to Arla and that's what I'll provide. I know nothing more, nor do I want to."

"Understood, Frank," smiled Kella. "When does our ship arrive?"

"It will arrive later today, refuel, and then set out for Arla Four. You will board during the stopover. You're replacing a number of the crew, according to the books. Make yourselves comfortable in the lunchroom. Food has been provided for you. I'll let you know when it is time to board the ship."

———— ◈ ————

WHILE KELLA AND FRIENDS relaxed, waiting for their ship, Nova Crew continued on towards home. Zartah was in the captain's chair as Micha, Lortax, and Lessa arrived on the bridge. He stood, giving the chair to Micha who sighed as he sat down. "Report, Zartah. What's our status?"

"We're topped up with fuel and weapons, Boss. We're about three weeks out from home at full burn, but we should meet up with our people well before that."

"Explain."

"Messages just came in. Gorda is nearly home and he sent messages on ahead. The viceroy's armada is already on the way here. Lady Marla is on the flagship. As soon as Gorda can drop off the families he will top up his crew with former mercs and join the armada."

"Very good, Zartah," grinned Micha. "I see you've been busy. Get some rest now." Zartah nodded and left for his quarters. A few others drifted in to replace the bridge crew and everything settled into routine. There was nothing else to do.

Assassins at Work

They boarded the old freighter without incident. Rathbone chuckled when he learned what the cargo was; antique weapons, some bound for President Garad's private collection. What a perfect way to smuggle their own weapons into Arlen space.

The five day trip was uneventful. They were stopped at three different check points, but even though the ship was searched each time, nothing was found. The false identities Kella had arranged passed inspection easily enough and eventually they arrived at the main spaceport on Arla.

As the cargo was inspected once again, then the crew was given a ten hour leave. The assassins slipped into the city with ease. Two hours later, they were in an apartment looking out over the walls of the palace. Kella went out for food while Rath and Keira studied the palace through binoculars.

Eventually they located what they wanted. They could see into a room that appeared to be a large living room. Keira's snarl brought them to attention. She pointed out the short balding man with the scar on his face. That was Garad. By the end of the day she had marked out the two sons as well. Both Rathbones studied the men until they were completely familiar with their faces.

They studied them for three days until they knew the men's routine. Each day, after the early evening meal, the three men would gather in that living room. The assassins had their field of endeavour. That living room would become the kill zone.

Early the next day Rathbone the Elder and Keira approached the servant's entrance of the mansion. They were dressed as cleaners. The armed guards checked them over, then waved them through. They spent the day working in and getting familiar with the layout inside.

After two days of this, Keira was getting frustrated, but the Elder Rathbone cautioned her to be patient. They needed to be certain of their escape route before they committed themselves to action. She bit her lip and endured two more days of exploring.

Three times the old fellow had led her into that living room on one pretext or another. Each time someone had ordered them back out. On the fifth day they made two different entries into the living room. By now they were being ignored. Garad even continued a conversation with one son, ignoring them completely. The time of reckoning had arrived.

As Keira and old Rathbone arrived back at the nest the next morning, the old fellow gave the nod. "All right, team," he said, "today's the day. They're having a meeting in the kill zone this afternoon. Today we strike." He shivered involuntarily at the wolfish grin on Keira's face. "Control it, Keira," he said as he gently squeezed her arm. "Let them see your hatred and we'll fail. You must remain controlled."

Keira looked into his eyes then she lowered her gaze, her face falling into the look of a down trodden house cleaner. As they approached the mansion Old Rath waved at the guards who waved back then ignored them, they'd become familiar faces and part of the daily routine of the palace. They set about their work methodically. Keira entered the empty living room and swiftly sabotaged the lights. With a grin she slipped out of the room again.

Once he had eaten, Rathbone set up his long range projectile weapon. Each day he had set it on the tripod and put one of the target men in the cross hairs. This time it was easy. He swept the room through the scope, but it was empty. He settled down to wait. He prayed Keira could stay focused for just a few more hours.

———●———

GARAD FUMED AND PACED about, his eldest son lazing in a chair looking bored. "Relax Father, he'll be right along."

"That boy has no sense," sighed the scarred dictator. "This is important. Everything has changed and this is an opportunity too good to pass up. We'll gain control over the whole sector if we play this right."

The son glanced past his father to the two cleaners, fussing with one of the switches, trying to repair the lighting. Garad waved a dismissive hand and snorted as though they didn't matter. At that moment the second son arrived. "I'm sorry, Father, but there was an urgent matter I had to attend to."

"A woman, no doubt."

"Indeed it was," grinned the arrogant fool.

"You can't spend your entire life between a woman's thighs, son."

"I can try," he joked. He looked away and sank into a chair as he realized his father wasn't laughing.

Garad sat facing his two sons, glaring at the youngest. "Listen carefully, both of you. The emperor has charged us with blocking the Borelian clans from going to the aid of A.S. Inc. He is sending us supplies as we speak. In two days' time six freighters will arrive carrying weapons and munitions."

"That'll last a week," sneered the elder son.

"That will be the first shipment, three more will follow. As soon as..."

He was interrupted as a man in uniform burst into the room. "Mr. President, we have an urgent message."

"Well, spit it out man."

"Sir, the viceroy and his entire armada are headed this way at speed. Sir, the high priestess and the Black Witch are with him."

"What??? Are you certain he is headed here?"

"Yes Sir, our spies have confirmed it. They have assassins on Arla Four right now. Sir, they're coming for you."

Garad's hand slapped the arm of his chair and blast shields dropped across the windows. "What do these assassins look like? Have you a description?"

The messenger swallowed hard before he spoke. He was trembling in fear. "Sir, it's Rathbone of Urn and Keira the Avenger."

The room was deathly silent for a moment, and then the eldest son laughed. "Well, Father, I'd say that either you're a dead man already, or, more likely, our spy has been discovered and fed misinformation. The viceroy obviously knows what's going on and seeks to throw us into confusion long enough for his armada to get here."

"Yes, you're probably right," sighed Garad. "Still, we'll take no chances. We'll stay on full alert until this is over. If there are assassins we'll find them. Actually, I'd like to see Keira again; see if the years have been kind to her." Both sons laughed at his joke.

Keira stiffened, but the grip on her elbow helped her stay still. She slowly turned to look at her companion and was surprised to see the merry twinkle in his eye. He motioned towards the door. Reluctantly, she nodded her agreement. She reset a switch and the lights came up.

"At last," grumbled Garad, "now get out." They left.

Old Rathbone and Keira headed straight for the gates. "Leaving a bit early, aren't you?" asked the guards as the siren sounded within the mansion.

"Split shift," grumbled Old Rathbone, "we get a few hours rest then we have to come back. Worse yet, we'll have to bring her brother as there will be no one to look after him."

"He'll need clearance."

"Come on, lad. The boy is built like a battleship, but he's a blank page, if you get my meaning. He can carry the heavy stuff for us."

The guard just chuckled and nodded. "All right then, I'll let the guys know you're coming. Damn, I hate these stupid lock down drills." The two cleaners nodded and walked out the gate.

Rath was waiting when they reached the hideout. "What happened?"

Keira slammed the door behind her and snarled as she signalled. "We were this close," she said, holding her thumb and forefinger close together.

"They have spies in the viceroy's camp," sighed Old Rathbone. "The viceroy has met up with his armada and they're on the way here. They also know we're here. That's why they slammed down the blast doors."

"All right, we need a new plan," sighed Rathbone, as he gently pulled Keira into his arms.

"We slipped away to give them time to search the mansion," grinned the older fellow. "As soon as it gets dark we'll go back in. I gave them a story as we left so there won't be any trouble getting inside. They'll have moved the search out to the city by then. We'll just have to hunt them down, one at a time."

"Why is it never easy?" sighed Rath, as he released Keira and sank to the floor, his back against the wall. She sat beside him and cuddled into his arms again. "Yes, dear, we'll get them. I promise."

"We'll have to move up the time table a bit," said the elder Rathbone, as he settled into a chair. "The emperor has given this lot orders to hold the viceroy back while he dispatches A.S. Inc. If that happens there won't be a safe place for the likes of us anywhere in the galaxy.

"There are six freighters of weapons and munitions headed this way with more to follow. We have two days to do what we came to do and throw this lot into disarray."

"I may not be a great assassin," grinned Rath, "but disarray I can do. We'll strike tonight. One huge batch of disarray coming up."

"What's the plan?" grinned the old fellow.

"I need to get inside first."

"We've got that covered. You come in with us. Just act blank when we talk to the guards. We'll get you inside, but what then?"

The elder Rathbone was enjoying this and Keira smiled in spite of herself. These men wouldn't cut and run like so many had before. These men were like Micha and the crew. They'd find a way to get the job done. She would find some closure at last.

"Is there a central security room? There should be a room where all the security forces hang out, monitor the vid feeds and eat junk food."

"There is," signalled Keira.

"All right, here's the plan. Get me to that door then disappear. I'll create some serious disarray. You find your quarry and dispatch them while I keep everybody else busy."

"Are you sure about this, Rath?" she sang.

"I am," he grinned. "These folks are bored security guards, not combat ready cyborgs. Now, are there weapons detectors to pass through going in?"

"Yes," replied Rathbone the Elder. "We'll have to improvise until we can borrow some weapons."

"Shouldn't be a problem," said Rath as he cuddled Keira closer. He shifted a bit to get more comfortable. "Get some sleep, my love. Tonight we go hunting." She fairly purred with contentment as she cuddled deeper into his embrace.

The mansion had been searched thoroughly three times, but nothing out of the ordinary was found. "Something big must be in the wind," groused one security guard as he slouched into a chair in the security office, "they're even more paranoid than usual." The other three men just snorted an agreement. "Ah well, it broke up another boring day. Where is everybody?"

"The president is in his quarters, reading. His first born and heir is already stoned on intoxicants, and you-know-who has another woman tied up in the basement dungeon. I wish we had put in audio too; I'd love to hear her scream."

"If anybody ever finds out we put that vid feed in there, it'll be us doing the screaming," said the first one. "Hey, who's that at the servant's gate?"

"Huh? Oh, that's that old cleaner and his assistant. I don't recognize the big guy though." He picked up a comm and called the gate. "Security here, who are those people entering the grounds?"

"Cleaners, Sir," replied the man at the gate. "They're on a split shift and brought their idiot brother to carry the heavy stuff. The guy is a real blank page; he doesn't breathe unless the old guy tells him. Should I detain them?"

"No, let them pass; I've had enough foolishness for one day." He turned to his companions before he spoke again. "Night shift cleaning crew." They nodded then relaxed back into comfortable boredom. It was no big deal anyway; they could see every move the cleaners made on the monitors.

They watched halfheartedly as the cleaners made their way to the storage room and gathered their tools. The big one was pushing a cart as they progressed along the corridor. "Hey, they're right here. Let's get them to clean up this mess." The speaker opened the door and barked an order. "You there, get in here and start cleaning up this mess."

Rath winked at Keira then pushed his cart into the security office. Once inside they attacked. The four guards were down and out before they knew what hit them. "Morons," snorted Rath, as he gathered the weapons from the dead security guards. "Now, let's have a look." He stepped over to the monitors, Keira right beside him. They easily located their prey.

"This is most fortunate," smiled the elder Rathbone. "This is a very modern set up. Look at all the toys, Rath."

"I see them, and I see our quarry. All right now, button, button, which one is it, ah, here it is. Knock out gas, just the thing. Okay, who's first on the list? How about that nasty piece of work torturing that poor woman?"

He hit the button and the door to the basement room locked, the vents closed, and the gas poured in. Keira watched with a wolfish grin as the man suddenly realized what was happening and frantically tried to escape. He called for security, but there was no help forthcoming from the security office.

Old Rath stayed at the security console while Rath pushed his cart along behind Keira. She led him down to the dungeon room then Old Rath unlocked the door from his position. The gas had already been cleared from the room. Keira smiled as she dumped the unconscious man into the cleaner's cart. Rath untied the woman and left the door unlocked behind them. With luck she'd escape once she awakened.

Once back in the security office Keira put her mortal enemy in a chair and bound him. She wedged a gag tightly into his mouth and secured it there. While she was waiting for him to awaken, Rath stripped off the largest of the security guards and donned his uniform. It was a tight fit, but it would do. Keira also took a security uniform.

Together they made their way to the eldest son's room. There were guards outside. "We've got to check on him," said Rath, as they approached the two men. "We've been watching the monitors and he's not moving. We just need to see if he's breathing."

"Probably stoned out of his mind again," sighed one of the men, as he opened the door for them. Rath and Keira struck, then dragged the two bodies into the room and shut the door.

"Hey, who're you?" asked a slurred voice. "What the hells did you do? Guards!"

His cry went unheeded then Keira was on him, her hand over his mouth preventing any further outcry. He struggled and flailed at her, but it was useless and he eventually stopped struggling. His mind began to clear as he stared at the woman's face.

"Do you know who this woman is?" Rath asked him. "Do you remember Keira the Singer who became Keira the Avenger?"

First recognition and then terror registered in his eyes. He tried to escape, but she snapped his neck and dropped the body to the floor. She spat on it, kicked it, and then turned away.

Outside the door they headed for the stairs and went up to the president's apartments. The blast doors were down and there were two guards standing by. The two assassins attacked at lightning speed, then dragged the bodies out of sight. They reappeared and took up the guard stations at the door.

Inside, a voice over the comm instantly caught the president's attention. "Mr. President, please come to the security office at once. Repeat, Mr. President, please come to the security office at once." He was out of his chair in a heartbeat. He swept up a weapon as he burst through the door.

"You two, come with me," he barked, as he hurried toward the stairs. Grinning, Rath and Keira followed close behind, weapons drawn. With the two guards in tow, Garad hurried down the stairs and along the corridor towards the security office. "What is it?" he demanded as he burst through the door.

It took a moment for his brain to register what his eyes were seeing. When it did, he felt the weapon pressed to his back. "Drop it," growled a deep voice. The weapon slipped from the president's hand and clattered onto the floor. "Hands behind your back." He complied and felt the bonds tighten around his wrists. "Who are you people? What do you want?" he demanded, as he was thrust into a chair. He gagged and twitched as he was hit with a low setting stunner, but didn't lose consciousness.

He was bound to the chair and turned to face the chair holding his youngest son. The man was just beginning to regain consciousness. As he did, Rathbone spoke. "To answer your questions, I'm Rathbone of Urn." Both men's eyes widened at that statement.

"I'm here under contract," Rath went on. "I've been hired by a woman named Keira to capture you so she could kill you herself. Do you recognize this woman?" Keira stepped closer so Garad could see her.

"You," he gulped, as he recognized the woman they had tortured so long ago. She nodded then turned a monitor so he could see the dead body of his eldest son.

"You tortured and maimed this woman and probably many more. Your son has paid for his crime with his life."

"I'll kill you all," he snarled, as he struggled against the bindings.

Keira met his gaze then shot the other son. He slumped lifeless in the chair. No emotion showed on her face as she slowly brought the gun around to him. Tears of terror ran down his face. "Please don't..."

"That's what she begged of you," said Rath. "Now you get the same response." Keira drove a blade deep into the man's heart, looking into his eyes the whole time. As his life slipped away, she turned and melted into Rath's arms, tears streaming down her face and her body trembling.

"It's over now, my beloved," he whispered softly. "It's done. Come, we have to get out of here now, and then sound the alarms." She nodded and wiped her face. She kissed his cheek then turned to remove the security guard uniform and don the cleaner's overalls again.

Once they were disguised as cleaners they made their way quietly to the back gate. "Done so soon?" asked the guard, as they approached his station.

"Piece of cake," replied Old Rathbone. "The place is as quiet as a tomb tonight. We finished up in good time. Now to get home for a cold one and some sleep."

"I envy you that," grinned the guard. "See you tomorrow."

"Tomorrow," he replied, and waved as the gate swung open and they walked away.

Once they were out of the guard's sight they moved swiftly. They couldn't go back to the hideout, so they hailed a taxi and went to the spaceport. They'd go to ground near there. Kella had given them directions, and she'd be there waiting for them.

As the taxi pulled up, old Rathbone stuck a weapon against the driver's ear. "Sorry, friend, but you'll have to come with us for a few days."

"That's okay, Poppa, I like your company," chuckled the driver as he peeled off his beard.

"Kella? Oh you rotten brat, I could have shot you." The old fellow was grinning and shaking his head. "Great disguise, but how did you know where we'd be and when?"

"I didn't. We've been taking turns cruising that area for the past four days. I got lucky. Come on, we'll hide this transport and catch up. There's hot food and warm beds in that old hangar." She pressed a button and a section of wall slid aside. She drove the transport through, then closed it again. It looked like any other old run-down hangar inside.

They stepped out and came around to Kella. "Watch yourself, keep your elbows in," she smiled. Suddenly the floor started to move downward. A few moments later they were in a large dormitory-like room with a kitchen at one end. They could smell the food cooking.

They stepped off the platform and it began to rise back into place. "So, you've managed to retrieve them," sang one of the three women who were busy in the kitchen. "Please tell me you people were successful."

"We were," said Rathbone. "Kella, what's going on here?"

"This woman is Nina," replied Kella. "Nina and the others are all former victims of the president and his sons. They help us from time to time as we do them when we can."

"There are quite a number of us really," said Nina as she steered them toward chairs at the table. "There's a large underground resistance movement ready to rise up, but we need your help. Did you truly kill that monster and his sons?"

"Keira did," replied Rath. "It was her due."

Keira looked at each woman in turn. She could see the scars on their faces and the pain in their eyes at what was done to them just as it had been done to her. "Are you truly Keira the Avenger?" asked Nina. "Did you really kill them?"

Keira nodded slowly then held up three fingers. "All three," said Rath. "You know about Keira?"

"Oh yes, Keira, your story has inspired us to survive. They hurt you the worst and you survived. Not only that, but you learned how to fight back, and you did. We're honored to have you here with us, and we can't thank you enough for what you've done." All the women had tears flowing freely now and Keira rose up to hold them. They all gathered in one big hug of release.

Rathbone smiled lovingly at Keira, then noticed his grandfather grinning at him. "What?"

"I'm proud of you boy. You handled this night's work like a real pro."

"I was taught by the best. Why, are you surprised?"

"Yes, I am, Rath. I expected you to kick in doors, blast away with weapons, blow half the place to the nine hells and back, leaving me to do the real work."

"You mean create disarray?"

"Exactly."

"Oh, I expect there will be lots of disarray once they find the bodies. I'll go back into the city and blow up a few things, shoot a few people, and make a nuisance of myself. You know, keep the folks entertained until the viceroy can get here."

"What have you got in mind?" asked Nina, as she and the others shyly released Keira. "Is there anything we can do to help?"

"Absolutely." He grinned as he reached for the fresh bread that had been brought to the table. "You said there's a resistance movement ready to rise up."

"Yes."

"Can they help me blow up a couple of things? Oh, and a decent hacker would be helpful too."

"I'm sure they can, and I can hack almost any system you want. Will you truly lead us, Rathbone?"

"Actually, I have something else in mind. If it works out, then there'll be no need for an uprising. The changes you want will come without bloodshed on a large scale."

"Tell us more," she said, as she and the others gathered round to hear his plan.

"Well, first, I want to scare the bejabbers out of the top military brass. Second, I want to capture those munitions that are coming in. Third, I want to have them in complete disarray when the viceroy gets here. If we get it right, he can walk in and take over without a fuss. The military will be thrilled to have someone in command once again. I love the military mind."

"Rath, how are we supposed to capture six freighters loaded with weapons and munitions?" asked Kella. "Even if we can manage it somehow, where do we hide them?"

Suddenly Keira started to laugh. She pointed at Rath's head and then at Nina. She then made a few swift signals. "Yes, my love," he grinned, "that is exactly what I have in mind."

"Care to share?" suggested Kella.

"Sure. Here's the plan. First we blow up a few things close to the military headquarters, and then Nina hacks into their comms. I go on the comms, announce myself as the dreaded Rathbone of Urn, take credit for killing the tyrants, and then threaten to kill anyone who tries to take command of the military."

"Fine," said Nina, "that'll cause confusion and fear, but what about the freighters?"

"Once we have things stirred up around here, you hack into the military system again. Message the freighters and warn them off saying we have an uprising here; there's no safe place to land and off load. Tell them to meet the fleet in space. Give them directions so they will run smack into the viceroy's armada. We'll message him to let him know they're coming. Then we'll start ordering the Arlen fleet to different quadrants; spread them out as thin as possible."

"I like it, Rath," grinned his grandfather. "It's a good plan. What's the backup plan?"

"The backup is I keep blowing things up until Lortax gets here to dig us out. I'm wide open to suggestions if anyone has a better idea."

"I can't imagine anything better than this," grinned Nina. "Come with me, folks." She stood and led them across the room towards a large display case. As she touched the case, it turned away silently and a door appeared. As soon as she stepped through the lights came on. Rath gave a soft whistle as he took in the array of electronic equipment.

"I built most of it myself," Nina said proudly, as she showed off her creation. She sat to the desk and pulled a board with dozens of strange symbols on it toward her. "So, here we go." Her fingers flew and images flashed on the vid screen and were gone so quickly they could not tell what they had seen.

"All right, here we are, the security system at the mansion. Just a moment and...yes, we're in." Several screens on the desk came to life and they had clear images of the president's mansion. The place was in chaos. In the living room, one man in an impressive uniform was trying to get things under control. Nina's fingers danced for a moment then she handed Rath a comm. "You're in," she said softly. "Make it quick so they can't trace it."

Grinning, he nodded then spoke into the comm. "Attention, attention. This is Rathbone of Urn. I suspect that by now you've discovered the results of my visit last night."

"Where are you? What do you want?" bellowed the uniform.

"I'm everywhere and I want you to listen. Last night I eliminated the three tyrants. Over the next few months I'll continue to eliminate anyone who tries to assume command of the military." Rath made a jerking motion and Nina cut the connection. They could tell by the uniform's display of frustration that they had been unsuccessful at tracing the hack.

"Any idea who that uniform was?" asked the elder Rathbone.

"That was Field Marshall Brill," sighed Nina. "He became field Marshall when the old Field Marshall declared himself president. He's as bad as the other three. If he takes over things could actually get worse."

"Can you get me close to him?" asked Rath.

"Probably not in the next few days. He's likely to have half the military guarding him."

"Good, then we've done our job," sighed Rath. "Can we message Viceroy Lortax from here?"

"Not a problem," replied Nina.

"Keira, can you work this thing? Send the message in code to Micha. He'll be with Lortax or I'll miss my guess."

Keira grinned and flashed a few signals and sang a note. Rath grinned and nodded. "She says she believes Micha will be there, too."

Keira looked at Nina who smiled and slid over to give Keira access to the controls. Keira looked confused for a moment. "Old fashioned keyboard?" asked Nina. At Keira's nod she pulled open a drawer and lifted one out. A moment later it was installed and Keira's fingers were flying over the board. Keira finished her message and Nina replaced the old keyboard in the drawer. "Now what?" she asked.

"Now we rest and feast," declared the elder Rathbone. "We've accomplished our mission, the target's been eliminated, we've thrown the enemy into disarray. I'd say that was a full night's work. I'm old now; I'll need to sleep for days just to recover from all the exertion."

There was a round of chuckles at that. "Come on, folks," grinned Kella. "I'll show you to the sleeping quarters."

As they followed Kella, Rathbone the Elder turned to Nina. "I always sleep better in the company of a beautiful woman. Care to join me?"

Her mouth dropped open and she blushed, and then turned away. "Are you truly that desperate?" she said harshly.

"What do you mean by that?" he asked gently, as he took her arm and turned her to face him again.

"I know what I look like with these scars. You might be older, but you can't be that desperate yet."

Old Rath gently pulled her closer. "It's the scars that attract me, woman. They speak of what you've endured. They speak of your strength, and your will to survive. They're badges of honor, every one of them. Girl, you're still here, still beautiful, and I mean what I say."

Nina gazed into his eyes for a long moment, then stepped closer. "All right, Sir, if you're certain this is what you want."

"I'm positive, pretty lady."

"Rathbone of Urn, Terror of the Galaxy, if you're half as good at sex as you are at killing people, I'm in for the night of my life."

"Damn," he said, as he let his shoulders slump. "This is where a reputation is more of a curse than a help."

"Oh no, there's no getting out of it now." She grinned as she slipped her arm around his waist. "Come with me."

"Why, that lucky old bugger," said Rath. Keira slapped him hard on the arm. He turned to her; she was glaring at him in mock severity. "Oh, but he's not as lucky as I am." She laughed then shrieked as he tossed her across one broad shoulder and carried her into the room they'd been assigned.

———— ◉ ————

A UNIFORMED MAN HURRIED into the meeting room of the viceroy's ship. Lortax was there, as was Lessa, her crew, and the High Priestess of Borealis Prime, Lady Marla. "Viceroy."

"Yes?"

"Sir, we've just picked up a signal on an obscure channel. It seems to be in code and is addressed to someone called, 'The Boss' aboard this ship."

"This ship?"

"Yes, Viceroy, it was sent to your flag ship."

"Looks like it's for you, Micha," grinned Lortax.

"Probably Keira," said Micha. "Can I see the message?"

"Of course, Sir," replied the man as he handed it over. "Is it in code?"

"It is," replied Micha. "Just give me a minute." He paused for a moment then smiled. "It's from Keira. Garad and his sons are dead. The Arlens are in disarray. Rath is trying to make that worse. There are six transport ships filled with Company weapons and munitions headed for Arla Four. Kella will attempt to send them on to meet us. It'll be an unpleasant surprise for them to meet us instead of the Arlen fleet.

"That's the gist of it, Chieftain. Rath was successful and he's sending us presents."

"He's such a good lad," laughed Lortax. "Well then, we should prepare to receive the gifts the emperor is sending to us.

FAR, FAR AWAY THE EMPEROR was troubled. He wouldn't admit it to anyone, but he was having small memory lapses. Worse yet, he was having strange dreams, strange but compelling dreams. In the dreams, his friend Jorm had a weapon of some sort. The weapon rendered the emperor helpless while the evil Jorm reprogrammed him. Could they be more than dreams? They were so vivid.

Jorm had been his good right hand and best friend for years. Of all the people he knew, Jorm was the only one he could trust, or could he? Of course he could. Jorm had stated many times he didn't want to be emperor. He had been well rewarded for his loyal service. He could trust Jorm. He could. But the dreams... those terrible, haunting, dreams.

Somehow he had to learn the truth. He called the chief of security and asked him to come quietly to the new temporary offices. When the man arrived, the emperor had a plan. "Hoaka, my trusted chief of security, I have a task for you."

"Command me, Sire," said the burly man, as he dropped to one knee.

Loran smiled. He liked this new level of respect he got as Emperor. It was far more satisfying than being the CEO of a company. "There are two things I need, Hoaka. First, I need secret surveillance on this office. Only you and I are to know about it and only I will be able to access the recordings. Second, I'll need a man here who will obey my commands without hesitation. I mean instant compliance within the space of a heartbeat. Do you have such a man on your staff?"

"I am that man, Sire. I'll gather the equipment needed then return and install the surveillance. What else would you have me do?"

"Shoot the door." There was only a split second hesitation while the man's brain registered the command then he whipped out his weapon, turned and fired. The door was blown outwards. "Very good, you'll do nicely. Now go fetch your equipment."

As the man hurried away the emperor sighed and returned to his small apartment off the office. "You must forgive me, Jorm. But I just have to know for certain that these are dreams and not memories."

Confusion on a Galactic Scale

K eira was in a fog; she had been all day. Rath was getting
concerned. "Keira, my beloved, are you well?" She just nodded
without making eye contact. Rath reached to tip up her chin with his
forefinger. "Talk to me, my warrior woman."

Keira favored him with a wan smile then began to sing and
signal. "I feel empty inside, my fierce man. For many years I've had
one main thought, one burning desire, one purpose in life; to find
and kill the men who maimed me.

"It's done. What do I do now? I feel like I've lost my bearings.
What do we do now?"

"Oh, but you do have a purpose, dear heart. Look at Nina and
the others who've suffered as you have. You've cut off the head of
the snake, but there are more in the nest. Now we have to destroy
that nest. Help me to tear apart everything those men built. Help me
destroy their legacy."

"You mean tear down everything they built; erase them from the
memory of the people completely?"

"Yes, let's destroy it so Lortax can build something completely
new. Put an end to the curse of the Arlen Alliance in this sector."

"Dear gods, do you truly believe that can be done?" asked Nina.

"Are you offering us a contract?" asked Rathbone the Elder.
"We've never failed to deliver on a contract." He was grinning at
Nina.

"How in the nine hells am I supposed to pay you if you succeed?"
she asked, a twinkle in her eye.

"Well, for me, you can pay me with sex," grinned the old fellow.

"What???"

"If we succeed, you bond with me and be my companion for as long as I survive. I'll expect plenty of sex."

"Are you crazy?"

"After last night? Absolutely besotted, but that's irrelevant. Do you agree to my price?"

"Just look at me, you old fool."

"I am looking at you, and I like what I see. Stop avoiding the question. Will you pay the price or not?"

She gazed into his smiling eyes for a long moment, then nodded. "I'll pay your price, Rathbone. How am I supposed to pay your two partners in crime?"

"Oh my dear woman, they owe me. I had no stake in any of this, yet I helped my grandson fulfil his contract with Keira. They owe me one, so they're honor-bound to help me with my contract. Right, Rath?"

"Absolutely right, Poppa," grinned Rathbone. "Keira?"

Keira sang a high sweet note and signalled with her hands. She raised her fist high. "Agreed," said Rath, as he raised his fist. "For the maimed, and a new day."

"For the maimed, and a new day," said the elder Rathbone as he raised his fist with them. He pulled Nina close and grinned. "Prepare yourself woman, you will soon be mine."

"You've truly never failed to deliver on a contract?" she asked, a mischievous smile on her lips.

"Never."

"Then I might as well pay up in advance," she grinned, as she offered her hand, fingers spread.

"Done," he chuckled as he laced his fingers through hers. "Rath, Keira, you're witness to the bond."

"We are witness to the bond," smiled Rath. He was beaming at Keira who had the fire back in her eyes. She had another purpose in life now, to help build something from the ashes of what she had wanted to destroy for so long.

"What's going on?" asked a yawning Kella, as she joined them in the common room. One of the other women passed her a steaming cup of something brown and she groaned with pleasure as she took a sip.

"Poppa and Nina have just sworn the bond," grinned Rath.

"What???"

"It was the price I had to pay," blushed Nina.

"Wow, that must have been some night," grinned Kella, "but I didn't realize you'd have to pay him."

"I didn't pay him for last night, you fool," laughed Nina, as she slapped Kella playfully on the arm. "I paid him for the contract."

"What contract?"

"It wasn't enough to just remove the dictator," grinned Rath. "Nina wants the entire government they built torn down and replace with something more civilized and people friendly. She offered the contract to Rathbone of Urn and he accepted. The price was the bond."

"Okay, so now we're going to bring down the whole damn government and replace it?"

"Well, he's going to try. Keira and I owe him a favor so we're going to help."

"I'll need your help too, Kella," said old Rathbone as he leaned across the table. "I understand that you're a business woman and I do understand the need for profit. What's the price of your assistance in this little adventure?"

Kella sipped from her cup and remained silent for a moment. They gave her time to think. Final she set the empty mug on the table. "All right, I'll agree to help you in this madness under two conditions. Father would skin me for taking such a big risk, so the reward must be equal to that risk.

"Understood." Said Old Rathbone.

"First, if we succeed, I expect my free trader's license to be honored throughout Arlen territory. I also expect a one year exclusive before any other licenses are issued.

"Second, should we succeed, you, Rathbone of Urn the Elder, must appoint yourself as governor for a five year term. That way I'll be assured of my price being paid in full."

"Me? Governor? Why for pity sake?"

Kella grinned broadly. She'd finally cracked that iron confidence of his. She'd finally caught him off guard. "The only way I can see this working is if there is a recognizable name to take the post. It also has to be a name with a reputation as strong and fierce as Garad's. You have that name, and you have a knack for organization, an attention to detail, that will be needed.

"Take a moment to think it over." She grinned as she rose, scooped up her mug and went to the kitchen for a refill. She was watching them out of the corner of her eye and grinning. Kella took her time refilling her mug then she returned and sat down. "Well?"

"You're completely mad, woman," sighed the elder Rathbone.

"It takes one to know one," she grinned. "Am I in or am I not?"

"Take the offer," said Nina. "I know you'd be perfect for the job."

"Nina, you're as crazy as she is," he sighed. "You've known me for less than twenty four hours and you've already bonded to me. Now you think I should be governor of the Arlen Alliance?"

"Yes, I've bonded to you. That means I'm now dependant on you to care for me, to provide for me. I need to know my companion has a good job. Take the offer."

"Oh gods," he grinned. "Am I going to be henpecked for the rest of my life?"

"Count on it," she laughed, "but only in the most loving way and only when it's for your own good."

"Rath, son, help me here."

"Looks like you're out gunned, Poppa. I'd surrender while you have the chance." Everyone was laughing now and the old fellow just shook his head sadly.

"Done, Kella," he smiled, as he offered his hand on the agreement.

She shook it then drained her cup. "All right, people, this is all fun and games, but it won't be easy. We need a plan."

"No problem," signalled Keira. "It seems pretty straight forward to me." Rath translated for her.

"Explain," said his grandfather.

"We do it Micha style," she replied with Rathbone translating. "Rath gets set up with the long range rifle, then you contact the Field Marshall. You announce yourself as the new Governor and start issuing orders. When he refuses to obey, Rath pegs him off. You then ask for the next man in the chain of command and repeat the orders."

"Oh, yes," laughed Kella, "that's classic Micha. What do you think, Governor?"

"I like it," he grinned. "Micha, eh? I liked that lad from the start. All right then, let's work with that. First we need to find the Field Marshall and then we need a snipers nest."

"Well, recon is our department," said Nina. "Come on, Leeza," she called to the woman in the kitchen, "we've got work to do. You folks relax until we get some information to work with."

"Yes, Ma'am," grinned the elder Rathbone. "Anyone for eggs? I'm cooking."

"Scrambled for me, Governor," laughed Kella. "I just have to go send greetings to the munitions convoy then I'll be right back."

THE YOUNG ENSIGN HURRIED across the bridge to the Captain. "What is it, Ensign?"

"A message from Arla Four, Sir. There's been a rebellion. The rebels control the spaceport and are hoping to capture this convoy for themselves."

"Let me see that." The captain read the message then sighed. "Dammit all, that's another six days on this trip. Ah well. Ensign, adjust heading to rendezvous with the Arlen Fleet at these coordinates. Signal the convoy of the course correction."

"Aye, Captain. Setting new course heading," replied the ensign, as he hurried back to his station. The captain continued to grumble as he sank deeper into his plush chair. Another six days, he wasn't happy.

———◦———

IT WAS HOURS LATER that Nina and Leeza surfaced from the computers. "This could be easier than any of us hoped," smiled Nina. Everyone gathered at the table once again.

"Tell me," said the Governor.

"The Field Marshall has taken over the President's mansion for himself."

"That didn't take long," grunted Rathbone.

"Better yet, since your attack came from the inside, he has made no adjustment to the security from the outside. Rathbone's sniper's nest is just as cozy as he left it."

"What? They didn't find it?" asked Rath.

"They didn't look," said Nina. "The Field Marshall has no desire to find the assassins, he's just happy they did their job."

"A practical man," grinned the Governor. "So we have a window and a nest. Can we get him into the right room?"

"He's taken that room as his meeting room," smiled Nina. "Tomorrow he'll be meeting with his top aides."

"Tell me about them," said the Elder Rathbone.

"There'll be admirals, Senka and Dixet, as well as General Tarnet, my darling companion. They'll have their own aides with them."

"Of course they will. That's not the problem."

"What is, my mate?" asked Nina.

"It almost seems too easy," sighed the Governor. "That always makes me nervous. Rath, What do you think?"

"I think we've been dealt a lucky hand, but it depends on one of them caving in to accept you as governor."

Keira sang and signalled. "She says she has seen Micha make this work many times. Micha's law, the shortest distance between two points is always a straight line. Keira says we should move on it."

"All right, it's a go," said the elder Rathbone. "Kella, can you arrange a shuttle with darkened windows and an empty hangar or warehouse?"

"I can. Are you planning to meet with military brass?"

"I am. We need them on side for this to work. First we get their attention then we convince them to follow our directions. We can get their attention with surprise and force, but we'll need persuasion for the rest."

"When do you need it?"

"If they're meeting tomorrow, I'll need it ready by then."

"Not a problem, Governor," she smiled. "I'll get right on it."

"Rath, you and Keira make your way back to the nest under cover of darkness. You need to be ready when that meeting starts."

"We'll be there. I'd rather take a taxi than a shuttle for this trip. Can I borrow yours, Kella?"

"Help yourself, Rath," she smiled as she worked her communicator in code. "The starter key is in it. Just leave it anywhere and I'll have somebody pick it up."

They left it several blocks away from the nest, but were ready as the day dawned. Rath set himself up at the window again while Keira stood guard. It was midday before the action began. Nina patched the comms in for them so they could follow what was going on.

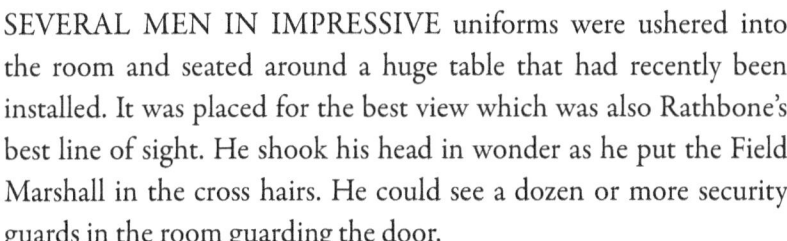

SEVERAL MEN IN IMPRESSIVE uniforms were ushered into the room and seated around a huge table that had recently been installed. It was placed for the best view which was also Rathbone's best line of sight. He shook his head in wonder as he put the Field Marshall in the cross hairs. He could see a dozen or more security guards in the room guarding the door.

They listened as the Field Marshall called the meeting to order and began laying out objectives for acquiring new territories. "Come on, Poppa, quit stalling. Let's do this before this guy makes me sick and I shoot him anyway," grumbled Rathbone.

Right on cue they heard the Governor's voice cut into the speaker system of the mansion. "Attention military leaders of the Arlen Alliance. This is Rathbone of Urn. I now declare myself Governor of the Arlen Alliance and all the territories. I now assume command of all military personnel and government employees."

Every man at the table leaped to his feet. "Where is that coming from?" bellowed the Field Marshall. "Get that shut off, now."

"Sit down and shut up, Field Marshall," barked Old Rathbone. "I give the orders here."

"The hells you do, Assassin. I'm in command. I give the orders."

"As governor I've given you a direct order. Will you comply?"

"I sure as hell will not," the Field Marshall bellowed at the ceiling.

Old Rath gave the signal. "So be it." Young Rathbone squeezed the trigger, the window of the meeting room exploded inward and the Field Marshall's body fell to the floor, a neat round hole in his temple. In a heartbeat the rest of the men were hiding behind the table they'd overturned.

The governor's voice came over the speakers once again. He was calm, almost as though nothing had happened. "Now then, who is the next ranking officer of the military? Speak up, your governor is waiting."

"What do you want?" asked a voice.

"Your acknowledgement, loyalty, and obedience are the first things I want. Your name and rank, Sir, if you please."

"This is Admiral Senka. I'm the ranking officer now that you've dispatched the Field Marshall."

"What's it going to be, Admiral? Do we work together or do I look further down the chain of command?"

"I think we can work together, Governor," replied the admiral. "I have no aspirations of dictatorship. I want to serve Arla. I believe a strong hand is needed at this time and you seem to have that. May we set the table back in place without getting shot?"

"Do it." There was a shuffling, then two men got the ends of the table and righted it. They seated themselves around it once again, but every man was nervous.

"Now then, Governor, you have the floor," said the admiral.

"Thank you, Admiral. Pay attention, people, here's the first order of business. I want you to recall all Arlen troops out of combat and pull them back to secure bases."

"Are you insane?" bellowed a General as he leaped to his feet. "Do you have any idea of how much territory we would lose if we do that? I won't stand for it." He was on the floor with a bullet in his skull before the sound of the shot reached them.

Everyone at the table sat still as stone. "Admiral, as ranking officer, you may now promote another man to the general's post." The admiral nodded and signalled a man who was standing by. The man gulped and took the general's seat.

"Now then," said the governor. "Let me continue. I'm well aware we'll lose territory, but we'll lose it anyway. Viceroy Lortax is on his way here with his entire armada. We cannot defeat him, and you know it."

"The Company will support us," said one man.

"The Company is no more. CEO O'Loran has declared himself Emperor Loran the First, and claims the entire galaxy. Viceroy Lortax has made a mutual defense pact with A.S. Inc. Together they can defeat the emperor and he knows this. This will keep him at bay. If we squabble with Lortax we'll lose and be absorbed into the empire. If we side with Lortax we'll lose some territory, but we'll remain free and a lot of Arlen soldiers will remain alive. We'll be a free state within the Borelian Free Alliance.

"Opinions, gentlemen." No one said a word. "Come, come, gentlemen. I won't shoot you for a dissenting opinion."

"That's good to know," chuckled the admiral. "Sir, I'm sure there'll be no further resistance from this room. However, I personally would prefer to meet face to face to discuss this matter in greater depth."

"Admiral, I will go public as soon as the viceroy's armada arrives. In the meantime, bring your two ranking officers and three security men. Step outside to the street where a shuttle will stop for you. Get on board and the shuttle will bring you to me."

The speaker system went silent. In an otherwise empty hangar Nina and her helpers swiftly packed up and fled the scene. The trace would be in, but there'd be nothing to find. Outside the mansion a shuttle with darkened windows pulled up and the uniformed men boarded. There was a heavily armed woman driving, a huge armed man at the very back, and an old man in a seat in the middle. They sat and the shuttle pulled away.

"Identify yourselves, now," barked one of the security guards as he rose to his feet and reached for a weapon. He was horrified at how fast Rath reached him and put a blaster to his temple.

"Sit down and shut up," snarled Rath.

"Yes, Sir, Governor, Sir," gulped the man as he swiftly resumed his seat.

"I'm not the governor," growled Rath. "I'm his current chief of security. All of you make nice and nobody gets killed. Understand? Good. This man is Rathbone of Urn, your new governor. You have the floor, Governor." He grinned and stepped back. Keira winked at him in the mirror as she drove.

"Now then, gentlemen," smiled the governor, as he turned in his seat to face them, "it's good to meet with you face to face. Let me be clear, my objectives are as follows. First, I want to keep as many Arlen soldiers alive as possible. Second, I want the Alliance to remain free and prosper. Third, I think Arla has had more than enough of tyranny, I mean to end that. There'll be no dictators, no military dictators, and no martial law. I believe it's time for the people of Arla to breathe without fear.

"You have an idea of how I see making this happen. I'm open to suggestions and opinions."

There were plenty, but old Rathbone had answers and convincing arguments for most of them. He also gave way on a few things, accepted the advice of the Admiral on a few others and in the end, although Rath and Keira were bored silly, the governor had the full support of the military leaders.

Within three days the Arlen Alliance had ceased all hostilities and withdrawn to safe territories. Many of the more brutal laws had been repealed, the general news media had been briefed and demolition of the former president's mansion had begun. Two days after that, the viceroy's armada arrived.

At first Lortax was elated to find the elder Rathbone as the governor and was more than happy to confirm him in that role. His joy faded swiftly as the negotiations began over territory, jurisdictions, military obligations etc. Old Rath was taking his job seriously and he was a skilled negotiator. Lortax was content to allow

Marla to take over and deal with him. In the end everybody was happy with the arrangements.

The governor chose to take himself and his mate onto a military ship and govern from space. He said it would be easier to inspect the territories that way. Lortax approved. There was also no word of impending action from the empire. They had gained some breathing room. The armada withdrew, leaving behind a number of ships and taking an equal number of Arlen ships with them.

Rathbone and Keira were shuttled up to Micha's ship. They were met by a welcoming committee of one. Jip. Rathbone barely stepped through the airlock when he was pounced on by the big dog, his tail wagging furiously and slobbery kisses being shared generously between Rath and Keira.

"Rathbone, Keira, report to the bridge."

"On our way, Boss."

As they entered the bridge there was a round of cheers. Edie hugged Keira while the men congratulated Rathbone. "We didn't have time to throw you folks a proper party before," grinned Micha. "Congratulations on your bond."

There were hugs and handshakes all round. "Deke," called Micha, "set course for Nova Prime and put her on auto. Everybody to the mess hall; we need to feast these folks properly. Besides, I want to hear how old Rath became governor of the Arlen Alliance." There was a round of laughter then they left the bridge. Deke set the course then followed.

⸺◉⸺

EMPEROR LORAN SAT BEFORE the monitor. It had been days since he'd had the special surveillance installed, but he hadn't been able to bring himself to check the recordings. Another of the dreams had driven him from his bed. It was time to learn the truth. He hit the switch and began the study. Several hours later he found it.

On the screen he watched himself rant and plan. It was a replay of the day before. Only he and Jorm were in the room. "I tell you, Jorm, now is the time. The Arlens can hold the viceroy back while we crush A.S. Inc. Once that's done, we hurl our entire imperial fleet at Sector Nine. We kill the witch and bring back my companion and daughter."

"Sire, please reconsider. This is a delicate time. Our forces are under equipped for an all-out assault on A.S. Inc. Sire, we need time to re-enforce the Arlens and then we need to up production of weapons and munitions. The supplies you sent to Arla Four have drained our resources somewhat. Be patient, Sire. Our time will come."

"You dare to gainsay me, Jorm? I should..."

He had frozen in mid-sentence. Horrified he watch as Jorm, playing with the remote control in his hand, walked around and around his still form. "Emperor, Emperor, Emperor, how many times do I have to tell you we cannot go to war right now. Listen closely. This is not the time for rash actions. This is not the time for war. Your daughter and companion have betrayed you. They are not worth your attention. We need to be patient and plan.

"Now, when I reactivate you, you will tell me that we have to be patient. This is not the time for rash actions." Jorm returned to his chair then pressed the button on his remote control. The emperor had come instantly back to life.

"Jorm, my old friend, this is not the time for rash actions. We dare not go to war at this time. We must be patient and plan."

With a howl of rage at his friend's betrayal, Loran hurled the monitor against the wall, shattering it completely. He began to pace about the room, muttering to himself. "Jorm, you traitorous little Selarian slime worm, you will pay for this. Oh yes indeed, you will pay.

"Doctor, what have you done to me? Were you not already dead I would take great pleasure in killing you myself. Steady, Loran, Steady, the first order of business is to get that remote away from him. Once we have that, then we will get some answers." He continued to pace and plan until the sun rose over the city skyline.

"Hoaka, I want you with me today."

"On my way, Sire." Hoaka hurried to the emperor's office. He sensed that something was about to happen. Today he might be expected to shoot without hesitation. He was ready.

As he hurried into the office the emperor stood and smiled grimly. "Set your weapon on stun." Hoaka instantly reset his blaster. The emperor reached for the interoffice comms. "Lord Dax, come to my office at once."

"Hoaka, as soon as he steps through the door, stun him."

"Sire."

Jorm didn't like the tone of the emperor's voice. He was reaching for the remote in his pocket as he stepped through the door of the office. Jorm didn't get a chance to use it. He was instantly hit by a blast from a stunner and lay twitching on the floor. He was vaguely aware as the emperor strode to him and retrieved the remote from his pocket.

As the effects of the stunner wore off Jorm Dax became fully aware that he was strapped to a table in the lower level labs. The emperor was observing him carefully, toying with the remote in his robotic hands. Jorm swallowed hard. The thing he had feared the most had happened. He could only hope to die quickly.

"Ah, Jorm, I see you are awake," smiled the Emperor. "You have some explaining to do."

"Sire, please..."

"First, you must tell me what the doctor has done to me and why."

"Sire..."

"Carefully, Jorm, I have you hooked up. I'll know if you lie, and if you do, this will happen." He flipped a switch and Jorm screamed as electricity surged through his genitals. The emperor waited patiently until the screams sank to whimpers then he hit the switch again.

This time when the screaming stopped, he spoke. "You will now tell me everything and you will tell the truth. You may begin."

"Sire," gulped, Jorm, "it was the doctor's doing."

"I'm well aware of who did it; I want to know how and why."

"Sire, I have no idea how, but he told me it was in case you malfunctioned. He built a fail-safe into your processor. Should you malfunction, it would put you in stasis until you could be repaired. He gave me one repair kit and he kept the other."

"There were two of these things?"

"Yes, Sire," sobbed Jorm.

"Where is the second? Tell me!"

"I don't know, the doctor kept it for himself. Please, Sire. I have only tried to serve you to the best of my ability."

Loran hit the switch again and Jorm screamed in agony. "I warned you I'd know if you lied." Something in Jorm's mind snapped and he was giggling as the pain subsided.

"What's so damned funny?" demanded the emperor.

"You are," snickered Jorm. "You know what that does, but you still haven't figured out what to do about it."

"I'll have that fail-safe removed."

"There's no one who can do it," replied Jorm, howling with laughter. "The doctor's work was too advanced and he's dead. There's only one person in the galaxy who can help you now."

"Who, tell me who it is," demanded the emperor.

"The black witch," giggled Jorm. "She fixed Rathbone. It's the only way he could have survived. Only her magic can fix this, and there's another one of those remotes out there somewhere." He was off in another fit of maniacal laughter.

Loran struck him a blow that crushed his skull. The body jerked a couple of times then lay still. "The black witch," snarled the emperor as he hurled the table and Jorm's body across the room.

"The doctor was a careful man," he mused to himself. "That thing must be in this room somewhere. I must find and destroy it." He tore the place apart, searched every shelf, desk, drawer, and possible hiding place. It was not to be found.

Finally he gave up and sank into despair. "The black witch," he muttered, "only she can help me. If Jorm spoke the truth, I'm doomed. I dare not attack Sector Nine now. Somehow I must find that second remote. Only then will I be safe."

———————⟡———————

RATHBONE WAS BACK IN his favorite place, the engine room of the ship. He loved being the chief engineer. He was relaxing back with his feet up on the bench and his back to the wall, a reading tablet in his hand. He was smiling.

A shadow fell across the doorway and he lowered his boots to the floor. "Welcome, Lady."

"Can't sneak up on you this time, I see," smiled Lessa.

"Fool me once, shame on you; fool me again, shame on me," he grinned. "I see you and Deke have met."

"We have and we have an agreement," she said, as she sat gracefully in the chair facing him. "He won't bomb Nova again and I won't turn him into a three tailed Arcalian toad."

"Sounds fair to me," chuckled Rath.

"You wanted to see me, Rath?"

"Yes Lady, I want to thank you for saving my life, and helping me find a place in your service. I also want to thank you for blessing my bond with Keira. Since I met you my life has gotten better and better."

"That flows both ways, my friend," smiled Lessa. "It was you who gave me the key to control."

"I'm quite proud of how well you mastered that," he grinned. "I've brought you a graduation present."

"Oh?"

"Yes." He grinned as he placed a small box on the desk and opened it. The box contained two small computer chips, a pair of long reach calipers, and a remote control. "It's a little something I picked up on Elliston."

"What's it for?"

"It's a repair kit for a robot. I awakened strapped to that table in the lab and I heard the doctor talking to O'Loran's personal assistant. If the robot is damaged or begins to act erratically, press the top button on the remote. This will put the robot into stasis. Once he is in stasis he can be repaired. Also, while in stasis the robot is susceptible to the power of suggestion. Once he is reactivated he will then act upon the suggestion as though it were his own idea.

"The doctor gave one kit to the assistant and kept one for himself. I took his after Keira killed him."

"It's very thoughtful, Rathbone; tell me the rest."

"It's a very special robot, Lady Arlessa. It claims to be the emperor of the galaxy."

Lessa thoughtfully closed the small box and placed it in her pocket as she rose from the chair. She gave Rath a friendly pat on the shoulder as she headed for the doorway. "Enjoy your romance novel, dear friend," she smiled as she walked away.

The End

And now for a peek at the next adventure faced by the Novans.

Beyond Nova

By
Prudence MacLeod
Book three of the Nova Series

Abandoned Secrets

All governments keep secrets, dread secrets. Secrets they do not want the general populace to know. Out at the very tip of the galaxy lies a secret, a secret well kept and then abandoned. Out beyond Nova lies Exile; where failures are buried deep.

<hr/>

GORDA SLOWLY STRUGGLED out of the downed ship; Zartah close behind him. "Was that exciting enough for you, Zartah?" he asked as he helped haul his friend from the smoking ruin of what was once a small fighter ship. They clambered away looking for cover, but the ship didn't explode.

Zartah put his back against a boulder and sank slowly to the ground. "That was a wild ride all right, Gorda. Any idea what hit us?"

"None, but I'm willing to bet it wasn't any random natural occurrence. We were shot down by an energy beam of some sort."

"Oh yeah, indeed we were shot down. What say we leg it out of here before whoever sent us the welcome comes looking for this ship."

"Agreed, my friend. Let's go." They headed into the forest, climbing steadily up the steep ridge. Zartah, knowing he was crashing and that he'd been shot down, had managed to steer the wounded ship into some difficult terrain. The idea was to slow down the enemy as much as possible while making an escape.

His comm unit crackled, sputtered, and then a voice came through. "Micha to Zartah, come in Zartah."

"Zartah here, Boss."

"Status?"

"We're alive and in relatively good shape, but the ship's lost."

"Extraction?"

"No, Boss, we're here, we might as well continue the mission. We were shot down though; I don't think we should leave that ship for an enemy to find and scavenge."

"Agreed. You clear?"

"Well clear, Boss."

"Zartah, report in every twelve hours, ship's time. You miss a report we'll come in. Call if you need anything."

"Understood, Boss. Zartah out." A moment later they heard the scream of an incoming shell. The remains of their poor battered ship were obliterated in the blast.

As the echo of the explosion faded, Gorda looked at Zartah and grinned. "Well, First Man, we have an entire planet to search for a single person. Where should we start?"

"Well, somebody shot us down, let's start by asking them."

"That sounds like a sensible plan to me. They'll surely come to investigate the blast; we could ask them then," chuckled Gorda.

They headed back towards the site of their less than elegant landing and found a vantage point where they could see the area and debris from their doomed ship. "Gorda, my old friend, how do we keep getting into these messes anyway?"

"It's all your fault, you keep asking for excitement."

"I guess I do at that," grinned Zartah. "Who could have guessed the day Lady Marla showed up that it would turn out like this."

———— ⬤ ————

THE ARRIVAL OF THE Viceroy's flagship bearing Lady Marla, High Priestess of the Temple of Borealis and all the Borelian Free Alliance, had generated a lot of excitement on Nova Prime. The new colony was thriving and with two powerful witches, as well as the dreaded Nova Crew, to defend them, slavers and raiders had stayed well away. However, the sudden unexpected arrival of the High Priestess herself meant something big was up.

Edie straightened up and eased the kinks from her back. They had just finished setting the last of the seedlings and she was smiling with delight. She might be a hardened warrior, but at heart Edie was still a farmer's mate. She blushed softly as she noticed Micha smiling at her, the love clear in his eyes. "Edie, you're so beautiful; I love watching you work the fields."

"You like looking at my backside, and you're not leaving me here alone. Forget it, Micha."

"What are you talking about, my lover?" Micha would try, but he already knew better. Lady Marla's arrival could only mean trouble. Trouble she would need a mercenary crew to solve. Edie knew it too. She'd stand at his side no matter what danger it put her in.

"You know very well that was Lady Marla's shuttle that landed. The Viceroy brought her himself. That means trouble, and trouble means a job for the crew. You call them in while I go clean up."

"Yes, Boss," he grinned.

"Yes I am, and don't you forget it," she replied tartly. She laughed as she marched away towards their small cottage, putting some extra sway in her stride for his benefit.

Micha watched her go for a moment, a warm smile on his young face, then pulled his communicator from his pocket and clipped it on his shoulder. "Micha to Crew, ready and man the ships just in case."

"Already on it, Boss," came Zartah's voice.

Micha grinned and headed for the cottage. He reached for the comm again then let his arm fall away. The farmer he wanted was already walking towards him. "Looks like you might be heading out," called the young fellow. "Does this mean I'll get no rest this season?"

"We've got it planted for you, Abel; what more do you want?"

"Well I guess I can watch it grow for you." He stopped as he reached Micha and became serious. "I'll keep the farm for you, Micha. Just remember to come back to it before harvest."

"I'm hoping I won't have to leave at all, but I've got a bad feeling about this. Thanks, Abel." Just then his comm squawked:

"Micha, we need you at the temple."

"On my way, Lessa."

———— ◉ ————

MICHA WAS MET AT THE temple steps by Lady Arlessa herself. "This can't be good," he thought to himself as she turned and led him into the building. They arrived at her office to find Brenna, Viceroy Lortax, and Lady Marla waiting with Lady Norlene. "So, where am I going and am I likely to come back?"

"That's what we love best about you, Micha," laughed Brenna. "Straight to the point."

"I'll lay it out for you, Micha," said Lady Marla. "Viceroy Lortax was going through some of his predecessor's files and made a terrible discovery. Do you know of, or have you ever heard of, Exile?"

"I know the meaning of the word, Lady, but I assume that's not what you mean."

"Correct. Exile is a planetary system out beyond the Galactic Rim. It is three systems beyond Nova."

"Lady there are only two systems beyond Nova."

"There is another, even farther out, Micha. Apparently, the old CEO of RIM Inc. used it to exile his political enemies. When O'Loran took over he continued the practice for a time. The former Viceroy was in charge of maintaining the prison, a task which he ignored for the most part. He simply dumped the prisoners there and forgot about them."

Micha just nodded and waited for her to continue. "When I made the sacrifice, my younger brother objected. As soon as the inhibitor was placed on my head he disappeared."

"He was sent to Exile?"

"We believe so, Micha," said Lortax.

"Do you have reason to believe he is still alive?"

"None," sighed Marla. "I only have hope."

"You want me to find him?"

"If possible," said Lortax. "Micha, he's Nara Clan; we're bound to help him. He's committed no crime against the Clans."

"How will I identify him?"

"This is our best guess of how he would look now, Micha," said Marla as she passed a vid screen to him. "He was still a boy when he was taken. His name is Kathan of Borealis Three, Nara Clan."

"Lessa?"

"I'll be ready to travel in a flash, Micha, if you decide to take the job."

"I'll pay your standard fee, Micha," declared Marla.

"I can't make any promises, Lady. I can only promise to do my best."

"Understood. Thank you, Micha. I know you were looking forward to a full season on the farm. I owe you one."

"It is always good to have the High Priestess owe you a favor," he grinned as he reached for his comm. "Zartah."

"Here, Boss. One ship or two?"

"One ship, but I want our Arcalian fighters on board."

"Understood."

Micha thought for a moment then went to his comm again. "Siemon Darks."

"Here, Boss."

You and your men will stay here with Lady Norlene to keep an eye on Nova."

"Understood."

"All right, Lady Norlene, should I leave Gorda here in command of the cyborgs?"

"I've warned you before about teasing an old witch, young Micha," she grinned, shaking a threatening finger at him. "Get out of here and get to work."

"Yes Ma'am," he smiled as he rose to his feet. Lessa and Brenna had already vanished.

Norlene reached out and gently laid a hand on Micha's arm. He turned to see the concern in her eyes. "Bring him back in one piece, Micha."

"Understood." He nodded as he gently patted the hand on his arm.

Micha made his way to the ship. It was the prototype intruder class Rathbone had acquired from the emperor. She had been renamed the Defender. "We set?"

"Set, Boss," replied Zartah.

"Take her up, Gorda. Standard orbit then we'll plan the mission before heading out. Put her on auto, then join us in the mess. This part always makes me hungry." He walked off the bridge, grinning at the laughter that followed him. He felt the ship rise beneath his feet then smooth out. A short while later the crew was gathered in the mess hall. Jip, as usual, was making the rounds, looking for snacks. Edie reached down to scratch behind a floppy ear.

"All here, Boss," grinned Zartah. "What have we got? There's not a lot of call for mercenaries these days."

Micha laid it out for them. He was a bit surprised that even Zartah's usual exuberance was dampened. "That's the mission, Crew. Options? Opinions?"

"Turn down the job, Boss," said Gorda quietly.

"Second that," agreed Zartah.

Micha was actually startled at the reluctance of his two most senior warriors. He sighed deeply and leaned back in his seat. "Can't boys. The man's Nara Clan and the Chieftain says go. Talk to me, Gorda."

"Just a few things I heard while in prison as a boy, Boss. I heard a man screaming in terror as he was dragged away. I asked one of the guards about it. He said the guy was being sent to Exile. He said it's a place out beyond the edge of the galaxy; a lone star system drifting away. He said nobody comes back from Exile. All the guards used to beg for the chance to go on that trip. It takes weeks and then they retire on Elliston with full pay for life. The thing is, even the guards who take that trip are never heard from again."

"Zartah?"

"I heard much the same thing. Point is, Boss, that system is drifting away and it's pretty far out there. Anything goes wrong, we might never get back. I'll confess that idea makes me a bit nervous."

Micha nodded but didn't say a word for a moment. Finally he spoke again. "Rathbone, tell me nothing will go wrong with the ship."

"Nothing will go wrong with the ship, Boss," chuckled the big cyborg. "I've brought spare parts for every vital system."

"Keira, are we fully armed?" She smiled and nodded.

"Provisions, Jorge?"

"As much food and water as we can carry, Micha. We could feed a full crew for months."

"All right, Lessa, we're ready to go, now tell us what you didn't want to tell me before we lifted off."

"Micha, are you suggesting I would withhold information vital to the mission of my crew?"

"Ena, is Lessa holding back?"

"Yes she is, Micha," laughed Ena.

"All right, I'll talk," sighed Lessa as she reached for Brenna's hand. "I have another reason for wanting to accept this job. In the years I was running from the old Viceroy I ended up in many strange places and learned some very unusual things. I learned of a planet where the failed genetic experiments of a secret Company lab were disposed of.

"The company had been experimenting for generations trying to breed super soldiers. They failed. The malformed mutants they created were shipped out in secret and dumped on a lonely planet far from the hub worlds."

"Exile," sighed Murtah.

"Yes," said Lessa. "Exile. Political prisoners were dumped there as well. Actually, I found there are two planets there. Wealthy prisoners were sent to one, the rest to Exile. I assume the wealthy got the more tolerable prison."

"So you want to see this for yourself, to see if there is anything you can do to help those unfortunate mutants."

"Yes, if any of them have survived. Perhaps I can heal some of them, or... I don't know, Micha, but I feel compelled to try."

Micha was silent for a moment. Edie squeezed his shoulder, knowing how he hated to put his friends in danger, but knowing he would anyway. "Anything further?" he asked at length.

"Ah, hells," sighed Zartah as he rose to his feet. "Let's do it. It should be exciting."

There was a round of laughter at that and Micha grinned with pride. His crew might have a few reservations about the job, but they wouldn't hold back. "Any questions?" asked Micha.

"Can I fly the first leg, Boss," grinned Jorge. "I always wanted to fly a ship this size."

"All right, Jorge, you're up. Set course for FarStar. We'll be able to get our bearings from there."

The crew filed out to their respective stations. Jorge grinning like a kid in a candy store, headed to the pilot's chair. "FarStar," muttered

Micha. "First we fly out to the very tip, the last star on the galactic arm, and then we go out to deep space looking for a ghost planet, a rumor."

"It could be worse," smiled Edie, as she linked her arm through his.

"Oh?"

"Zartah could get bored."

"Yep, that would be worse," he chuckled, as he settled into the captain's chair.

Two weeks later they reached FarStar, a small star with six planets, none inhabitable. There was a marker satellite beaming a constant warning to go back. Lessa leaned over Jorge's shoulder and tapped in the heading. It was straight out from the galaxy. He set the course and the ship turned into the new heading, but didn't move.

"Nothing out there on sensors, Boss," said Murtah as he stared at the screen before him.

"Lessa?"

"That's the heading Lortax gave me, Micha."

"Jorge, one half speed for one day then full stop and hold. If we don't see anything then we go back."

"Aye, Captain," sighed Jorge as he engaged the engines.

No one spoke, if fact they hardly breathed as the minutes slowly ticked by with nothing appearing on the screens. Eventually they succumbed to the boredom and went to rest. It was mid-day the next when Jorge brought the ship to a full stop.

Micha was in the Captain's chair again. "Murtah?"

"Nothing there, Micha," he replied as he gazed at the sensor screen.

"Behind us? Still see FarStar?"

"Very clear."

"All right, Jorge, half speed, one more day." Micha rose and headed for the mess. Waiting always made him hungry.

"Aye, Boss. One more day, half speed."

Another day of silent tension passed then Jorge stopped the ship again. "Murtah?"

"Yes. There's a star out there, but just barely visible on sensors."

"FarStar?"

"Still there, but barely detectable."

"Jorge, continue on heading, three quarter speed."

"Aye, Boss. Three quarter speed." Murtah flicked the image up onto the large screen and they all watched as the lonely star slowly grew in the view. The next day they arrived.

There were ten planets around the dwarf star, but most were just rocks without atmosphere. Three seemed like possibles.

"Well, I'll be damned; there is something out here after all," muttered Micha. "Anything on sensors, Murtah?"

"There's life on two of the planets, Boss. Looks like they were terraformed at one time."

"Which one, Lessa?"

"I don't know, Micha."

"All right crew, I guess we'll have to look them over. Rathbone, you and Keira take a small fighter and check out the nearest planet. "We'll drop scouts off at the next one and come back to pick you up."

"On our way," signaled Keira. They hurried away and soon a small fighter ship dropped out into space.

"Ship's away, Boss."

"All right, Jorge. Move us over to the next one. Zartah, you and Gorda want to go down for a look?"

"Oh yes, indeed. Come on, Gorda, this'll be exciting."

"Oh, wonderful," groused Gorda as he winked at Micha.

"I've still got a bad feeling about this," sighed Micha as the small fighter ship dropped out of the belly of the Defender. He watched the screen as the craft descended into the atmosphere. A few moments later he heard the call on comms.

"We're under fire! Dammit, we've been hit. I'm losing control. We're going in hot! Hang on, Gorda."

"Zartah, Zartah, come in." There was nothing but static on comms.

Don't miss out!

Visit the website below and you can sign up to receive emails whenever Prudence MacLeod publishes a new book. There's no charge and no obligation.

https://books2read.com/r/B-A-ZKBBB-DCURC

BOOKS 2 READ

Connecting independent readers to independent writers.

Also by Prudence MacLeod

Forgotten Worlds
Suvi
Echo of the Past
Survivors
Ship
Fleet
Unite
IGEN
T.E.N.

Nova series
Novan Witch
Assassin of Nova

Watch for more at https://www.prudencemacleod.com/.

Telling a story is like knitting a sweater. Start with a ball of possibilities, pull out one small thread and begin. With luck and patience you will create something quite wonderful.

About the Author

On a far off windswept island Jennifer Crandall sits with her dogs and cats creating fantastic stories for all to enjoy. She publishes as JL Crandall, Prudence MacLeod, and Jenni Leigh.

Read more at https://www.prudencemacleod.com/.

www.ingramcontent.com/pod-product-compliance
Lightning Source LLC
Chambersburg PA
CBHW020232260626
47156CB00002B/643